NECESSARY
EVILS

NECESSARY EVILS

BASED ON THE BEST-SELLING

LEFT BEHIND® SERIES

NEESA HART

TYNDALE HOUSE PUBLISHERS, INC.   WHEATON, ILLINOIS

Visit Tyndale's exciting Web site at www.tyndale.com

TYNDALE is a registered trademark of Tyndale House Publishers, Inc.

Tyndale's quill logo is a trademark of Tyndale House Publishers, Inc.

Discover the latest about the Left Behind series at www.leftbehind.com

Copyright © 2005 by Tyndale House Publishers, Inc. All rights reserved.

Written and developed in association with Tekno Books, Green Bay, Wisconsin.

Cover photograph © 2004 by Getty Images. All rights reserved.

Designed by Alyssa Force

Scripture quotations are taken from the *Holy Bible,* New Living Translation, copyright © 1996. Used by permission of Tyndale House Publishers, Inc., Wheaton, Illinois 60189. All rights reserved.

Published in association with the literary agency of Alive Communications, Inc., 7680 Goddard Street, Suite 200, Colorado Springs, CO 80920.

Published in association with the literary agency of Sterling Lord Literistic, New York, NY.

Library of Congress Cataloging-in-Publication Data

Hart, Neesa.
  Necessary evils / Neesa Hart.
    p. cm.
  ISBN 1-4143-0039-5 (sc)
  I. Title.
  PS3558.A68357N43 2005
  813'.6—dc22
                                                    2004022001

Printed in the United States of America

10   09   08   07   06   05
 6   5   4   3   2   1

What People Are Saying
about the Left Behind Series

"This is the most successful Christian-fiction series ever."
Publishers Weekly

"Tim LaHaye and Jerry B. Jenkins . . . are doing for Christian fiction what John Grisham did for courtroom thrillers."
TIME

"The authors' style continues to be thoroughly captivating and keeps the reader glued to the book, wondering what will happen next. And it leaves the reader hungry for more."
Christian Retailing

"Combines Tom Clancy–like suspense with touches of romance, high-tech flash and Biblical references."
The New York Times

"It's not your mama's Christian fiction anymore."
The Dallas Morning News

"Wildly popular—and highly controversial."
USA Today

"Christian thriller. Prophecy-based fiction. Juiced-up morality tale. Call it what you like, the Left Behind series . . . now has a label its creators could never have predicted: blockbuster success."
Entertainment Weekly

Tyndale House products by
Tim LaHaye and Jerry B. Jenkins

The Left Behind® book series
Left Behind®
Tribulation Force
Nicolae
Soul Harvest
Apollyon
Assassins
The Indwelling
The Mark
Desecration
The Remnant
Armageddon
Glorious Appearing

Coming Spring 2005:
The Rising
Left Behind® 10th Anniversary Edition

Other Left Behind® products
Left Behind®: The Kids
Devotionals
Calendars
Abridged audio products
Dramatic audio products
Graphic novels
Gift books
and more . . .

Other Tyndale House books by
Tim LaHaye and Jerry B. Jenkins
Perhaps Today
Are We Living in the End Times?
Embracing Eternity

For the latest information on individual products, release dates,
and future projects, visit www.leftbehind.com

**Tyndale House books by
Tim LaHaye**
How to Be Happy Though Married
Spirit-Controlled Temperament
Transformed Temperaments
Why You Act the Way You Do

**Tyndale House books by
Jerry B. Jenkins**
Soon
Silenced

1

His clothes smelled terrible.

The acrid scent of burning fuel and rubber from the exploding limousine clung to everything Randal Arnold was wearing. He ignored the piercing gaze of Harmon Drake, head of the Secret Service office at the White House, and sniffed his arm. It wasn't just his clothes. His skin smelled, too. He reeked of that horrible burnt-hair odor he'd experienced only once before when he'd recklessly ignited a propane grill with a too-short match.

The scent made his nose twitch. "I need a shower," he muttered.

Drake gave him a hard look discernable even in the small dimly lit room where a bank of television monitors showed the frenzy of activity that now engulfed the White House. "Are you amused by this, Mr. Arnold?"

"No. No, I'm not." Randal rubbed his hands on his trouser legs and tried not to squirm. "I just noticed that I smell like the inside of an ashtray." His gaze darted to the monitors where he could see the still-burning wreck.

Minutes ago, a limousine designated to carry the presi-

dent to the National Press Club for a major announcement
had exploded near the White House portico. Acting on a tip
from his boss, White House Chief of Staff Brad Benton, and
information from his father, Senator Max Arnold, Randal
had narrowly prevented the president and Nicolae
Carpathia from boarding the bomb-laden limousine just
seconds before the blast. Spouting a story about a missing
security log on the lead limo—it was the truth, but not the
real reason he was panicked—Randal had managed to persuade the Secret Service agent in charge of loading the
motorcade to pass up and park the first car and load the
president and Carpathia into the second vehicle.

The president's motorcade had barely left the White
House gates when the parked limo had exploded. The force
of the blast had scattered pieces of the armored vehicle
across the White House lawn and knocked Randal and several other bystanders to the ground.

Still shaken, Randal had found himself plucked from
the pavement and hurried to Drake's office by a Service
agent. Within seconds of the blast, while White House
security was still scurrying around to ensure that the president's vehicle was safely on its way to the National Press
Club and had not been sabotaged too, the guard had all but
shoved Randal into the hard chair near the bank of security
monitors.

Randal suspected that Drake wanted a crack at him before Conner Trellis, the head of White House security,
worked him over. Territorial feuds between White House
security and the Service were common. It was no secret that
Drake and Trellis were bitter rivals. Since the day a sniper
had taken shots at Brad in the secure White House parking
lot, both sides had been scrambling for jurisdiction of the
case. Reggie Lawton, Drake's second in command, was
heading up the Secret Service investigation, and Conner

Trellis had roundly criticized both Lawton and Drake for their lack of progress in the case.

Praying earnestly for wisdom and discernment, Randal had tried to gather his composure for the coming interrogation. He'd quoted every verse of Scripture he knew to keep himself calm, but the adrenaline rush from the blast had left him feeling boneless and weak. He could hear the steady pounding of his blood echoing in his ears. The longer he sat there, the more aware he became of the ache in his head and the sting in his shoulder. Now he tried to ignore the pain as he focused on Drake. "You know how it takes a while after a big shock like that before you start to notice stuff. Well, I knew my head hurt, and I was sure that my shoulder's killing me, but I hadn't noticed until now that I stink. Did you notice?"

"Yes. But I don't care." Drake's exasperation was evident. "I'm going to ask you again," he said. "But I have something I want you to look at first." He punched a button to rewind a security tape. Images moved across the monitor in an accelerated blur—like reading microfiche at the library.

Randal's stomach churned in queasy discomfort as his head began to swim. He closed his eyes until he heard the tape grind to a stop. Drake had paused it on a frame that showed Randal and Brad stepping into an elevator. "You entered the elevator with Mr. Benton here." Drake pushed another button and indicated a second monitor. The screen showed Randal and Brad in the elevator. "What was on that piece of a paper he handed you?"

God, please, Randal prayed wordlessly, *I need Your help. I need Your wisdom.* He didn't want to lie, but he didn't want to tip his hand either. Until he talked to Brad, he had no idea how much he should reveal to Harmon Drake—not when he knew someone was trying to kill Brad and had already failed three times. Brad's would-be assailant could be a White House insider whom Brad was close to implicating in the murder of former press secretary, George Ramiro.

Or even worse, it might be one of Carpathia's own operatives who knew that Brad hadn't been fooled by the secretary-general's cover-up of his assassination of international financier Jonathan Stonagal and Joshua Todd-Cothran, the former head of the London Exchange. Carpathia had murdered both men the morning of his installation as secretary-general of the UN. Impossibly, he had apparently managed to brainwash all the eyewitnesses into believing that Stonagal had killed Todd-Cothran and himself in an unexplained act of violence.

Brad had witnessed the event via closed-circuit feed to the White House Cabinet Room and, unlike the other White House officials watching with him, had not succumbed to whatever evil forces Carpathia had used to alter the memories of the witnesses. Fantastic as the story seemed, Randal believed that God had supernaturally protected Brad from Nicolae Carpathia's power.

With that knowledge, however, came the very real possibility that Carpathia knew about Brad's resistance. Brad and Randal had often discussed the fact that it was highly possible George Ramiro's murderer wasn't the only person who wanted Brad dead. The chilling truth was that the Antichrist himself might be after Brad. And with good reason.

Randal rubbed his palm over the tight spot that had developed in his chest, then dragged his fingers through his tousled hair in a futile attempt to straighten it. Drake was still watching him intently. "It's like I told you," Randal said. "Mr. Benton told me earlier he'd be really tied up today with the Carpathia visit. He asked me to check on some things for him. Did I tell you already that I went to see Emma Pettit this morning?" Randal had driven to Loudon,

Virginia, to deliver a message from Brad to his friend and assistant. Emma was recovering at home after being shot two weeks earlier in the White House parking garage.

"Yes."

"Oh." The flat answer told him the other man's patience was waning. "I'm feeling a little confused. Like I said earlier, I whacked my head when I hit the ground. Maybe I've got a concussion or something."

"The paper, Mr. Arnold."

"Oh. Yeah. That. It was just a reminder note. Something Brad had asked me about. It's personal, you know. I don't really feel like I can tell you what it is without talking to Mr. Benton first."

Drake frowned slightly. "You know, Arnold, ever since Benton returned from Kansas, people have been commenting on the fact that you seem to be more like his assistant than his driver."

Randal shrugged. "Well, with Mrs. Pettit out and all that—I'm just trying to help out."

Drake looked unconvinced. "And I don't suppose that in your role as his substitute secretary, you might have come across any information that we'd find useful in this investigation?"

"I really don't pry into Mr. Benton's business. You'd have to ask him about that." For a moment, Randal thought he'd demand more details, but the older man hit another button on the remote control instead. "But whatever it was, that note sent you running from the elevator to the pay-phone bank outside the Press Room."

Randal had watched his own image hurry down the long hallway near the Press Room and duck into the phone booth. He'd never realized he was quite that tall. It was weird looking at himself like this. "I had to make a call. It wasn't a big deal."

"So you used a pay phone? Not an inside phone."

"It was a personal call. I don't like to make personal calls on House phones."

"I appreciate your conscientiousness," Drake said with unmistakable sarcasm. "Your cell phone wasn't working?"

"I don't get good reception downstairs. Maybe I should look at switching carriers. Does your cell phone work down there?"

Drake crossed his arms over his broad chest and propped one hip on the edge of the monitor rack. The only light in the room came from that bank of monitors. Limned in the glow from their screens, he looked menacing. "You are aware, of course, that every phone in the House is on auto record?"

"I guess so. Yeah."

"That includes the pay phones. You might as well tell me now. I'll have the tapes of your conversation in a few hours."

Randal didn't respond. By the time Drake got the tape of the call, Randal would be able to talk to Brad, who would know what to do. In the meantime, Randal was going to keep his mouth shut.

Drake turned his attention to the monitors again. The tape showed Randal hurrying down the hall toward the portico doors where the motorcade was parked. The president, Carpathia, and their contingent were moving steadily toward the doors when Randal rushed past. Studying the tape intently, Drake asked, "Do I need to point out to you that if anything I discover on those tapes implicates you, Benton, or whomever you called, in that limousine explosion that criminal charges will be filed?"

Like I'd have risked my neck to save the president and Nicolae if I'd been involved. But I don't think it'd be smart to say that just now. "No, sir. You don't need to point it out. I'm aware of that."

"And there's still nothing you want to tell me?"

"I've told you everything I can." Randal watched Drake's profile. The man was obviously suspicious, and though Randal's interactions with him had always been pleasant in the past, something told him that he couldn't trust him now. The Holy Spirit, Randal had to believe, was prompting him, guiding him to hold his tongue. *Please, God, please show me what to do.*

Randal rubbed the knot on the back of his head while long seconds of silence stretched into agonizing minutes. As Harmon Drake watched, rewound, and watched the tapes again, Randal begged God to get him out of here so he could talk to Brad.

What Drake couldn't seem to understand was that even if Randal had wanted to talk to him, he didn't have many answers to give. In fact, with the very clear evidence that someone had tried to murder the president, perhaps Brad Benton as well, Randal had nearly as many questions as Drake did. That piece of paper that Brad had handed him had a single name scrawled across it: *Major Nuñez.* Randal had asked his dad for information about the guy. And that had cascaded into the whole chain of events that had led him to derail the assassination attempt, which had led him to this chair. What did the name mean? How had that name led Max Arnold to discover the assassination plot in time to stop it?

The shrill ring of Randal's cell phone startled him. Drake's gaze swung from the monitors to the phone clipped on Randal's belt. "It seems that your phone is functional again. You have a call."

Randal looked down at his cell. The phone rang one more time.

Drake met his gaze. "Answer it, Mr. Arnold. You never know. It might be important."

Randal pulled the phone from his belt. His fingers were shaking. "Hello."

"Randal? Thank God!"

"Mom?" It was his mother, Mariette, and she sounded really upset. Mariette was the deputy director of FEMA, and she'd headed into work unusually early this morning to avoid the inevitable traffic jams and road closures Carpathia's visit to the White House would cause. She didn't have any reason to call—unless she'd heard about the explosion. By the tone in her voice, she'd heard.

"Yes, this is your mother. Honey, I just saw the news. They showed footage of you getting blasted across the White House lawn. I was worried sick. Are you all right? Why didn't you call me?"

"Yes. I'm fine. I can't talk right now," Randal said.

"Company, huh?"

"Yeah."

"I see." Mariette paused. "Do you need anything?"

"No. Like I said, I'm fine. Look, I'll call you later."

"Does Brad know what's going on?"

"I'm not sure."

"Okay. I'll see what I can do about that. And I'm going to call Marcus," she told him, referring to their mutual friend and pastor, Marcus Dumont. "I'll let him know what's happening."

"Thanks."

"I'm praying for you."

"I need it."

"Be careful."

"Mom—"

"Okay, okay. Sorry. Call me when you can."

"Yes, ma'am. Bye." He flipped the phone shut and looked at Drake. "My mom. She caught the news."

Drake hesitated for a moment, then tossed the remote

onto the control table. In two long strides, he was towering over Randal's chair. His dark gaze had turned menacing, soul-less even. Randal's head ached too much to tip it backward. Instead he stood, bringing himself to eye level with the security chief. Though Drake was uncomfortably close to him, neither man backed away. "All right, Mr. Arnold. If you're sure you have nothing else you want to say . . ."

Randal held his gaze for long seconds, then shook his head. "No, sir."

"Then get out of here." Drake waved a hand toward the door. "If you want someone to take you to the infirmary . . ."

"It's okay. I know the way."

"Fine. Have them check out your head. Maybe tomorrow you'll feel less . . . *confused*."

The subtle emphasis on the last word was not lost on Randal. "Maybe."

"In the meantime, if you find yourself being questioned by Conner Trellis, you'd be wise to remember that he may think this is his House, but the president is my responsibility. And when it comes to his security, I can be a real pain in the—"

The door of the control room swung open before he could finish. The shaft of bright light sent a spike of pain through Randal's head. "Mr. Drake?" The agent who had ushered Randal to the control room stuck his head into the room. "Eagle is on his way back to the nest."

Drake nodded. "I'll be right there."

Randal understood the code. The president's press conference was completed and the motorcade was en route back to the White House. That was good. He'd be able to talk to Brad soon.

"Get out of here, Arnold," Drake said. "I'll let you know when I need to talk to you again."

★ ★ ★

Brad checked his watch for the tenth time as the president tried, once again, to wrap up questions from the media. They'd heard the news about the explosion shortly after the president's limousine had turned off Pennsylvania Avenue. Brad, who had already been struggling with the fact that he was seated less than ten inches from Nicolae Carpathia inside the president's limo, nearly lost his composure when Carpathia started gushing about his profound thanks for the president's excellent security and their narrow escape.

Fresh in Brad's mind was the vision of Carpathia executing Stonagal and Todd-Cothran at the UN barely a week before. Though Carpathia certainly oozed the humble charm that had made him a media darling, Brad was more convinced than ever that the man was the embodiment of evil. With eyes as blue as the Caribbean waters where Brad had spent his honeymoon on a cruise with Christine, Carpathia was handsome, smooth, sophisticated, and almost irresistibly boyish. Even now, as Nicolae listened to President Fitzhugh field questions about the United States' involvement in and its position on his proposed reforms and UN programs, he appeared slightly humbled and overwhelmed by the attention paid to him by America's head of state. Had Brad not known better, he too might have fallen for the act.

Already today Fitzhugh had issued a statement to the press announcing that he was going to lend Carpathia the new *Air Force One* for the treaty signing in Jerusalem next week. All who were close to the president knew how shocking the offer had been. Fitzhugh was like a kid in a candy shop when it came to the new plane. To give up the right to make the aircraft's maiden voyage had been a major concession on the president's part.

But only those closest to the administration knew what Fitzhugh had gotten in exchange for the offer: Carpathia had finally agreed to allow the U.S. to chair the International Nuclear Disarmament Committee. Though he'd made allusions to his willingness for the U.S. to play such a prominent role, Carpathia had never formally promised Fitzhugh the chairmanship until today.

Gerald Fitzhugh's critics would be surprised to learn that the man was capable of putting the best interests of the U.S over his own personal agenda.

As far as everyone at the White House was concerned, the meeting with Carpathia had been productive. The U.S. had given little but gained much in the game of international brinkmanship, but Brad found the entire thing highly suspicious. He alone seemed to remain immune to Carpathia's feigned naivety and false humility. Brad had noticed something odd—Fitzhugh seemed to personally dislike Nicolae when he talked about him in closed circles, but their interaction today had been nothing but cordial and warm. And it didn't feel like politics as usual.

Brad's blood chilled each time he made eye contact with Nicolae Carpathia and felt the cloak of evil that surrounded him. Ever present in his mind was the thought that Carpathia might know that Brad had not been duped by his efforts to cover up the assassination of Todd-Cothran and Stonagal. Though he strongly suspected that the same men who had murdered George Ramiro were behind the recent attempts on his life, it was not beyond reason to believe that Carpathia could count him as an enemy as well. After all, as a child of God and a follower of Christ, he was at war with the evil Carpathia served.

Brad was grateful he'd prayed with his pastor and close friend, Marcus Dumont, this morning. Marcus had prayed for a hedge of protection around Brad that would shield

him from Nicolae's evil. Both men were aware that Brad
might find himself in serious danger before Carpathia's
visit concluded. If, indeed, Carpathia knew that Brad had
witnessed and remembered the murders at the UN, there
was no telling what kind of revenge he might exact. Though
Brad had discerned no animosity in the secretary-general's
countenance, there was something chilling, a certain
understanding in the man's eyes, that made Brad wary.

The feeling had only gotten worse when news of the explosion at the White House had come. Brad had itched to
call Randal for a full report, but knew he wouldn't have the
time or the necessary privacy until the press conference
ended. He'd taken some comfort in the information from
the White House that no one had been injured in the blast.
Randal was fine, and the fact that the president's limousine—the vehicle that would have carried President
Fitzhugh and Nicolae Carpathia to the Press Club—had
been sabotaged, was compelling evidence that Carpathia
or one of his people had not been the likely assassin. Brad
found small, ironic comfort in knowing that whoever
wanted him dead, it apparently was not the man who was
the center of evil in the universe—at least not today.

"Mr. President," a reporter called from the back of the
room, arresting Brad's attention, "about the explosion—"

President Fitzhugh held up his hand as a Secret Service
agent stepped onto the dais with him. "Please. We don't
have any information on that. Forrest Tetherton will keep
you informed as we get the details."

"Do you think it was an attempt to stop you from signing the treaty?" another reporter demanded.

At the urging of the Service agent, Fitzhugh turned to
leave. A third reporter yelled, "Was it some kind of protest?"

The president stopped to look at the crowd of reporters.
His mouth was turned up in amusement. "Protests take

place in Lafayette Park across the street from my office," he said caustically. "Assassination attempts, if that's what this was, are treason."

"Do you think they were after you, or Mr. Carpathia?"

"Hard to say," Fitzhugh responded. "When you do what we do for a living, you make a lot of enemies. The Bible might call peacemakers blessed, but there are a lot of people who'd like to argue the point."

Another barrage of questions followed, but the Secret Service agent prompted the president with a hand at his elbow. "Mr. President, please. We've got to get you to a secure facility."

Fitzhugh shot Brad a look as he exited the platform. Brad understood the wordless communication and mounted the dais in an easy stride. Holding up his hands to quiet the clamor as the president and Carpathia left the room, he squared his shoulders and glanced at the faces in the crowd. He'd faced this same bunch hundreds of times, taken their questions, engaged in their banter, traded wit for wit and jibe for jibe. He respected them, and they seemed to respect him.

But today, the crowd looked different, more frustrated, desperate. He'd been noticing that same look of desperation on faces a lot lately. He'd mentioned it to Marcus. Marcus said it was the dawning of a collective understanding of the dismal state of the human race. In a world where all of God's children had disappeared, a world where now only a few new believers were struggling to bring light to the ever-encroaching darkness, people were only beginning to understand the absolute misery of life outside the Garden of Eden.

Brad rubbed a hand over his face. He was weary. The stress of the morning had taken its toll. He hoped he was projecting his usual confidence—for he was far from feeling it just now. "Ladies and gentlemen, please." He waited for the room to still. "Please." His voice was lower now. "We're thankful that no one was hurt today. The president and Secretary Carpathia have made significant strides, as you know, but we have an evening of long meetings and a state dinner ahead of us." He managed a slight smile. "And I've still got to change into my tuxedo."

That won a slight laugh. The reporters often called him Fitzhugh's Fashion Plate. They didn't know that his reputation for sartorial perfection was a product of his wife's good taste, not his own. Now that Christine was gone, taken in the Rapture, Brad was on his own in more ways than one. It was, however, the least of his current problems.

Brad motioned behind him for the rest of the White House contingent to file from the room. "As soon as we have any additional information, we'll let you know."

2

Marcus switched off the television with the remote. "I don't know," he told Mariette on the phone. She'd called to tell him she'd spoken to Randal. "Did you see the press conference?"

"Some. I turned off the TV to call Randal."

That brought a slight smile to his lips. "Who cares if the future of the world is being mapped out on TV; you've got to check on your kid?"

"I thought about driving over there."

"They're in lockdown. You couldn't have gotten in—not even with your clearance."

"That's what David told me," she said, mentioning her assistant at the FEMA headquarters. "He talked me out of it. Barely."

"Did you get through to Randal when you called?" Marcus glanced out his office window. From his vantage point, Washington looked peaceful. It was difficult to believe that the most evil man in history was prowling the city's streets as he campaigned for his plan of terror and global domination. "The news says no one was hurt, but it looked like he took quite a spill."

"He says he's okay. He couldn't talk. I think he was being questioned by White House security."

"No surprise there," Marcus told her. "They can't like the fact that they've had a sniper in their parking lot and now an attempt on the president's life in less than a month."

"Do you think that bomb was meant for Fitzhugh?" Mariette asked. "Or Carpathia?"

"Or Brad?" Marcus mused. "It's hard to say."

"Marcus, I'm really worried about Randal working down there. With everything going on—"

"Mariette," Marcus said quietly, "we've talked about this. God has put Randal in a position to serve Him in a unique and significant way. Today proved that. You have to trust God to take care of him."

She was silent for a moment. "It doesn't mean I have to like it."

That made him laugh. "No, I don't suppose it does."

"I've got to go. I don't want my line tied up if Randal tries to call. I just wanted you to know what was happening."

"I appreciate that." He glanced at the clock on his desk. "Are you and Randal still planning to meet me at the house tonight?" The three friends, knowing Brad would be spending his evening at a state dinner with the president and Carpathia, had agreed to meet and pray for him, for his safety, for God's wisdom, and for Brad's discernment.

"I am. And I'm sure Randal wants to be there. We'll have to see how he's doing. He said he wasn't hurt, but—"

"You're not sure?"

"You saw the tape of the explosion. Didn't you see him slam his head on the pavement?"

"You told me his head was hard," Marcus pointed out.

"Not *that* hard," she muttered. "If he has a concussion, I'm not sure he should go out tonight."

"Well, let me know. I can always come to your place."

Because Mariette, Brad, and Randal all worked in downtown D.C., the four prayer partners usually met in Marcus's Georgetown brownstone.

"I appreciate that."

"All right. Let me pray with you for a minute before you hang up," he said.

"I'd like that."

"Lord, thank You for protecting my young friend. Thank You for Your continued providence and guidance in our lives. I ask that You put a hedge of protection around both Randal and Brad as they struggle to be Your servants in a hostile environment. Let Your will be played out today, no matter what the outcome, and please give us the grace to accept it. Thank You for loving us. Thank You for Your grace and the gift of Your Son. Amen."

"Amen," Mariette responded. "I'll call you when I hear something."

"I'll be here."

★   ★   ★

"Mr. Arnold."

Randal fought his way through several layers of sleep. Whatever the nurse had given him for his pain had knocked him out cold. His head felt like someone had stuffed it full of cotton.

"Mr. Arnold, we're going to move you now."

"Move?" He wasn't sure if he'd managed to say the word out loud. He did manage to open his eyes. The shadowy forms of a pair of EMTs loomed over him. Randal felt the world shift as they lifted him off the infirmary bed and transferred him to a gurney. "Move where?"

"George Washington Hospital," came the reply. "You've taken quite a hit on your head."

Randal struggled to sit up, but quickly abandoned the idea when his stomach lurched. "Hospital. Don't need a hospital." His head swam slightly. "I need to talk to Brad Benton."

With a firm hand to the shoulder, one of the EMTs pressed him back onto the gurney. "Just lie still."

"No. Mr. Benton. I need to talk to Mr. Benton." Randal wiggled one hand from under the sheet and reached for his cell phone. Clarity was beginning to return in a rush of hideous images that had him frantic to know where Brad was and how he was doing.

"What you need is rest." The EMT pushed him back on the gurney.

If he'd had the strength, Randal would have grabbed the man by the collar and shouted, *"The Antichrist is trying to kill my friend, you moron, and I'm not going to the hospital until I know where he is!"* As it was, the best he could do was shake his head and say, "I need to talk to him. It's important."

The EMT brought his face close to Randal's ear. "Everything's taken care of, Arnold. Just shut up until we get you out of here."

Stunned, Randal froze. Those words seemed to be more than the simple statement they appeared to be on the surface. It felt more like a secret message being passed. He searched the now expressionless face of the EMT, but found no clue. The two technicians were racing him down the hall toward a back exit of the White House. Ahead he saw Harmon Drake looming near the doorway. Secret message or no, Randal was going to play along. He shut his eyes as the gurney bounced over the rough marble flooring.

"How long do you expect this to take?" Drake demanded of the EMTs. "I still need to ask this person a few questions. When will he be available for interrogation?"

"Hard to say," one of them responded. "We'll know more once he's been examined by a doctor."

A blast of cool air washed down the hallway when a security guard pushed open the door. Randal dared to sneak a look outside and saw the swirl of red and blue emergency lights atop an ambulance. Pops of white light indicated the presence of media photographers. Vaguely, Randal heard the din from the gaggle of reporters yelling unanswered questions at Harmon Drake. With dispatch, the two EMTs loaded him into the back of the ambulance, then slammed the doors.

Randal opened his eyes to find Brad Benton seated inside the ambulance studying him with concern. "Brad."

"Hey, kid." Brad gave him a slight smile. "How you feeling?"

Randal collapsed against the pillows with a sigh of relief. Whatever had happened in the hours since the limousine explosion, Brad was okay. "Like crud. Saving your sorry neck nearly knocked the snot out of me."

Brad laughed softly. "So I hear. Your head killing you?"

"Not much. The nurse gave me some kind of horse-sized painkiller. I feel like I'm fighting my way through fog."

"I'll bet. Sorry for the melodrama with the ambulance. I just needed to get you away from all those eyes and ears so I could talk to you, and this seemed like the best plan."

"Yeah, well, just hope my mother doesn't see a picture of me on this gurney on the news. She'll be climbing all over your case."

"Too late for caution there, buddy. Your mother saw you whack your head on the driveway on national television. The ambulance was her idea."

Randal groaned. "Great. Are we really going to the hospital?"

"Yes."

"Is she meeting us there?"

"I had to practically restrain her to keep her from riding in the ambulance."

"Thanks for that, anyway."

Brad put a hand on Randal's shoulder. "I'm sure you're fine, but it's not going to hurt to have a doctor check you out."

"All I really need is a shower and a super large value meal from a burger joint. I haven't eaten since this morning. I think that's the real reason I've had such a headache."

That won a genuine laugh from Brad. "I should have known. My son was just like that. His mother used to say that when he turned thirteen, he went from three meals a day to one—it started at 7:00 in the morning and ended at midnight." He rapped his knuckles on the small window behind the cab of the ambulance.

The window slid open. "Everything okay?" The same EMT who'd warned Randal in the infirmary gave him a measured look. "You sure you don't need me to come back there and check him out?"

"No, Jerry. He's fine. Maybe a mild concussion. And a bad case of malnutrition. Hasn't eaten since breakfast. Any chance we can go through a drive-thru on the way to the hospital?"

Jerry chuckled. "Sure thing, Mr. Benton. We'll have to kill the lights, though. It looks bad when we've got hot lights on top and we're sitting at a take-out window."

"No problem."

"Okay, but you've got to explain it to his mama." Jerry shut the window.

Randal groaned. "You didn't say Mom *arranged* for the ambulance. Are these her people?"

"Not exactly. But she's tight with emergency and medical personnel in just about every locality in this country. Stands to reason she'd know a few here in the District."

"She has a way of making me feel like a six-year-old."

"She's your mother. That's her job." Brad leaned closer and lowered his voice. "The only way I kept her out of the ambulance was by telling her there were some things we needed to discuss privately about what happened today. It was a tough sell, but I bought us a little time. Tell me what you know."

Randal glanced around the inside of the ambulance. "I guess we're safe here."

"Relatively."

"You don't think they put some kind of bug on me or something while I was in the infirmary."

Brad shook his head. "Drake never imagined you'd be leaving the White House until he had what he wanted. You're okay."

"Did he question you?"

"He wanted to, but by the time we returned from the Press Club, he had his hands full with the investigation. It's going to take several hours for the Secret Service and White House security to finish deciding who's in charge."

"I can believe that. You should have seen the way Drake's guy hauled me up to his office. I wasn't even off the pavement yet."

"What did you tell him?"

"Nothing, really. I just played dumb. He asked about that paper you handed me in the elevator—but I told him it was something personal you'd asked me to do and that he'd have to ask you about it."

Brad leaned back and stroked his chin. "He accepted that?"

"Yeah. I thought that was a little weird." Randal frowned as he replayed the conversation in his head. "I think he wasn't too uptight about it since he said he could get the recording of my phone conversation with Max."

"You called your father?"

Randal nodded. "When you gave me that name, I didn't know what to do with it. I just figured Max could find out the quickest who the guy was. I placed a call on a pay phone outside the Press Room."

"And Max told you about the bomb?"

"Yeah. I told him I needed to know who this Nuñez guy was."

"He knew him?"

"Not at first. He asked Helen—she's his . . . assistant." Randal never knew exactly how to refer to the woman who'd been at the center of his family's conflict for so many years. "I heard her place a phone call in the background. Then she said something to Max. He told me that whatever I did, I couldn't allow the president to get into the lead limousine in the motorcade. I started to ask what he was talking about, but he just got really insistent."

"So you don't know how he knew," Brad mused.

The ambulance swayed slightly as it moved over the poorly maintained District roads. Randal tried to ignore the lurching sensation in his stomach. He felt weird lying down during this conversation, but he didn't dare try to sit up. Food, he hoped, would knock the edge off his nausea. "How *did* he know?" he asked Brad. "Who is this Nuñez guy anyway?"

"I'm not sure. When I was downloading Gray Wells's files this morning, a security message popped up on the screen. I'm sure Gray knew that if anybody was after those files, it had to be because something had happened to him. He must have programmed the security prompt as a tip."

"You think Wells knew someone wanted him dead?"

"I think so, yes," Brad stated. "I found several indications in his e-mails that he was keeping a paper trail, but I haven't had time to go through everything yet. As soon as I get back to the White House, I'm going to lock myself in my office and see if I can make any sense of the information Jane Lyons sent me from George's desk and the stuff I downloaded today from Gray's computer. I'm hoping that between the two, I'll have enough evidence."

Randal thought that over. "Was there anything else besides Nuñez's name in that security prompt?"

"No," Brad told him. "All it said was 'Find Major Nuñez.'"

The ambulance rocked slightly as it turned into the entrance to a fast-food restaurant. The small window slid open again. "What's he want?" Jerry asked Brad.

"A burger with everything, extra-large fries, and a Coke." Brad dug into his pocket and handed Jerry a twenty-dollar bill. "And whatever you guys want."

"Anything for you?"

Brad shook his head. Jerry shut the window again as the ambulance eased forward in the line.

Randal continued to ponder the cryptic message on Wells's computer. "So, if Wells was looking into the crash of that Galaxy you were on, then Nuñez could have been Wells's contact at the Pentagon."

"Maybe." Brad pursed his lips. "Or, he could be involved with whoever tried to kill the president today. I haven't told you this, but the night of the Rapture, I had a conversation with Grayson Wells about what had happened. He was looking into the military response for me, and we had discussed the possibility that there was a supernatural reason for the disappearances." Brad's expression turned grim. "That was before I met the Lord—before I knew the truth."

"What did Wells think?"

"He had good reasons not to believe this had been a military strike or an environmental disaster. His sister and her family were believers. He'd heard them talk about the Rapture, but wasn't ready to go there yet himself. He was going to look into some things for me."

Randal's eyes widened. "You think he got killed because of it?"

"I think he was digging around and somebody got wind of the fact that he was helping me. I think that's what got him killed. Especially if he uncovered a plot to assassinate the president."

"Brad, do you really think someone at the Pentagon could want to off the president?"

"It's possible. The Joint Chiefs of Staff haven't made any secret of how they feel about the way he's handling this. Marsden, especially, is furious about this meeting with Carpathia."

"Yeah, I can imagine. He and Max kind of see eye to eye on stuff like this. Bomb 'em now; ask questions later."

"There are several key leaders at the Pentagon who think the president is risking our national security by not taking a more aggressive stance. Given the current political environment, it's not hard to believe that some of those leaders think the U.S. would be better off if Gerald Fitzhugh weren't president."

"I know, but *assassination?* Seriously?"

"A month ago, I would have said it's ridiculous. Now I'm not so sure." Brad leaned closer. "I'm not even so sure that Victor Rudd isn't partially responsible for what happened today. Rudd makes most of his money off the American war industry. I doubt he's very thrilled at the idea of world peace. It's possible he played a role in trying to kill the president."

"Or you," Randal pointed out. "You would have been in that limo, too."

"True, and if Rudd had anything to do with George Ramiro's murder, then it's more than possible that they were after me."

Randal's eyes widened.

"We got news of the explosion in the limo on the way to the Press Club. The whole time, all I could think about was how we know that Carpathia isn't the one trying to kill me—at least not today."

"So what are we doing to do?" Randal asked. "By now, Drake has got to know that I called Max."

"Probably. But all he knows—for the moment anyway—is what you and I know. You asked him about Nuñez, he had Helen place a phone call, and then he warned you not to let the president into the limousine. He might be able to run the tape through forensics and eventually hear who Helen spoke to and what she told Max, but that'll take a while, and my guess is, your father's not going to be very forthcoming with that information. That'll buy us some time."

"He's going to know you got Nuñez's name from Wells's computer, though. Don't you think?"

"He probably would anyway."

The ambulance pitched forward again. Jerry slid open the window and passed Brad a drink and a sack. The aroma made Randal's mouth water. "I'm starving," he said. "I'm queasy from all that pain medication, but I'm starving."

Brad thanked Jerry as he slid the straw into the soda top. The window slid shut and Brad handed Randal his drink, then reached into the bag for the burger. "The proof I need right now," Brad continued as he peeled the wrapper from the burger, "is whether or not the people behind the bomb in the limousine also sabotaged my flight from California."

Randal choked slightly on a sip of his drink as he suddenly remembered his conversation with Liza Cannley that morning. "Uh-oh, I forgot to tell you. Everything got so crazy . . ." He set the drink aside and struggled to sit up. "I talked to that reporter this morning."

Brad helped him with a steadying hand at his shoulder. "Liza Cannley?"

"Yeah. She called me when she couldn't get you."

"I was in those meetings with Carpathia. What did she say?" He handed Randal his food.

Randal took a huge bite of the burger. "Sorry," he muttered around the mouthful, "I know this is rude."

"Don't worry about it. Tell me about Liza."

He wiped his mouth with the back of his sleeve. His clothes still smelled like smoke. "She was looking into Rudd's ties to Constantine Kostankis. She found the link you were looking for."

"You're kidding."

"Uh-uh." Randal quickly told Brad about Liza's discovery at the Interstate Commerce Commission, about her theory that Kostankis and Rudd had conspired to secretly ship gold out of the South Range security facility for illegal distribution to foreign allies of the Fitzhugh administration, and how the evidence seemed to show that upper-level White House and Pentagon officials had been behind the deal.

"So the White House used Rudd's facilities to process the gold bars and Konstankis's ships to move it worldwide," Brad said. "Someone in the administration must have decided to make an end run around congressional approval to finance a covert operation overseas."

Randal recalled a story he'd read in the paper earlier that year. "Wasn't Max's committee looking into allegations that someone at the Pentagon was encouraging covert action in Syria against the regime there?"

"There were hearings in January," Brad confirmed. "Nothing came of it."

"Do you think it could be tied to this?"

"I wouldn't doubt it. Several of the Joint Chiefs have made no secret of their dislike of Fitzhugh's policy in the Middle East. They think he's dragging his feet on ending the war by not sending a bigger American presence over there. They don't like the way the peace talks have been going."

"So you think they took matters into their own hands."

"It wouldn't surprise me. It also wouldn't surprise me to find out that if George Ramiro had discovered this—then that's why he ended up dead." Brad had been steadily investigating the death of the former White House press secretary since shortly after the Rapture. The closer he'd gotten to the truth, the more danger he'd found himself facing.

Randal knew that Brad had already survived at least three failed attempts on his life. If the bomb in the limousine had been meant for him, that made four. The man's determination to press on and trust God to take care of him inspired and impressed Randal tremendously. "Brad—" he lowered his voice to a near whisper—"isn't Rudd supposed to be at the state dinner at the White House tonight?"

"Yes."

"Carpathia's the guest of honor. So if Rudd's there, and whoever's representing the Joint Chiefs, and Charley Swelder—" Brad was convinced that Swelder, the president's head policy advisor, was implicated in Ramiro's murder—"you could conceivably have everyone who's after you under the same roof."

The ambulance tilted again as it turned into the emergency entrance of George Washington Hospital. Brad shot Randal a slight smile. "At least it won't be boring."

3

Brad climbed out of the ambulance as the two EMTs guided Randal's gurney through the bay doors of George Washington Hospital. He was tossing the empty food sack into the trash can when he heard his name.

"Brad." Mariette was hurrying down the sidewalk from the waiting-room entrance. Marcus followed at a more leisurely pace. "Brad, how is he?"

"He's going to be fine, Mariette." He put his hands on her shoulders to prevent her from rushing though the doors. "He may have a slight concussion."

"I want to see him."

Marcus shot Brad a dry look. "She's about to take over the hospital."

Brad didn't doubt it. As deputy director of the Federal Emergency Management Agency, Mariette knew how to handle a crisis—and people. She was known as a center of the calm in disaster situations, national tragedies, and potentially fatal crises, but seeing her son thrown to the pavement by an explosion that could have killed the president of the United States had rattled her. "He's all right," Brad said again.

"I want to see him." She met his gaze. "I need to see him."

"Just let the doctor check him out." Brad wrapped an arm around her shoulders and began to guide her back to the waiting room. "I don't think it'll be long."

She hesitated, but finally yielded. Brad glanced at Marcus. "Guess that hedge of protection we talked about this morning was pretty powerful. When did you get the news?"

"Mariette called me not long after it happened."

"I was in a meeting," Mariette explained. "My assistant came in to tell me what was going on." She shuddered. "Have you seen the film?" she asked Brad.

"Not yet. We got the news in the motorcade on the way to the Press Club. As soon as the president finished making his statement, the Service was in a hurry to get him out of there."

"I can imagine," Marcus said.

They entered the emergency room waiting area. The place was packed, Brad noted. He'd be unable to talk freely with his two friends. "I had to take questions at the press conference about the nuclear treaty and the U.S. role," he told them. "So I didn't get back to the White House as quickly as I would have liked." He'd called Mariette en route to let her know that he'd learned Randal was in the infirmary at the White House. He'd asked her to arrange for the ambulance pickup.

Marcus indicated a relatively empty corner of the waiting room by the vending machines. "Over here."

"Maybe I should ask to see the doctor," Mariette said, glancing around the room.

Brad shook his head. "You won't get any answers. They don't take White House patients to the examining rooms down here. He's on the second floor. We've got a doctor on call who handles these things."

"Will he know—"

"Where to find us?" Brad interrupted Mariette's question. "Yes." He gave her shoulders a reassuring squeeze. "It won't take long."

The three friends made their way through the sea of people to the small haven where Brad sank wearily onto a hard chair. "I'm beat," he said, shooting a quick look at his watch.

Marcus glanced around at the disinterested faces in the waiting room. "Is there anything you can tell us?"

"Not here," Brad said. "In the ambulance Randal told me what he knew." He looked at Mariette. "I know it was hard on you letting me have that time with him. Thank you."

"I haven't decided yet what I'm going to make you pay for that," she told him. "It's going to cost you, though."

Brad was relieved to see the spark of humor in his friend's eyes. She'd sounded frantic when he'd spoken to her earlier. Marcus had obviously been a comfort to her. "I'm sure it will."

"Mariette's considering canceling her trip to New York," Marcus informed Brad.

"I don't think you should do that," he told her.

"I've already decided to cancel it," she said.

Mariette's meeting, Brad knew, was with a select group of officials Carpathia was gathering at the UN to form an international relief organization patterned after FEMA. The world was still realizing the global effects of the Rapture, and there were certain areas of the developing world in desperate need of assistance. For reasons no one knew, but that they'd all agreed had to be divinely appointed, Carpathia had invited Mariette, and not her boss, to attend the session.

The group of friends had prayed together over the possibility of her involvement. While she didn't like the idea of working for Carpathia—the man they knew to be the Antichrist—she had also seen the hand of God in placing her in such a strategic position of influence. Today, Brad had learned during the president's meetings with Carpathia that Carpathia was considering tapping Mariette as the head of the new agency.

"Randal can't be home alone," Mariette objected.

"He can stay with me," the two men said simultaneously. Brad shot an amused look at Marcus. "Great minds—besides, aren't you going to New York tomorrow, too?" At Brad's suggestion, Marcus had been asked to represent the United States evangelical denominations at a global religion summit Carpathia was also holding in New York.

"The meeting's been pushed back to Thursday. There were several representatives who were having trouble making it in. Air service is still unpredictable in most of the world."

"It doesn't matter," Mariette insisted. "I'm not leaving Randal alone."

"Mariette—" Brad shifted in his chair—"do you think Randal would want you to miss the meeting just to stay home and baby him? We can handle it."

"This from a man whose idea of a square meal is a can of soup and a bag of pork rinds," she shot back.

She sounded so much like his wife, Christine, at that moment, Brad's heart squeezed in a fist of grief. "How'd you know about that?"

"Because I broke into your secure pantry and took pictures with my infrared camera." She swatted his arm. "Randal told me he picked up groceries for you the other day."

Brad held up his hands. "I promise not to let your kid live off junk food while you're gone." He was glad he hadn't mentioned the stop at the drive-thru on the way to the hospital.

Marcus placed a hand on Mariette's arm. "Randal would be the first to tell you that you need to make that meeting. You know he would."

She looked unconvinced. "I'll have to see how he is first."

With a slight twinge of grief, Brad recognized her expression and her tone as similar to responses he'd received from Christine. Loosely translated, it said, "I'm not really considering this, but I don't want to talk about it anymore." Christine had been among the faithful believers who'd been raptured, and Brad missed her, along with his three children, fiercely.

"Brad?" Marcus was looking at him curiously. "You okay?"

Brad swallowed the sudden knot in his throat. "Fine. Sorry. Just living in the past for a minute."

Before either of his friends could question him, the nurse at the admitting station called Mariette's name. "Mrs. Arnold? Mariette Arnold?"

Mariette jumped up. "Yes. We're here."

"The doctor will see you now." The nurse indicated the elevator with a sweep of her hand. "Second floor, third room on the left."

A commotion outside the door drew Mariette's attention. Several male voices were engaged in a heated conversation. Randal still slept peacefully, his hair a dark tumble against the stark hospital pillowcase. She brushed a curl away from his forehead, then headed for the door. The security guard Marcus had posted there was a member of their church. After consulting with Randal's doctor, Mariette, Brad, and

Marcus had agreed that he should spend the night at the hospital. Mariette had insisted on staying with him. Marcus planned to join her as soon as he could.

Brad had left a half hour ago to shower and change for his requisite attendance at tonight's state dinner at the White House. Marcus had offered to fetch clean clothes and some personal supplies for Mariette and Randal, but no one had felt right about leaving Mariette at the hospital alone. Marcus had provided the solution. He made a quick phone call to a young man who was a newly baptized member of the church he pastored—the church where Mariette, Randal, and Brad all attended. A former bouncer in a local bar, Nero Jefferson had lost his young wife and their two-year-old daughter, his mother, and two sisters in the Rapture. Grief-stricken, devastated, and terrified, he had turned to the church for answers. His mother had been a member of Marcus's downtown D.C. congregation before her disappearance.

After meeting with Marcus several times, Nero had prayed to receive Christ as his Savior and been baptized the following Sunday. Determined to put his old life behind him, he'd quit his job at the trendy Georgetown bar on Monday morning. Still unemployed, he'd welcomed Marcus's call—for both the income and the opportunity to help members of his new church family. At a towering six feet six inches, with a heavily muscled physique, a shaved head, and a gold hoop earring, he looked like a charming, amiable Mr. Clean.

She'd hugged him fiercely when he'd knocked on the door of Randal's hospital room and informed her he was there to make sure her son spent an uninterrupted night. Not for the first time since the Rapture and the weeks that followed, Mariette had marveled at the way the dramatic events had turned her life upside down. She now had a cir-

cle of brothers and sisters in Christ that included men like
Nero Jefferson, and she was closer to them than she had
ever been to the social and political circles she'd maintained during her years in Washington.

Now, as she approached the door, she heard the low
rumble of Nero's bass voice denying someone entry to the
room. "I don't care if you're Julius Caesar," he was saying as
Mariette pulled open the door. "That boy is sleeping and
you're not going in."

Mariette swallowed hard as her eyes adjusted to the
harsher hallway lighting. Standing in a tight semicircle
around Nero were three of the most powerful men in the
universe: President Gerald Fitzhugh; his chief policy advisor, Charley Swelder; and Nicolae Carpathia. *Like an unholy
trinity*, Mariette thought with a shudder as she looked beyond the tuxedo-clad trio to quickly scan the bevy of Secret
Service agents who prowled the corridor looking slightly
flustered. Several nurses looked nervously on as the confrontation unfolded. Only Nero appeared unimpressed.

Mariette took a deep breath and edged around him.
"Problems?" She met Charley Swelder's gaze. "Hello, Charley."

"Mariette," he said tightly. "I'm glad you're here." He indicated the president with a wave of his hand. "I believe
you've met President Fitzhugh."

"Yes."

Gerald Fitzhugh gave her hand a vigorous shake. "Good
to see you again, Mariette. I understand you've had your
hands full over there at FEMA. Bernie's been keeping us
apprised."

"I'm sure he has," she said dryly. Her boss, Bernie
Musselman, had made no secret of his political aspirations
or his lack of interest in the day-to-day operations of the
agency.

"I don't think you've met Secretary-General Carpathia," Charley continued.

Nicolae Carpathia stepped forward, his blue eyes full of charm, his handsome face the picture of humility. "Mrs. Arnold, I am such an admirer of your work." He took her hand in both of his. "I was looking forward to meeting with you and the other members of the relief-agency formation team this week. I had hoped it would be under happier circumstances."

Mariette slid her hand from his grip and fought the urge to wipe it on her slacks. "Me, too," she said.

Charley gave his watch a meaningful and obvious look. "The president and the secretary-general wanted to express their appreciation to Randal for his heroism this afternoon." He looked at Nero with disdain. "We managed to jam a trip over here into the meeting schedule this evening."

"I appreciate that," Mariette assured him.

Nicolae's expression was a mask of concern. "How is your son?" he pressed. "I understand he was thrown to the pavement by the blast."

"He's resting."

"Surely he can stand a two-minute visit," Charley insisted.

From the corner of her eye, Mariette saw Nero's jaw tighten. "You know," she said, "I'm so flattered that you came by—"

"I insisted," Nicolae said. "My good friend President Fitzhugh suggested that he might not be well enough to receive us, but I was so impressed by his bravery today. I wanted to offer my personal thanks."

The president spoke up. "I told you, Carpathia, that my only concern was that our report from the hospital said he wasn't receiving visitors."

Nicolae tipped his head apologetically. "Forgive me. I

did not mean to insinuate that you did not wish to come. My English sometimes fails me." He met Mariette's gaze. "What I meant to say was that Fitz warned me that we might not be able to see Randal, but I thought I would like to try."

Mariette was thankful for the solid, warm presence of Nero behind her. Despite Nicolae's charm, she felt a decided chill as she realized exactly why he was so dangerous. Had she not known who he was and the evil he perpetrated, she could have easily fallen for his casually elegant charm. "He's resting," she told them. "The doctor has decided to keep him overnight just to be sure he's okay. It's probably only a mild concussion, but we're not sure."

Charley looked at his watch again. "We'll only need a moment."

Two of the Secret Service agents near the nurses' station began to approach them. Mariette recognized the man with them, who had a large camera around his neck, as a member of the White House Press Corps. "So you thought you'd turn it into a photo op?" she asked Charley.

"For the love of—" Charley wiped a hand through his thinning hair. "Everything in this town is a photo op, Mariette. You know how this works."

"Randal's not up to receiving visitors," she said. Behind her, she felt Nero shift and cross his broad arms over his chest.

"It'll take thirty seconds," Charley insisted. "I'm sure you realize what a sacrifice this is for the president and the secretary-general."

"I'm not going to let you turn my son into a campaign ad," Mariette shot back.

"You're being unreasonable." Charley took a step closer. "I think you should consider the political consequences—"

"All right, all right," Fitzhugh grumbled. "Back down, Charley. We knew we might not see Randal."

Mariette recoiled when the pop of the cameraman's flash momentarily blinded her. "I'm sorry." She had to stifle a laugh at Charley's threat of political consequences. With any luck, the consequences would be so dire that she'd get out of her scheduled trip to New York to meet with Nicolae's United Nations relief team. "I really can't let you see him."

"Mariette," Charley grated out, "I'm sure we could get clearance from his doctor. We're wasting time. We've got a state dinner in less than an hour."

"You might get clearance from his doctor," she assured him, "but you're not getting it from me. He's heavily drugged. He's out cold. And he needs his rest." She looked disdainfully at the photographer, who snapped another picture. "Not fifteen minutes of fame."

Nicolae's laugh was soft. "You know, my mother would have done the same thing. Any mother would." He held up both his hands in a conciliatory gesture. "Just assure us you will pass on our thanks to your son and let him know we are in his debt. Hmmm?"

"Of course."

Nicolae looked at a clearly irritated Fitz Fitzhugh and an enraged Charley Swelder. "My conscience is assuaged, gentlemen," he told them. "I have paid my respects. I am ready to get back to work." He clapped an arm around the president's shoulders. "We still have some details to work out on the Jerusalem issue. Perhaps we can settle that matter on the ride back to the White House so we both can relax at dinner tonight."

The two men started down the hall followed by several Secret Service agents and the photographer who was busily snapping photos.

Charley remained behind. "The political stakes have never been higher, Mariette. I'd think that you of all people would understand that." As a high-level political operative, Charley had enjoyed a front-row seat to the spectacle of Mariette's divorce from Senator Max Arnold. He knew exactly what kind of price she'd paid for playing with political fire.

"I do, but that doesn't mean I'm going to put my son at risk."

"He's a hero. He deserves a little recognition."

She couldn't suppress a bitter laugh. "He doesn't deserve to be used as a political bargaining chip or a public relations campaign."

"Get smart, Mariette. He could use this as his ticket up if he wanted to."

"He doesn't."

"Don't make that decision for him."

"I'm his mother. Right now, it's my right and my responsibility. When he's well, he can decide for himself."

Charley looked like he wanted to argue, but Nero leaned forward and gave him a shrewd look. "The lady asked you to leave." His deep voiced seemed to rumble down the corridor.

Charley frowned but backed away. "At least your gatekeeper is doing his job," he said. "Don't be surprised if this costs you later."

"I won't."

Charley nodded to the remaining Secret Service agent, and the two hurried down the hallway in the direction of the elevator.

Mariette exhaled a long breath and turned to face Nero. "Thanks. I'm not sure I could have handled that without you."

He shrugged his broad shoulders. "I didn't do much, Ms. Arnold. Just looked mean and stood my ground."

She managed a slight smile. "Well, it worked. You got rid of them."

"You know," he said, "I don't got a lot of education, but I know bad manners when I see 'em. My ma used to say that the only difference between a gentleman and a jerk was lack of home training, not lack of breeding."

Mariette laughed. "I suppose that's true."

Nero tipped his head toward the door. "So you go on inside and take care of Randal. Nobody but the reverend, Mr. Benton, or the doctor is coming through this door without coming through me first."

She laid a hand on his forearm. "Thank you, Nero. You're a good friend."

"Randal's my brother," he said with a slight shrug. "I'd do it whether you or the reverend paid me or not."

Randal had taken an interest in Nero since his baptism. Marcus had asked Randal to play a role in discipling Nero, so the two young men had met regularly to study the Bible together. "He feels the same way about you," Mariette assured him.

Nero nodded. "I know he does. I'm just thankful to Jesus that he's all right."

"Me, too," Mariette told him. "Me, too."

★ ★ ★

Brad snapped on the desk lamp in his office. Daylight Savings Time was still two weeks away, and the sun still set fairly early. The only illumination in the office came from the ever-present lights that lined Pennsylvania Avenue and lit the Ellipse.

Once he'd left the hospital, he'd used the White House

locker-room facilities to shower and change into his tuxedo for tonight's state dinner. Given the buzz of activity downstairs, the last-minute scurrying of the White House staff to prepare before the guests began to arrive, and the inevitable hustle of the press office, Brad knew no one would be looking for him. His opinion on the day's events couldn't be more irrelevant to members of the Fitzhugh administration.

He paused for a moment to pick up the picture of Christine he had on his desk. She had been so beautiful, with her warm smile and the laughter that always seemed to light her eyes. During their marriage, Brad had often wondered what gave Christine that spark that had first drawn him to her—where she had found that inner light that made her so appealing. Only now that he'd accepted Jesus as his personal Lord and Savior did he understand. Christine's inner light had been the person of Christ living inside her. *"I myself no longer live,"* the apostle Paul had written, *"but Christ lives in me."*

"I'm going to try not to fail you again," he told the picture. "This time, I'm going to get it right, sweetheart."

He rubbed his thumb over the glass that covered her face. How he longed to touch her, to laugh with her, to feel the comfort of her arms wrapped around his waist. Brad closed his eyes and fought tears. Lately, they'd begun to flow easily. Every night when he went home to the sterile little suite he'd rented since the blast had destroyed his apartment, loneliness rushed over him in a flood of longing. He found some comfort in knowing that the Bible said this separation from his family was only for a little while—that, at the very most, he had just seven years to wait until he could spend eternity with them.

Seven years of this tense, miserable existence with danger behind ever corner; fear, anxiety, and what he was beginning to think was paranoia, driving him forward. Brad shuddered and gently placed the picture down on his desk. What he'd told no one was that he would have welcomed the opportunity to die in that explosion today. The blast would have killed him instantly, sending him straight to the presence of God and the welcoming arms of his wife and kids. Then all this would be over.

But God wasn't through with him yet, or at least that's what Marcus would say. There was a secret part of Brad that wondered if the real truth was that God wasn't through making him pay for all the years he'd lived in rebellion, refusing to surrender his heart to the Lord.

The thought filled him with guilt. God had cared for him enough to sacrifice His Son to save Brad's sorry soul. How could he question God's perfect love and timing for his life? Deliberately, he shook off his melancholy and crossed to the small safe in his office. This was getting him nowhere, and he since he'd pulled Randal and Liza and Emma into this circle, he owed it to them to see things through.

He pulled the documents he wanted from the safe and carried them back to his desk. For the next hour, he'd search for whatever clues he could find—connections, evidence, anything that would tell him who had pulled the trigger and murdered George Ramiro and, more importantly, who had taken photos of George's body and sent them to Brad. Why had someone wanted him to know that George had been killed and not merely disappeared in the Rapture? That question haunted him more than all the others.

★   ★   ★

"How is he?" Isack Moore asked Marcus as he watched Marcus pack his briefcase full of the day's correspondence and most pressing issues demanding his attention.

"Banged up," Marcus told him, "but generally all right. The Lord spared him." He didn't miss the tightening of Isack's jaw.

Of all the members of his staff and ministry who had missed the Rapture, Isack was clinging most stubbornly to his anger and bitterness against the Lord and against Marcus. He had not yet forgiven Marcus for deceiving his followers, and held him at least partially responsible for the loss of his wife and children. "I'm glad to hear he's okay. I'm sure his mother was worried."

Marcus tossed the final file into his briefcase, then picked up a stack of pink phone messages. He began to quickly sort them. "She is. Brad Benton and I are still trying to persuade her not to cancel her trip to New York."

"If it were my kid," Isack said, "I'd want to stay here until I knew he was well."

Marcus didn't point out all the times that the business of the ministry had taken them all out of town, the times that he knew Isack had missed his kids' piano recitals, soccer games, and church plays because he'd been on "the Lord's business." Too late, Marcus had discovered that the business of the Lord was not enough to secure a man's place in eternity, and that God would have been the first to tell a man like Isack Moore—and like Marcus Dumont—to make sure their priorities were in place. "I believe he's going to stay with Brad for a couple of days," he told Isack as he continued to look through the phone messages. "Randal's got a mild concussion, but nothing more serious. I think after tonight, Mariette will realize—"

He stopped abruptly when he came upon a message from Sanura Kyle, the attorney Brad had recommended to him to defend him against Theopolus Carter's lawsuit. Theo Carter, Marcus's former attorney, had filed a civil suit on behalf of the families of some of Marcus's high-dollar

donors alleging that the monies their relatives had willed
the ministry before the Rapture had been gained under
false pretenses. Now that the courts had ruled that insurance
companies must treat the disappearances as deaths and pay
out on life insurance policies, New Covenant Ministries
stood to gain hundreds of millions of dollars in estate set-
tlements if the court ruled in their favor.

Marcus folded the message and slipped it into his shirt
pocket with a twinge of guilt. Sanura had, thus far, provided
excellent counsel. Her legal brilliance had successfully
negotiated Marcus's ministry through the stickier parts of
the case, but Marcus had been avoiding her for personal
reasons. The attractive young attorney whom Brad knew
from the White House was nearly twenty years younger
than he, and Marcus had been distinctly uncomfortable
with the almost immediate kinship he'd felt to her. She was
too young, he was too old, and the world was far too unset-
tled for him to even contemplate something as ill advised
and ill timed as a personal relationship with the woman.

Worse, he had been forced to admit that he'd deliberately
shut his heart and his mind to the possibility of companionship since losing his wife to cancer several years ago. No
matter what Brad said, he wasn't ready to consider what
role Sanura Kyle might have in his life.

But her message was marked *urgent*, and Marcus felt like
a coward for avoiding her for so long. Tonight, he'd call her
from the hospital—which, he admitted to himself, was no
less cowardly. He could hardly have a personal conversation with the woman while he sat by Randal's bed and kept
Mariette company. "Coward," he muttered.

"What?" Isack asked him.

Marcus shook his head. "Nothing. Nothing important."
He finished sorting the messages and picked up his briefcase. "I think that's everything."

"You're headed to the hospital?"

"I'm going to sit with Mariette tonight."

"I see."

Marcus studied the younger man for a moment. The deep-rooted anger was still there, causing the lines at the side of his mouth to deepen. "Isack—I've been busy the last couple of days getting ready for the trip to New York, but you know my door is always open to you."

"Of course."

Marcus set the briefcase on his desk. "Is there something we need to talk about?"

"No, Marcus." Isack crossed his arms over his chest. "There's definitely nothing for you and me to talk about."

Marcus drew a weary breath. "Since the White House asked me to participate in this religious meeting in New York, you've seemed . . . frustrated."

"I don't know why you'd say that."

That won a slight smile from Marcus. "You've worked for me long enough that I know a few of your habits. When we've got a big speech coming up, or some kind of event, you've got a lot of responsibility. The closer the event comes, the more your tension level rises." He paused. "And the more your tension level rises, the more you pace in front of your desk. Velma tells me you've just about worn a hole in the carpet this week."

Isack dropped his gaze. "I've got a lot on my mind."

"You don't want me to go to New York, do you?"

Several seconds of tense silence ticked by. When Isack met Marcus's gaze again, his eyes burned with anger. "I don't want you to go to New York and embarrass yourself and us by looking like a religious zealot. What are you going to tell them? That if they'd listened to you before, they wouldn't be in this mess, but now, since they didn't and you didn't either, the only choice they have is to believe we've all got seven years of horror and disaster left before God wipes us off the face of the planet? They'll laugh you right out of the UN for that, Marcus."

"I hadn't planned on putting it quite like that. . . ."

"Do you think this is funny? You know, a year ago, this is exactly the kind of opportunity you'd have wanted. You would have had all of us working on this twenty-four hours a day. We'd have been lobbying every senator and congressman we know to get you an invitation to this meeting. The exposure. The publicity. The prestige. You would have wanted all of it."

"Yes," Marcus admitted, "that's probably true."

"And now that you have it—now that it was *handed* to you, you're going to go and make a fool of yourself."

"I have to tell the truth, Isack."

His lips twisted bitterly. "You never felt that way before."

Marcus accepted the accusation as his due. "I always told the truth," he said softly. "I just didn't choose to surrender my life to Christ. I knew the truth then just as I do now. I chose this path."

"But what about the rest of us?" Isack burst out. "Where does that leave us?" He muttered something beneath his breath and stalked across the office to the window where he stared out at the city. "Is it easy for you to stay up here in your tower and rain down judgment on the rest of us?"

"Isack—"

"I mean, really, what has this cost you? You didn't lose a family. You didn't even have to face your friends and tell them you'd been a liar and a cheat for the past thirty years. You got it all, Marcus. The money, the power, the fame—everything you ever wanted. You got every bit of it." Isack turned on him, his face a mask of hurt. "And it didn't cost you anything, did it?"

Marcus briefly closed his eyes and prayed for wisdom.

Isack was among the few remaining members of his staff who had not been raptured. And, like all of Marcus's remaining people, Isack had lost family and friends in the Rapture. That night he'd railed at Marcus for deceiving them all. A part of Isack still blamed Marcus for not holding him accountable for his faith. After all, even though Marcus had preached the truth, he had not believed it himself. Isack had a point, in a way. If Marcus had believed, he would have disappeared with all the believers. "I suppose you could look at it that way," he admitted.

Since his wife had died, Marcus had made a point of emotionally cloistering himself. Until he'd been forced to turn outward after the Rapture, he'd had no close friends and no family. His personal grief and loss had been minimal. "I didn't lose anyone close to me."

"My wife is gone, Marcus," Isack choked out. "My kids—every night I go home to an empty apartment. My mother, my sisters, everyone I cared about. I've got no one left. But you—you keep telling us that the book of Revelation is all about hope, that we're supposed to see God's great plan and love for mankind in all of this. That a God who would allow this kind of suffering isn't really just some mean-spirited bully who enjoys making us miserable." He shook his head. "I'm sorry, Marcus, but I don't see a whole lot of hope in all this. We've got seven years to live—isn't that what you said? And those seven years are supposed to be full of terror and disaster? Where's the hope in that?"

"I'm sorry," Marcus said. "I'm sorry for your loss. I'm sorry for your grief. I'm sorry I wasn't a better friend and pastor to you before all this happened. I'm sorry I failed you, and I'm sorry I failed to be the man I should have been." He wiped a hand over his face. "If I hadn't been so stubborn and spent the better part of my life shaking my fist at God, I could have been a better man."

Isack turned back to the window.

Lord, Marcus prayed silently, *he needs You. He needs to know You care about him. Help me show him that.* "But I wasn't," he said aloud. "I failed you. I failed every person who believed in this ministry and what I claimed to be about. I failed my staff, I failed myself, and I failed God. And I guess to answer your question, that's what it cost me: I had to come face-to-face with the fact that I had no one to blame but myself for the fact that I was publicly humiliated into admitting that I'd been a fraud for my entire adult life—that'd I'd used God and His Word as an economic and personal opportunity. I have to look myself in the mirror every morning and know that I failed people like you, Isack, that because of my arrogance, I failed to care enough about you to make sure you had a personal relationship with Christ."

Isack didn't answer. In the window, Marcus saw the reflection of his angry young face. He crossed the room to stand next to him. "When I look at this city," he told Isack, "I see all those hurting people, people who desperately need to know that God is still in control of this world, and that there's an end to this pain.

"But I also see a city filled with evil men who are serving the forces of darkness. The view out this window hasn't changed that much since the Rapture, but what I see is dramatically different. The world is different."

He put a hand on Isack's shoulder. "We no longer have the luxury of riding the fence. We're going to have a brief window of peace—about eighteen months—to choose one side or the other. Either we will spend what time we have left living for God, or we will marry our souls to Satan. I have no idea how many more breaths God is going to allow me to draw before He takes me home," he admitted. "Frankly, I don't understand His grace or why He'd let me have this second chance. In His shoes, I don't think I could have been so forgiving of a man like me, but in whatever time I have left, I plan to do all I can to atone for squandering the better part of my life. God loves me enough to give me that chance. I don't want to waste it."

Isack remained perfectly still, his eyes fixed on the city. "Then I guess that's where we disagree, Marcus. I don't see this as a second chance. The fact that God stripped everyone from me and left me here to deal with this—" he finally looked at Marcus, his eyes fathomless and hollow. "It's worse than dying. It's like dying all over again every morning. There's no relief from it. There's no way out."

Marcus's heart clenched at the despair in the other man's voice. "God will give you hope if you'll let Him, Isack. But you've got to let go of this anger."

The bitterness returned to Isack's gaze. "It's like you said; God may be full of grace and willing to forgive, but I don't think I am. I don't have it in me."

Marcus studied his friend a moment longer, then dropped his hand. "All I can do is pray that God will help you see your way through that. Whatever you're feeling, He can handle listening to it. He won't turn His back on you simply because you rail at Him. If that were the way He worked, He'd have given up on me years ago."

"I'm through railing," Isack said, his tone bleak. "I don't have any more fight in me."

"Isack—"

He held up a hand. "Forget it, Marcus. I'm sorry I bothered you with this. You've got enough on your mind."

"It's not a bother."

The shudder that ran through Isack reminded Marcus of a dog shaking off water. "Well, it's not going to get solved tonight anyway." Isack turned away from the window. "One of those files in your briefcase has your speech notes for your trip to New York. If you have a chance, you should probably go over them."

Marcus studied him closely. "What are your plans for the next few days?"

Isack's laugh was harsh. "The same as they always are. I'm going to work. That's what I do. It's what keeps me sane and makes me get up in the morning."

"If you don't want to go home alone tonight, you're welcome to come sit with us at the hospital. I know it's not ideal—"

Isack shook his head. "Forget it. I'll be fine. I've got a frozen dinner and a date with cable TV waiting for me."

Marcus still hesitated. He didn't like the look of utter hopelessness that seemed to have settled over Isack. "Just promise me you'll call someone if you start to feel overwhelmed."

"What? Do you think I'm going to do myself in or something? I promise you, Marcus, I'm not that desperate. I'm just angry."

"I need your word, Isack."

"Sure. Whatever."

"You have my cell-phone number."

"Yes."

"And Velma is concerned about you too," he said, referring to the young woman from their bookkeeping office whose husband and infant son had vanished in the Rapture. "You know she is."

"Yeah."

"If you're not willing to turn to God for comfort, then at least turn to the people who care about you. None of us should have to go through this alone."

Isack wiped a hand through his hair. "Look, Marcus, I'm

okay. You asked me what I thought, and I told you. Yes, I'm frustrated that you're going to New York and probably undo years of work on our part. Yes, I'm frustrated that you're going to make us look like fools to the world. Yes, I'm angry that we're all going through this horror while you seem to have gotten off scot-free. And frankly, you're not going to talk me out of any of it." He shook his head in exasperation. "Look, I'm sure Mrs. Arnold is waiting for you at the hospital. Go be a good friend to someone who cares, Marcus. Because I'm not sure I do anymore."

Marcus watched Isack stalk out of the office. He closed his eyes and dropped his head against the cool glass of the window. *Lord, I'm so worried about him. I can't reach him. Only You can reach him. Please watch over him, protect him, and send someone his way who can help him through this.*

From the corner of his eye, Brad saw Harvey Mellman, the White House chief usher, hurry through the State Dining Room, his expression intent. That was never a good sign. Something was wrong in the kitchen or somewhere, and it was Harvey's job to fix it.

Brad took several deep breaths and schooled his face into a careful mask of indifference. White House staff and the press were already beginning to speculate on why the president and Carpathia had not yet descended from the residence, and he knew the moment he made his way into the crowd, he'd be expected to have answers. No one, he expected, would want to hear the answers he had. After nearly an hour of poring over the information in his office, he was now virtually certain who was responsible for George Ramiro's death: Victor Rudd.

In the weeks before his death, George had evidently

seen the same evidence Liza was sending Brad that implicated Rudd and Kostankis in an international plot to use
U.S. gold reserves to finance covert military operations in
Abkhazia—a region of the former Soviet Republic of Geor-
gia. There, in the small town of Sukhumi, a former Soviet
nuclear research facility still held uranium deposits and a
stockpile of nuclear weapons. An ethnic rebellion in the
area had temporarily given control of the facility to Hizb
ut-Tahrir al-Islami, an Islamic extremist group with strong
sympathies toward several international terrorist groups.
Currently, rebel fighters were struggling to regain control of
the region, but with limited resources and waning international support, the war was turning into a long and bloody
conflict.

The U.S. had been monitoring the situation closely, but
many Pentagon and congressional officials felt that the
Fitzhugh administration had remained too long on the
fence. Already, several top-level Soviet arms inspectors
claimed they could not verify if any of the uranium had
gone missing. Though Congress had steadfastly refused to
authorize any action in the area, George had somehow discovered that Rudd, Kostankis, and several other top-level
officials had taken the matter into their own hands by fi-
nancing the rebels with U.S. gold reserves from the South
Range facility.

Kostankis had used his international shipping and
banking contacts to effect the transfer, while Rudd covered
the movement of the gold bullion inside U.S. territory. The
plan had been to replace the gold reserve once the coup
succeeded by using profits from the sale of the uranium to
legitimate sources, but, like Brad, George had not yet
pieced together which White House, Pentagon, and maybe
congressional insiders had made the illegal transfers possible. Who had initiated the deal, who had known about it,

and who was going to be implicated when it fell apart? Those questions had gotten George killed.

According to the notes Brad had received from Jane Lyons, on the day of his death George had met Major Nuñez for an early morning run near the Pentagon grounds. Nuñez must have given George some crucial evidence against top-level Pentagon officials that tied them to the illegal operation. That evidence was not anywhere in the information Jane had supplied, nor did Brad find any names in Gray Wells's files. Colonel Wells, Brad suspected, had stumbled on the plot when he began investigating what had happened to the military flight Brad had boarded last week in California. No one at the Pentagon had a record of the flight, nor was there any evidence of a C-5 Galaxy transport plane experiencing mechanical difficulties or crash-landing in the Midwest, yet Brad had narrowly escaped with his life when he was pushed out of the plane.

He was now certain that the flight had been yet another attempt to kill him and stop his investigation into George Ramiro's death. With the world now in financial and military chaos, Brad wasn't surprised that Rudd and his supporters were feeling desperate. If they knew what he did—that Nicolae Carpathia had murdered two of his key supporters in cold blood for reasons that still remained a mystery—their anxiety would no doubt heighten. With a psychotic killer soon to rule the world, Rudd, Kostankis, and the like weren't going to want to find themselves on the wrong side of justice.

"Brad." Forrest Tetherton, Ramiro's successor as Fitzhugh's press secretary, brought a hand down on Brad's shoulder. Brad flinched. Forrest looked at him through narrowed eyes. "Any idea what's keeping them? They're not still haggling over who's going to sit where at the treaty signing next week, are they?"

Brad grabbed a water glass from a passing waiter, using the excuse to shrug Forrest's hand away. "I don't know," he admitted. "I think the president is still holding out for several promises of U.S. oversight into some of Carpathia's initiatives."

"Still?" Forrest darted a nervous glance around the room. "I thought we'd agreed earlier today that POTUS was going to chair the Disarmament Committee."

Brad squelched an irritated sigh. POTUS was an acronym for President of the United States. White House insiders like Tetherton tended to use the acronym as a way of stressing their access to the president and the Oval Office. Brad thought clarity was more important than status, so he rarely used the acronym. "They did, but there's more at stake here than the Disarmament Committee. The secretary-general hasn't budged on the issue of consolidating global currency, and we're not going to commit to that until we know it won't affect the strength of the dollar," Brad responded.

He caught sight of Harvey Mellman again. The man had emerged from the kitchen hallway and was deep in conversation with one of the protocol officers. Brad indicated the scene to Forrest. "Something's wrong."

Tetherton glanced at the chief usher. "I'll say. The protocol office is having fits over the seating arrangement. Carpathia's the guest of honor, but there's no protocol to determine precedence for seating."

Brad felt the tension in his neck building. Upstairs, decisions were being made that would change the course of human history. Here in the White House, men who had murdered at least two White House officials—and possibly plotted to assassinate the president himself—were milling about in relative freedom. On the international stage, a plot that could possibly put nuclear-ready uranium into the hands of terrorists and dictators was being played out. And the chief concern in the dining room was whether the Antichrist should sit to the president's left or right. Brad lost what remained of his patience. "Excuse me," he told Forrest, "I need some air."

In long strides, Brad made his way across the dining room toward the long hallway that led to the terrace. At moments like this, his isolation at the White House oppressed him. Painfully aware that he could trust no one, that somewhere in this building were men who wanted him dead, his soul ached as he thought of the warm circle of fellowship at Mariette's house tonight where Marcus, Mariette, and Randal were praying earnestly for his safety and well-being.

His heart twisted as he thought of Christine, how much he would like to have her on his arm tonight, how he hoped—*prayed*—that he'd given her a reason to be proud of him. He missed her. He missed his kids. He felt the sting of tears as he slipped outside into the chilly night air. For reasons he couldn't define, he'd felt the loss of his wife and kids more acutely in the last two days than he had in the weeks since the Rapture. A mantle of depression had settled on his soul, and Brad was increasingly aware that he didn't have the strength to face what lay ahead. Only God could get him through that. Beneath his breath, he quoted, "For I can do everything with the help of Christ who gives me the strength I need." He and Marcus had discussed the verse— and the way Brad was learning to embrace it—this morning on their daily run through Rock Creek Park.

The acrid scent of a clove cigar carried on the night air and intruded on his thoughts. The unmistakable scent assailed Brad's memories and sent his adrenaline racing. He knew only one man who smoked clove cigars and had a reason to be at the White House tonight. He gathered his composure and turned to face Victor Rudd. "Victor. I didn't see you earlier."

Rudd was leaning against a column, his face partially concealed in the shadows. "That was intentional." Rudd took a long puff of his cigar and the orange glow illuminated the harsh angles of his face. He looked like a man, Brad thought, who wouldn't hesitate to murder an enemy. Victor regarded Brad through narrowed eyes. "I always head straight for the bar at these blasted things. I can't get through the night without a scotch or two under my belt."

Rudd's face told the story of exactly how he'd become one of the most powerful men in the world. With razor-sharp features, piercing gray eyes, and a perpetual down-turn at the corner of his mouth, he'd let greed, cynicism, and ruthless business acumen forge his worldview as well as his success. Though Brad had met him several times before, and had never particularly liked him, he'd never sensed menace in him. Had he been deliberately blinded by Victor's well-publicized charitable contributions and his well-documented support of political allies?

Marcus called this new awareness Brad felt a sense of discernment, something the Holy Spirit had gifted him with after he'd accepted Christ as his Savior. Whatever it was, his heart was pumping so hard now, he could hear the pulse in his ears. He schooled his expression to remain neutral even as he considered that the man standing barely three feet away might easily be the one who'd ordered the attempts on his life. "I can sympathize with the sentiment," Brad told him, "if not the methodology. I'd rather be home mowing my grass than enduring one of these dinners." He slipped a finger beneath the collar of his shirt and tugged at the band of his bow tie. His clothes felt suddenly hot and constricting. He resisted the urge to shoot a quick glance over his shoulder to see if the marine standing guard seemed aware that Brad was facing a potential murderer.

Rudd dropped the cigar to the pavement where he ground the orange embers with his patent-leather-clad foot. "This one's worse than most." He leveled a knowing look at Brad. "As you probably know, I've got more riding on it."

There was an unmistakable threat in his tone. Brad didn't doubt that Victor was feeling the pressure of the evening. As Brad's investigation had begun to hone in on the most likely suspects, Victor had certainly grown increasingly nervous. Exposure would mean financial and political ruin. Victor would face the threat of a congressional inquiry and even imprisonment if found guilty of defrauding Congress and conspiring to illegally use U.S. gold reserves. For that matter, even if he weren't referring to the investigation, he still faced a potential partnership with the Antichrist that offered a one-way ticket to hell. How much higher could the stakes be? "Oh?" Brad asked.

"Hmm. Believe it or not, I've got enemies here."

And friends. Friends and allies who'd murder for him if necessary. "Fitz is one of your biggest fans," Brad countered.

"As long as I benefit him politically and financially. And Fitz is only as good as his staff anyway. Got to tell you, Benton, there aren't but a couple of 'em I'd even consider hiring to work for me. Useless, lazy, and self-impressed. That pretty much sums up Fitz's crew."

Rudd shook his head as he folded his arms across his chest. "I didn't get where I am in business by trusting anyone but myself." He flicked a speck of lint from his immaculate black sleeve.

Brad noted the man's perfectly manicured fingernails with a sense of irony. His life, the fate of the U.S., and the future hung in the balance, and Brad found himself suddenly entertaining a long-forgotten memory from childhood that seemed to perfectly sum up the moment.

He'd never been close to his father. The salt-of-the-earth North Carolina farmer had died before Brad's fourteenth birthday, but Brad had never forgotten the day his father— a deacon at their church—had come home from a meeting of the pastoral search committee. They'd interviewed a new candidate that night, and Thomas Benton's only answer to his wife's queries had been, "When a man has profession-ally manicured fingernails, you just have to wonder how well he'd do in a crisis."

Thomas Benton was just one of the few people Brad was looking forward to getting to know better when he finally made it to heaven. Looking at Victor Rudd now, he recalled his father's assessment of that preacher they hadn't hired and figured his father had probably made the right call. Vic-tor wasn't a man to dirty his hands. When he'd needed to murder George Ramiro and Gray Wells, he'd gotten some-one else to do the deed for him. Brad wouldn't even be sur-prised to learn that Victor had no personal knowledge of the details. Men like Rudd didn't leave themselves open to prosecution by getting involved in the day-to-day racket of their organization. They paid someone else for that.

Victor was not only a ruthless self-preservationist, but a shrewd and practical businessman who knew how to con-trol his organization and his supporters.

Brad took a deep breath as he prayed for wisdom. "So what's your agenda tonight, Victor?"

Rudd gave him a knowing look. "Same agenda I always have. To look out for me, my interests, and my future." *And*, his cold gaze said wordlessly, *to make sure no one stands in my way.*

"Everyone seems to agree that the future lies with Nicolae Carpathia and his initiatives. Even the people who don't agree with him can't deny that he's holding most of the cards right now."

Rudd swore softly. "Seems like it," he conceded. "But I've got to tell you, he may be a hit with the peace-loving tree huggers and the media's star of the month, but there's not a lot of profit in peace on earth. Believe it or not, the man's got enemies."

And he dispenses with them, Brad thought, remembering Joshua Todd-Cothran and Jonathan Stonagal, *with a cold-blooded precision even Victor would have to admire.* At least Victor Rudd and his war-loving friends could take comfort in the news that the world was now facing an impending disaster of unimaginable proportions. The business of war was about to enter a bull market. "Do you think so?" Brad asked. "It seems to me that Carpathia's public-relations team is getting their job done. We haven't seen this kind of fervor surrounding a state visit in decades."

"I've got a multibillion-dollar empire that depends on the business of war. I think you can understand why an international peace treaty that turns Jerusalem over to the Israelis and tosses all the nukes into the sun for inciner-ation isn't my idea of a profit center."

"You probably aren't alone in that."

"But you want to know what really burns me?" Victor took a step closer. Brad stood his ground. "Do you have any idea how much money I've given Fitz in the last twenty years?"

"Roughly," Brad said. "I've seen the campaign finance reports."

Rudd's laugh was unpleasant. "More than the FEC knows, I'll tell you that much. I made that man who he is. Swelder would still be running city-council campaigns in Vermont if it weren't for me and my money." Rudd crossed his arms over his chest. "And when I need one simple thing, one problem to go away, I can't count on Swelder to take care of it."

"You ought to know," Brad told him; "in politics, problems can take on a life of their own."

"This one needs to die a quick death," Victor shot back. His gaze narrowed. "I thought I had it taken care of, but somebody is intent on digging up the past."

"Oh?"

"And evidently, I haven't made it clear enough that I'm not going to let anyone in the White House take me down. I was around before Fitz was elected, and I'll still be around when he's got his feet propped up in his presidential library. Are you following me?"

"Am I supposed to feel threatened?"

"Do you?"

"No," Brad assured him.

"Interesting." Victor gave him a speculative look. "I can't quite figure you out, Benton, you know that?"

"I'm not so complicated."

"What I can't figure is if you're here to cover for Fitz's indiscretions, or if you're here to be his conscience."

"I'm my own man. I'm here to do whatever I feel led to do. Whatever God calls me to do."

Disdain registered on Rudd's face. "That kind of thinking can get you in trouble." He paused. "George Ramiro used to think like that."

Brad went perfectly still. "What about George?"

"He liked to dig around," Victor said. "Asked a lot of questions that weren't his business. Had trouble leaving well enough alone."

"Then you're probably glad he's gone."

Rudd shrugged. "Doesn't matter to me either way. Some underling like Ramiro isn't going to stand in my way simply because he gets a yen to change the world." Victor leaned closer to him. "In fact, I'd have to say just about nobody stands in my way."

Brad didn't miss the implied warning. "Maybe," he said, "but I guess I've got a little of George in me. Once I start looking for answers, I can't stop. It's who I am. I don't change that for anyone."

"It could kill you, you know—that kind of thinking."

"Maybe. But at least I can live with myself knowing I did the right thing."

Victor's laugh was harsh. "That's rich, Benton. You might be six feet under but your conscience will be clean."

"Something like that."

"Then let me make one thing perfectly clear. If I think my business is threatened, I can be ruthless in protecting my interests. I'd advise you to remember that."

"I will," Brad assured him. Coming from the dining room, the distinct sounds of "Hail to the Chief" sounded. Brad tipped his head toward the glass doors. "That's our cue," he said.

Rudd held out a hand. "After you, Benton. I'll watch your back."

★   ★   ★

Liza Cannely tucked a priority delivery envelope under her arm as she hurried down the busy street toward the FedEx office. She'd considered using the drop box outside the *Los Angeles Times* building, but had changed her mind at the last minute. The information she was overnighting to Brad Benton was so inflammatory, she'd feel better about it if she personally put it into the overnight pipeline.

A warm wind had developed this afternoon, bringing with it the balmy smell of the ocean and the promise of summer. Around her, the city still showed signs of the destruction wrought by the strange events of that horrible night. It was hard to believe it had been just over three weeks since the world had turned upside down and a third of the population on the planet had disappeared into thin air. "The Rapture," Brad called it. An act of God. Liza hadn't told him, but that's exactly what she had feared. If God would unleash something so horrible and so devastating on the world, then what else would He do?

She shook off the sense of foreboding as she reached the end of the block. She shaded her brown eyes and checked the traffic, then hurried across the street toward her goal. When she'd heard the news of the explosion at the White House that day, she'd been stunned to learn that Brad's driver, the same young man she'd spoken to this morning, had been instrumental in preventing the apparent assassination of the president and Nicolae Carpathia.

Liza knew better. The same people who'd stalked Brad in Los Angeles, who'd managed to sabotage his return flight to Washington, who he believed had bombed his Alexandria, Virginia, apartment and sent a sniper gunning for him in the White House parking lot, had now managed to penetrate White House security and rig a presidential limousine to explode.

She clutched the envelope a little tighter against her side. She had told no one, but she suspected they were also the same people who'd been watching her movements for the last few days. She wasn't sure exactly when or why, but it had become apparent to her that she was being watched. The same keen instincts that made her good at her job told her that someone was monitoring her movements. She'd noticed a series of small things: the rubber band missing from her morning paper yesterday; her mail, which her slightly obsessive-compulsive postman always stacked from largest to smallest piece in her box, had been scattered as if searched; the doorman in her building had left on vacation and had been replaced by a stranger. All things that could be explained, yet they all left her with a sense of foreboding.

She'd considered calling the police, but had dismissed the thought as she pictured herself trying to explain why a missing rubber band had made her feel ill at ease. Overworked before the events of the other night, and now struggling just to maintain a sense of order with a recent spike in crime, the police would laugh her off as another nut who'd been driven to the edge by the global crisis.

Liza shot a quick look over her shoulder as she darted into the FedEx office. She was relieved to find someone she recognized behind the counter. The young woman had worked this shift for as long as Liza had been coming to this office. "Hi. Did I catch you in time?" she asked.

"Oh, yes, ma'am. Our last drop-off isn't until seven at this office."

Liza handed over the envelope. "It's already labeled."

The woman gave it a cursory look. "Okay. We'll get it there."

I hope so, Liza thought grimly as she muttered her thanks and left the building. She considered returning to the parking garage where she'd left her car, but changed her mind. The idea of going home to an empty apartment where she sensed menace in the corners and watchful eyes in the shadows had her clutching her arms across her chest despite the warm breeze. She turned instead and headed down a side street. There was a small, private hotel there where her editor often put up guests of the paper. The place was secure, quiet, and outfitted with the latest in technology and business services. Maybe tonight, safe within the walls of the hotel, she'd get a decent night's sleep while she waited for Brad to return her call.

4

Liza let herself into the third-story hotel room and turned the safety lock. She was glad she'd thought to make a large cash withdrawal from her savings account a couple of days ago. She'd been able to exist without using her credit cards for nearly seventy-two hours now. She was sure if she told anyone about the new prepaid cell phone in her pocket or the five-hundred-dollar cash deposit she'd put down on this room where she was registered under a false name, they'd think she was paranoid. But as soon as Liza had seen evidence that Victor Rudd might have played a role in George Ramiro's murder, she'd known that she couldn't be too cautious.

If Rudd was capable of murdering a man as high profile as Ramiro, it would take next to nothing to make a midlevel reporter at the *Los Angeles Times* disappear.

She moved quickly to pull the lined drapes shut and check inside the closets, behind the bathroom door, and behind the shower curtain. Finally satisfied that she was alone, she sank onto the bed and chastised herself for watching too many suspense movies where would-be assassins leaped from hiding places to kill their victims and terrify movie audiences.

Wiping a hand through her hair, she slipped off her shoes and lay back against the pillows. She reached for the remote. Tonight's state dinner at the White House was going full throttle, she suspected. The cable news stations would have updates on the assassination attempt, any agreements the White House had reached with Carpathia, and with luck, she might catch a glimpse of Brad that would give her a clue about how he was faring.

She was still reeling from seeing the news footage of Randal being thrown to the ground by the force of the limousine blast just hours after she'd spoken to him.

She crossed her legs on the bed as she found the news channel. Nothing to do now but wait. Maybe later, she'd risk ordering room service, but for the first time in days, she planned to get a decent night's rest cocooned within the anonymity of this hotel room.

★   ★   ★

An hour later, Liza found herself fighting through layers of sleep. She'd drifted off during the monotonously repetitive news reports, too many restless nights taking a toll on her. But something on the news had arrested her attention and awakened her.

Outside, darkness had fallen. The only light in the room came from the bluish cast of the television and the digital clock on the nightstand. She switched on the bedside lamp. The harsh light hurt her eyes, but Liza sat up and rubbed them vigorously as she reached for the remote. Evidently lacking substantive news, the channel now featured a society reporter who was showing earlier footage from the steady parade of VIPs at the White House state dinner. Liza's mouth went dry when she saw Victor Rudd and his unidentified young date stop to talk to Charley Swelder as he entered the White House.

Brad was in the White House with Victor Rudd and Nicolae Carpathia—not to mention most of the Joint Chiefs of Staff, one of whom Brad seemed sure knew something about the sabotage attempt on his last return flight from California.

She rubbed her upper arms as she felt a sudden chill. Brad had told her often in recent days of his supposed newfound faith in God. He claimed that the disappearances had been part of God's plan for the future of the world. Though the cameraman on the TV had shifted his view to feature a movie star and her husband making their way into the White House, Liza's gaze remained fixed on Victor Rudd, who still conversed with Charley Swelder in the background. For the moment, she hoped Brad's God was real. She'd known and written about enough politicians in her career to know that Brad Benton was a rare find—a politician who seemed to care as much about getting a job done as he did about keeping his job in the first place. Though he'd been merely a professional contact before the disappearances, the shared experience of the last few weeks had tightened their friendship.

The image on the television shifted, and she lost sight of Victor Rudd as he entered the White House. A sliver of fear worked its way down her spine as she thought of Brad seated at a State dinner surrounded by his enemies. "I hope your God is watching out for you," she said quietly. She punched a button on the remote to change to another news station. There was nothing she could do now but wait. And she hated it.

★   ★   ★

"Mr. Benton, there's an old friend the president would like you to meet in the mural room."

Brad set down his fork and gave the young man leaning over his shoulder a measured look. Jordan Trask, the president's personal assistant, was arguably one of the most powerful young men in Washington. Though his duties included everything from toting the president's suitcases to picking out Christmas gifts for Fitz's friends, associates, and political allies, Jordan enjoyed unprecedented access to a man who, until three weeks ago, had been the most powerful man in the world. Now, Brad thought, as he caught a glimpse of Nicolae Carpathia's golden head at the guest of honor's table, Fitz's role on the global stage was waning almost daily.

"Mr. Benton?" Jordan prompted him.

Brad excused himself to the three ambassadors, their wives, and a U.S. senator and her husband seated at his table and pushed back his chair. "I'll be right there." Like every senior official at the White House, he instantly recognized the double meaning of Jordan's message. An "old friend" in the White House meant a highly sensitive issue had arisen. Jordan used the phrase to summon any member of the White House staff the president required without arousing suspicion.

Brad followed Jordan through the dining room, pausing periodically to answer a question or offer a greeting to a guest. Despite Jordan's inscrutable expression, Brad sensed the younger man's tension. As they finally made their way toward the less crowded South Portico, Jordan studied the historic paintings on the wall to avoid making eye contact with Brad.

As Brad walked with Jordan along the colonnade toward the West Wing, the crunch of their footsteps on the flagstone seemed unnaturally loud. Still reeling from his conversation with Victor Rudd, Brad found himself remembering Marcus's prayer for his protection this morning. As the evening progressed, he felt evil beginning to close in on him. Not since the morning in Rock Creek Park when Marcus had led him to the Lord had he felt so oppressed.

Lord, he prayed silently, *wherever I'm going tonight, no matter what lies ahead, I know You're with me. Give me the strength to trust You.*

They reached the French doors that led to the mural room—a mural-painted receiving room adjacent to the Oval Office where the president often received guests and important visitors. The marine on guard made eye contact with Jordan, then eased slightly aside to allow Brad entrance. Jordan indicated the door with a wave of his hand. "The president is waiting for you," he said.

Brad entered the room alone. The lighting was so dim, it took him a moment to identify the president at the far end examining a detail in one of the murals that covered the walls.

"You wanted to see me, sir?" Brad asked.

Fitzhugh turned to face him. Brad wondered how the man could look a decade older than he had this morning. "Benton," he said, his voice slightly gravelly. "How are things going in the dining room?"

"I'm not close enough to the head table to say." Brad shoved his hands into his trouser pockets. "As far as I know, the ambassadors from the Congo, Nepal, and Taipei are having excellent conversation with Senator Jamison."

"Your table?"

It was no secret that state-dinner seating was reflective of power and access. Brad had not been seated within six tables of the head table since coming to the White House. "My usual," he said nonchalantly. "I'm just grateful I don't have any Hollywood types this time." At the last state dinner, Brad had found himself seated with the director and three actors from a recent Hollywood blockbuster. "It never ceases to amaze me that an actor thinks starring in a hit movie suddenly makes him an expert in foreign policy."

Fitzhugh laughed. "Jordan assures me that we get frequent requests for invites from the studios. I guess they figured you'd know how to talk to them because you're from California." He moved away from the mural and headed for the small drink cart. "You want a drink?"

"No thanks."

Looking pensive, the president poured himself a scotch. "That's right. You don't indulge, do you?"

"I don't enjoy alcohol," Brad told him. "Never have."

"Even before you became a religious fanatic?" The question held an unmistakable bite.

Brad ignored it. "Was there something you wanted to discuss with me, sir?"

That won a muttered curse. Fitzhugh indicated the two sofas with a slight wave of his scotch glass. "I managed to get away from listening to Carpathia's drivel for a few minutes. I've got to tell you, Benton, the man is slicker than motor oil."

"I've heard that." Brad took a seat across from the president.

"I think we're making some progress on this idiotic nuclear disarmament plan, though. He's at least agreed to let us chair the committee. We'll have some control over how that develops, anyway."

Brad wondered how Fitzhugh would respond if he told him that, in the long run, it would make little difference. Nicolae Carpathia was going to rule the world in an empire of evil, deceit, cruelty, and satanic power. He leaned back and crossed his legs. "I'm sure you're pleased," he said, deliberately noncommittal.

"Hmm." The president plunked his glass on the coffee

table. "Actually, I'd like to tell the guy to take his hare-brained ideas for peace and goodwill on earth and crawl back under his rock. This is the United States of America. We don't answer to the UN."

"It's a new world," Brad countered.

"Yeah, well, I liked the old one."

For all his frustrations with Gerald Fitzhugh, Brad had always appreciated the man's candor. "In some ways, I did too," he admitted. Though he was grateful that through his loss and grief he'd found the Lord, he missed Christine and his children fiercely. Brad's greatest regret was not being able to share the news of his faith and salvation with the people he had most loved. He found comfort in the knowledge that their separation was not forever. He had eternity to spend with them.

"The way I see it," Fitzhugh was saying, "I've got about ten minutes before I've got to go back in there. So let's cut to the chase. Tell me what you were talking to Rudd about."

Brad's heart rate kicked up a notch. "World peace," he told the president.

His gaze narrowed. "You think that's funny?"

"No, sir."

"Rudd's a big ally of this administration."

"I know that."

"He's a powerful man."

"I know that, too."

"We can't afford to alienate him."

"You may not be able to avoid it," Brad told him.

The president's expression darkened. "He's made his objections to this treaty very clear."

"There's no profit in peace."

"He told you that?"

"Yes."

"That doesn't surprise me." He reached for his drink. "Rudd's pragmatic if nothing else."

"True enough." Brad studied the other man's face for a clue to what he was thinking.

"I'm not going to mess with you, Benton. Charley's fuming that you talked to Rudd tonight. We've got a lot riding on this meeting with Carpathia, a midyear election to worry about, and next year we've got to launch a campaign." He shook his head. "Carpathia blackmailed me into offering him the new plane for the treaty signing in Israel, but I think we got some important concessions in exchange. Still, we need Rudd on our side. He's going to be tricky. He enjoys wielding power. Charley's not sure you're the best person to represent our position in conversations with him."

"I wouldn't sabotage your campaign," Brad said honestly.

"But you wouldn't necessarily support it either."

"We both know why I'm in this job, Mr. President. We also both know that as soon as the dust settles from my predecessor's scandal, I'll be asked to resign. You're using me."

"And you get to be White House chief of staff out of the deal. It's not such a bad exchange, don't you think?"

"No. I never said it was."

"But you resent it?"

"No," Brad said honestly. "I came here with my eyes open."

Fitzhugh studied him a moment. "Things could have been different, you know. George liked you."

At the mention of George Ramiro, Brad's senses kicked into high gear. "I liked him."

"What do you think happened to George, Benton?" Fitzhugh asked.

The scene seemed to grind into slow motion for Brad. "He's dead," Brad said quietly.

Fitzhugh leaned forward and braced his forearms on his knees. "Dead?" he pressed. "Is that the word we're using now for all those people who disappeared?"

"No, sir," Brad said carefully. "George didn't disappear." He took a deep breath. "He's dead."

"What makes you think so?"

Lord, Brad thought, *this is the valley of the shadow of death. I need Your wisdom and Your guidance.* "I've seen pictures of his body."

Several tense seconds of silence ticked by. Fitzhugh sat perfectly still. Brad waited, watching him carefully. Finally, the president uttered a dark curse and slammed his glass on the table with such force that the liquor sloshed onto his hand. "Pictures? You have pictures?"

"Yes, sir."

"Who the— Who knows about this?"

"Six people including you. Colonel Grayson Wells knew, but he's dead."

"Who's seen these pictures?"

"Besides me, the LA county coroner, a reporter, and whoever sent them to me."

Fitzhugh cursed again as he surged to his feet and began to pace. "That idiot. I told him he was playing with fire."

Brad felt his heart rate begin to return to normal. "Sir?"

"George and I had a conversation the afternoon before the disappearances. He was working on—" he stopped abruptly. "It doesn't matter. It was something delicate and politically charged. Let's just say he wasn't going to make a lot of friends with it. Where did you get the pictures?"

"I don't know who sent them. I have a theory."

"George had a theory too. He followed it and it got him killed. He and I had a conversation a lot like this one the day before he died. Am I going to hear tomorrow night that you've disappeared too?"

"Maybe."

"And why are you telling me this?"

Brad considered that for a moment. "Because, sir, I think there are some people in your inner circle who are involved in some activities you wouldn't personally condone. I never suspected you had anything to do with George's murder, and I still don't." He rubbed his eyes with his thumb and forefinger before continuing. "You know, I voted for you."

Fitzhugh managed an unpleasant laugh. "Thanks for that, I guess."

"I voted for you because I believed then, and I still believe, that you wanted to accomplish something while you were here."

His expression turned angry. "And you don't think I have."

"I don't think you've done all you could, sir."

"Two years of economic growth aren't enough for you?"

Brad shrugged. "I also think that you may have an idea who's responsible for George's death—or at least have your suspicions."

"What if I do?"

"Then it's up to you what you do with that. I've come too far to let this drop. I'm going to find out who murdered George, and I'm going to make sure they pay for it."

"I don't think you know what you're dealing with here, Benton."

Brad suppressed a slight smile. After nearly being murdered by a sniper, a bomb in his apartment, being pushed from a military aircraft that no one at the Pentagon was willing to identify, and an assassination attempt on the president's limousine, he knew exactly what he was dealing with. "I'm willing to take the risk—" he paused—"I have to."

Fitzhugh looked at him narrowly. "A wise man would probably let it drop, you know. Common consensus is that George disappeared with everyone else. No one's looking for him."

"I am."

"What if this destroys you? Don't you think that if someone was willing to murder Ramiro, they'd be willing to murder you to keep you from exposing them?"

"Yes, sir."

"Most people would call you a fool for that."

"It won't be the first time." Brad stretched his arms across the back of the sofa. "But I can respect myself for standing for something."

Fitzhugh stopped abruptly and faced him, his expression a mask of frustration. "And that's exactly what you have against me, isn't it? You think you stand for something and I don't."

Brad carefully considered his next words. "Mr. President," he said, "you live in a house where men like Abraham Lincoln, Franklin Roosevelt, and Lyndon Johnson determined the future of the world. They slept under this roof. They made decisions in this building. Abraham Lincoln signed the Emancipation Proclamation and went to war because he believed it was the right thing to do. It cost him half the country and ultimately his life. Franklin Roosevelt sacrificed the lives of six thousand U.S. soldiers on the beaches of Normandy to stop Hitler. It cost him the support of the electorate who thought that a war in Europe was none of our business. Lyndon Johnson refused to back down during the civil rights movement because he was disgusted by the way our nation treated some of our citizens. It cost him the American South. All of them made unpopular but important decisions because they viewed their role as president as an opportunity to make history and do the right thing." Brad paused. "I'm not sure anymore that you'd be willing to make an unpopular decision if you thought it would cost you something as insignificant as the Iowa caucus."

Fitzhugh's shoulders tensed. "I see."

Brad stood. "I'm sorry if it sounds disrespectful, sir," he said. "It's not that I think you don't stand for anything. I just think you're not willing to fight for the things you stand for."

He crossed his arms over his chest. "That's a strong accusation."

"I'd love to be proven wrong."

The president held his gaze for a moment then waved a hand toward the doors. "I think we're done here. Don't be surprised when Charley grills you on your conversation with Victor Rudd."

"Nothing Charley Swelder does surprises me."

"Including murder?"

Brad slid his hands into his trouser pockets. "Nothing."

Liza snatched her ringing cell phone off the nightstand in the hotel room. She was starving, but she hadn't dared venture out—nor would she, not until she heard from Brad. With a sigh of relief, she recognized his number on the caller ID. "Hi," she said. "I wasn't sure you'd have a chance to call me tonight."

"I don't have long. I'm on my way back from the West Wing to the dinner. Where are you?"

"Some place safe." She pulled her knees to her chest. "Brad, I think someone's been following me for the last couple of days."

"It wouldn't surprise me. Randal told me what you found."

"I overnighted everything to you—I got it wrapped up

and out this afternoon." Outside, the wail of a police siren carried above the din of the city.

"Good. I'm sure it will help. I spent a couple of hours tonight going over things. I think I've got the entire puzzle just about pieced together."

"Be careful," she warned. "I saw Rudd arriving at the White House on the news tonight."

"I'll be fine. God's watching out for me."

"I hope so," Liza assured him. "I hope He's looking out for all of us. Is Randal all right? I saw the report earlier."

"He's fine—just a concussion."

"Do you think someone was after the president?"

"I'm not sure yet. Could be."

Liza tipped her head back against the headboard and closed her eyes. "I'm scared. It's kind of weird, I know. I've broken a lot of stories about a lot of bad people, but—" she paused—"it's like you said. These people could make us disappear. Enough people are already gone. I don't want to join them."

"I know. Look, Liza, just keep your head down a few more days. Are you sure you're in a safe place?"

"I think so. I'm pretty sure I shook the person tailing me. No one knows I'm here. I've been living on cash, not using my credit cards. I think I'm as safe as I can be under the circumstances."

"Do you need anything?"

"A good night's sleep," she said, knowing how unlikely it was.

Brad paused. Liza could hear the din of the crowd through his cell phone. The clank of dinnerware and glass suggested he'd reached the dining room. "I'm sorry I dragged you into this, Liza," he said quietly.

"If you remember, I insisted on butting in. You weren't going to tell me anything. It was my choice, not yours."

"You could be in serious danger—"

"Yeah, yeah, I know. Been there. Done that. Often, even.
I've got that crazy snooping gene every reporter is born
with. My Native American name should have been Nose
Where It Doesn't Belong."

Brad laughed. That made her feel better. "Just be careful," he said. "If you see anything out of the ordinary or
even *feel* uncomfortable, get out of there. I'll call you tomorrow. I think we've got to get you to Washington so you
can finish breaking this story. As soon as we're sure of our
facts, we've got to get this out to the public. That's the only
way we're going to survive this."

"I agree."

"And, Liza?"

"Yes?"

"Don't trust anybody; do you understand?"

"Yeah. I get it."

"Good. That'll keep you alive."

It was after midnight—late by D.C. standards. D.C. was a
power breakfast kind of place, and the official nightlife
rarely went past midnight. No politician wanted constitu-
ents to think their elected representative was wasting their
tax dollars partying late. Even in the light of recent events,
some old rules still held.

Brad rubbed his eyes with his thumb and forefinger as
he hurried toward one of the ubiquitous official black sedans. With Randal in the hospital, he'd been assigned a
driver from the motor pool for the night. He'd always hated
the formalities of state dinners, and he'd never been glad-
der to see one end. After five hours of being trapped in the
same building with Victor Rudd, Nicolae Carpathia, and

Charley Swelder, he'd barely mustered the strength to say a civil good-bye to everyone as he'd all but bolted from the building.

Right now, what he wanted was to get out of his monkey suit into some comfortable clothes, and put his feet up somewhere so he could tell Mariette and Marcus everything that had happened. The idea of being with close friends he could trust, friends who made it safe to let down his guard, had never been so alluring to him. Since he couldn't go home to Christine anymore and lay his head on her shoulder and unburden his soul, this was the next best thing.

Brad found his designated car in the secured lot by scanning the identification numbers ghosted on the vehicles' rear windows. Fifteen. That was his car.

Brad exhaled a weary sigh. In the driver's seat, the uniformed chauffer was slouched down with his cap pulled over his eyes, stealing a quick nap while he waited. Brad rapped his knuckles on the glass, startling the man awake.

The driver sat upright, then reached for his door handle. Brad was already rounding the car to slide into the passenger seat. As he'd told Randal the day he'd come to work for him, he considered having a driver a convenience, not a necessity or an ego trip. Brad never sat in the backseat. He always sat next to the driver.

He pulled open the door, tossed his tuxedo jacket into the back, then slid in.

"Sorry, Mr. Benton. I shouldn't have dozed off like that."

The man's voice made Brad freeze. With his right foot still on the pavement, he turned to look at the man in the dim light. It wasn't the same driver who'd picked him up at the hospital to bring him to the White House. "Where's Justin?" he asked carefully.

"Just—? Oh. Did Justin drive you earlier tonight?"

"Yes. Where is he?"

"I don't know. The pool's pretty much maxed out to-night," the man told him. "You know we lost a few drivers with that whole disappearing thing a few weeks ago. After the explosion today, I heard that a couple more quit. It's all we can do to keep the bases covered. Justin's driving some-body else home, I guess."

"He said he'd be here for me tonight."

"Well, we don't always get to pick our assignments, you know. I'm sure Randal's told you how it works." The man reached for the keys hanging in the ignition. "You want me to take you back to the hospital or home?"

Lord, am I being paranoid? Brad wondered. "Look, I know this is going to sound a little strange, but do you mind if I take a look at your log sheet?"

"The log sheet? You mean my assignment book?"

"Yeah."

The driver shifted warily. "Well, normally I wouldn't mind, but things are so crazy tonight, we didn't have time to do all the logs before the pickups. They sent us out here a half hour ago and I forgot to bring my paperwork."

There wasn't a single driver in the pool, Brad knew, who simply forgot his or her security papers—especially not when the White House was still on a heightened security alert from this afternoon. He pulled his cell phone out of his pocket. "Then I'll just call the control—"

The driver quickly held up his hand. "No, wait. If you do that, I'll get in trouble. I could lose my job. I got a wife and kids. I—it was just an honest mistake."

Brad's nerve endings were now on full alert. Around him, he saw other guests make their way out of the White House and enter vehicles. He reminded himself that here, out in the open, he was relatively safe. If he let this man drive off with him in the car, anything could happen. Brad made a quick decision and levered himself out of the vehicle. "Look," he told the driver, "like you said, you're short-handed tonight. Since I'm just headed over to George Washington Hospital, I think I'll catch a cab."

The man started the car. "Mr. Benton, I really think you should get in."

Brad shook his head. "No, I'll be fine." From the corner of his eye, he saw a high-ranking member of Congress and her husband walking toward him. "You can report back to Dispatch and tell them to check with me tomorrow. I'll let them know you were here on time."

The man's expression turned grim. Brad saw him slide his hand beneath the seat. "I really can't let you do that, Mr. Benton. You're going to have to come with me."

The amber glow of the streetlights glinted off something metal and round as the driver moved his hand from beneath the seat. Brad gauged the distance from the car to the approaching congresswoman. "I don't think so," he said succinctly.

The man leveled the pistol at him. "I don't think you understand—"

"Congresswoman," Brad called to the approaching couple, "I didn't see you earlier tonight." Representing the thirty-seventh district in California, Gloria Dempsey had known Brad and his family for years.

The unsuspecting woman and her husband stopped, and Brad took a couple of steps forward. His friends were now blocking the gunman's aim at Brad, just as he had planned. Brad was pretty sure that the man in the car didn't want a scene on the White House lawn. He was almost certain that they'd all get out of this alive.

"Hello, Brad," Gloria said cordially. "It's been a while." She put her hand on his shoulder. "I've actually been meaning to call you. I was so sorry to hear you lost Christine and the kids."

Brad stole a quick look over her shoulder at the driver. He still had the pistol pointed in Brad's direction, but with the congresswoman in his way, he was forced to wait out the confrontation. Brad deliberately looked away from the driver and returned Gloria's embrace. "It's a difficult time for all of us," he assured her. "I appreciate your concern."

"Is there anything we can do for you?"

"Actually, my driver was just saying how shorthanded the motor pool is tonight. I'm headed over to George Washington Hospital to see a friend. Do you think you could give me a lift? It would give us a chance to catch up."

"We'd be glad to," Congresswoman Dempsey said. She looked over her shoulder at her husband. "All right with you, Bill?"

"Sure, sure." Bill Dempsey extended a hand to Brad. "Brad, good to see you."

"You, too."

Brad looked back at his driver. "Problem solved," he said. The man glared at him, but lowered the gun. "You can tell your boss I took care of myself." He linked one hand beneath the congresswoman's elbow and started across the parking lot, careful never to present a good target.

His heart pounding, he slid into the backseat of their vehicle and shut the door on the dangerous world outside. Gloria gave him a shrewd look. "All right, Brad. What's going on? Since when do top-level administration officials need rides from lowly members of Congress? Especially when they are standing right outside their own official limo."

"They do tonight." He wiped a hand over his forehead. "It's a long story, Gloria. But I've never been so glad to bum a ride in my life. Thanks for accommodating me. I owe you one."

Bill started the vehicle and merged into traffic. "This wouldn't have anything to do with that explosion this afternoon, would it?"

"I can't say," Brad said. "If I told you anything, I'd be putting you at risk."

"Are you in some kind of trouble, Brad?" Gloria asked.

"Probably not the kind you're thinking of, but I'm not safe company anymore." He looked at his friends. "You might want to avoid me for a little while."

"You may have a point." Bill turned out of the security gate, eased his way past the police barricades, and drove onto Pennsylvania Avenue. He checked the rearview mirror with a slight frown. "Well, whatever you're into, you'd better watch your back. It looks like it's getting crowded behind you."

Brad looked back to see a half-dozen security vehicles descending on the gated lot. As Bill turned the corner, Brad saw a Secret Service agent pull his "driver" from the sedan and push him up against the vehicle's hood. A gun glinted in the lights as it fell from the man's hand. Clearly somebody had noticed his predicament and called it in.

"Brad, what's this about?" Gloria said.

"This one's bigger than me or you." Brad shook his head. "Trust me, you don't want to know. Just get me to the hospital, okay? And forget I was in your car. If anyone asks, you didn't see me."

★ ★ ★

"You've had quite a night, Brad," Marcus said. He leaned back in the hard chair in Randal's hospital room and studied his friend, who stood staring out the window. Brad still wore his tuxedo pants with his shirt half unbuttoned, his tie loose around his neck, and his eyes bloodshot.

"You could say that. It could have been worse. I'm still here." Once Brad had gotten safely inside Randal's guarded room, with Nero Jefferson still diligently standing watch outside in the hallway, Brad had spilled everything—all that he'd learned that night about Victor Rudd, his allies, his enemies, and George Ramiro's murder.

Mariette tucked the sheet around Randal's shoulders. "What are you going to do?" she asked Brad.

"Wait until I get Liza's package. If the evidence she found can conclusively link Kostankis and Rudd to South Range, then I have enough to confront them with."

"But not enough to take to the authorities," Marcus mused.

"I don't know. Can we trust the authorities?" Brad turned from the window with a heavy sigh. "I still don't know who sent me the pictures or why. Someone wanted me to know that George was murdered. I don't know if sending those pictures was a threat to my life or a plea for help. Tonight, somebody called in the troops when that phony driver tried to kidnap me. Seems to me that the authorities are of two minds about what to do with me."

"Yeah—but the ones who want you dead are certainly out there." Mariette thought that over. "Do you think it's possible that whoever killed George wanted you implicated and out of the way?"

"Yes," Brad concurred. "It's possible. I've considered that."

Marcus drummed his fingers on the arm of his chair. "Maybe we're looking at this the wrong way."

"What do you mean?" Mariette asked.

"Maybe we're trying to attach some sinister or hidden motive to the pictures when actually, whoever sent them wanted the truth exposed." Marcus looked closely at Brad. "And given your reputation at the White House, this person, or persons, figured you were the only one who could be counted on to see that mission through."

Brad leaned against the windowsill and stroked his chin. "But who would have a motive like that?"

"Someone who knew George was murdered and was too scared to act on it himself."

Randal coughed and mumbled something none of them understood. Mariette quickly poured him a glass of water and held the straw to his mouth.

Brad shot the boy a look. "What?" he said, making his way toward the bed. "What did you say?"

"Maybe," Randal said more clearly, "whoever sent those pictures participated in the murder and suffered a nasty case of guilty conscience."

"Randal has a point," Marcus mused. "The Los Angeles county coroner confirmed that the pictures were taken within a few hours after the murder, yes?"

"Yes," Brad said.

"Then whoever took them," Mariette continued, "knew where the body was at the time of the murder. They couldn't have simply stumbled on it a few days later."

"So what if," Marcus said, "they helped dump the body, then returned to the dump site to take the pictures."

Brad frowned. "The only reason I can think of for someone to do something like that is to cover his tracks."

"If they were an unwilling participant—," Mariette added.

"Or following orders . . . ," Randal said.

Marcus met Brad's gaze. "Like a member of the military."

Brad rubbed his face, almost too tired to think. "Or a member of the Secret Service."

"The Service?" Mariette pressed. "You think the Service could have had something to do with this?"

"It's a possibility, anyway," Brad confessed. "How else does someone murder a top-level administration official and no one at the White House has wind of it? Who else but the Service has the power to cover up something like that?"

"Things were a bit confused at the time," Mariette pointed out.

"Not until later that night," Brad said. "The cover-up was in place well before the Rapture, and enough people knew about it that they had to stick with their story, or they'd have blamed George's disappearance on that."

"So you think this goes all the way to the top?" Marcus asked.

"Yeah. I'm just not sure where the ultimate power is. I know that if a senior administration official was involved in a murder that might in any way implicate the president, then yes, it would go all the way to the top. The Service would be expected to cover it up, keep it quiet. That scenario explains all the breaches in security—and it explains why the people who want me dead seem to know every move I make. It also explains why Rudd has been able to get away with his scheme with Kostankis. Rudd would have to have a top-level insider to make that work, someone who could cover for him with Congress and hush up anyone who might question what's going on."

"Think he's got a cabinet member in his pocket?"

"Probably at least one. I would think that someone high up at Treasury would have to be involved as well, and someone at Defense who could contact Kolsokev's people without arousing suspicion."

"The Russian president?" Mariette asked.

Brad nodded. "I'm virtually sure from looking over

Gray's notes that Kostankis and Rudd are using U.S. gold reserves to help Kolsokev put down a revolt in Abkhazia. There's an old Soviet nuclear facility there that's fallen into the hands of Hizb ut-Tahrir al-Islami."

"That Islamic extremist group," Marcus said. "I remember hearing about this in the news. Russian scientists haven't been able to confirm whether or not there was uranium at the facility."

"There was," Brad told them. "Or at least U.S. intelligence indicated there was. Of course, our intelligence people have made a few mistakes in their day. I know that Fitzhugh's been under considerable pressure from the Joint Chiefs to take some kind of action in the area. Dave Marsden's been pushing especially hard." The general had been one of the president's most outspoken critics since the Rapture, and had, at one time, advocated a first strike on the Russians in response to the disappearances.

Mariette nodded. "That makes sense. We were asked months ago to provide the administration with a response plan in the event of a nuclear attack on the U.S. There's been speculation that the president has been expecting some type of terrorist attack using former Soviet nuclear weapons."

Brad scrubbed a hand over his face. "Given Dave Marsden's personality, it wouldn't surprise me to learn that he got frustrated with the administration's lack of activity and took matters into his own hands."

"Without presidential or congressional approval?" Marcus asked.

Brad shrugged. "If Marsden seriously believed the security of the U.S. was at stake, then I don't think he'd hesitate to conduct a covert overseas operation. Given Rudd's contracts with the Pentagon, it makes sense that Marsden would turn to him with the plan."

"And Rudd would have brought Kostankis into the picture."

"Rudd's shipping connections would have led him to Kostankis. It's no secret that Kostankis is pro-U.S. and anti-terrorist. The Greeks have supported us on this since before 9/11."

"Sure," Randal said. "They've been fighting with Turkey since the world began. Just another way of striking an enemy, I suppose."

"All right," Marcus said, "So Rudd, Marsden—you think?" He looked at Brad with raised eyebrows.

Brad nodded. "All I found in Gray's files were references to high-ranking military officers at the Pentagon. He didn't name names."

"Then why Marsden?" Marcus asked.

"Gray and I discussed Marsden, Mayweather, and Cranston the night of the Rapture. Several members of the Joint Chiefs of Staff were among the missing, and Marsden had made a power play to take over the council. To my knowledge, the national security advisor and Admiral Stein were the only dissenters at the time."

"Palatino doesn't like Marsden?" Mariette asked, referring to the national security advisor.

Brad shook his head. "*Dislike* is too soft a word. Hates the man. And the feeling is mutual. Security briefings are like verbal sparring matches with those two."

Marcus stroked his chin. "So Marsden is a likely candidate, but you can't prove it."

"No," Brad concurred, "I can't."

"Okay, it's a reasonable hypothesis. We don't have enough proof to pin this on anyone, of course, not in a court of law. Who else do you think is implicated?"

"Drake," Randal said firmly. "Harmon Drake."

"What?" Brad frowned. "I don't know, Randal. Drake's a

hard nut, there's no question on that, but I don't think he'd do something illegal, not even to protect the president."

"You didn't see him today," Randal insisted. "I did. He's hiding something. And he's sweating bullets about it."

"He might be, but Harmon Drake's been the head of the Secret Service for the last three presidents. He's not about to get himself jailed over this one."

"But," Mariette added, "you *do* think a member of the Service is involved."

"I think a member of the Service has information," Brad stressed. "I think it's highly possible that if George Ramiro had discovered evidence linking Rudd to the theft of the gold reserves at South Range, and that if he were murdered in the White House the night of the Rapture, that Harmon Drake's men would have been called in to clean up the mess. I think Drake might know what happened, but I think that if he does, he's equally as interested in finding the perpetrators as I am."

Mariette dropped into her chair. "I am definitely not going to New York tomorrow."

"Mom," Randal said, "you can't do that. I'm fine."

Marcus reached over and gave her arm a squeeze. "There's nothing you can do here."

"I can look after Randal," she insisted.

"I'm fine."

Mariette ignored him. "And if Brad is right, he's got the most powerful men in the world ready to kill him. There's no way I'm leaving town with this going on."

Randal exhaled an exasperated breath. "Oh, Mom."

Marcus moved quickly to head off the pending argument. "Nobody has to make this decision tonight," he pointed out. He gave Mariette a knowing look. This afternoon he'd counseled her on the necessity of giving her son space to be a young man and not the little boy she still longed to protect. "Give it some time." He saw the indecision and anxiety in her eyes. "Some space."

"I'm okay, Mom," Randal said. "You can't protect me forever."

"I can try," she muttered.

Still standing near the window, Brad exhaled a long sigh and crossed to the bed. "You can't understand it, Randal. You don't have children. You probably won't have them now."

The sudden silence that settled on the room was thick with grief and understanding. The seven-year Tribulation clock had begun to tick audibly again, reminding them all that time was short and even though their eternal futures were secure, their immediate futures were uncertain. More people would die before the Tribulation was over.

Brad cleared his throat to break the silence. Reaching into his pocket, he produced a flat brass key. "I have a feeling," he told his three friends, "that this has something to do with the answers I need." He dropped it on the white sheets.

"What's it for?" Randal asked.

Brad sighed. "I'm not sure. It was in the package I received from Jane Lyons. She said it was with the files George had given her before he died."

Marcus picked it up and examined it. "It's not marked. It's not a post office key."

"I think it's a safe-deposit box or a private mailbox."

"But where?" Mariette asked.

Brad shook his head. "I haven't figured that out. I have a feeling that whatever evidence got George Ramiro killed is locked away somewhere. And I think this is the key. I just have to find the lock it fits."

"How are you going to do that?" Randal asked.

"I have to—" Brad stopped short when his cell phone

rang. With a frown he pulled it out of his pants pocket. "This is probably bad news. I have never gotten a good phone call at one o'clock in the morning," he said as he flipped it open. He pushed the Receive button and lifted the phone to his ear. "Benton."

Marcus watched the play of emotions across his friend's face. Though Brad seemed to be coping admirably with the stress, Marcus had begun to notice a recklessness about him that he found worrisome. He knew from their recent conversations that Brad had begun a slow slide into serious depression. Maybe even clinical depression. Brad missed his wife and children. His lingering guilt that he'd deceived them for so long gnawed at him. In unguarded moments, he'd confessed to Marcus that he would even welcome death. With death would come heaven; a reunion with his family; and an escape from the stress, uncertainty, and fear of the changing world in which they lived. Brad had begun to talk about the Tribulation the Bible said was coming as his punishment for having rejected God before the Rapture. Though Marcus worried, he continued to pray that God would give Brad the peace that could only come from Him.

"I'll be right there," Brad said. He slapped the phone shut and thrust it back into his pocket.

"What's wrong?" Randal asked.

"That was Harmon Drake. They just found Forrest Tetherton's body splayed out on the floor of his office."

Mariette gasped. "Oh, Brad."

"Dead?" Randal asked. He pushed up on his elbows. Brad nodded.

"May God save his soul," Mariette prayed quietly.

"Suicide?" Marcus asked.

"Possibly. Or, more likely, murder," Randal guessed.

Brad drew a steady breath as he massaged the muscles in

his neck. "Either way, it's one more casualty in this whole mess." He pinned Marcus with a bleak look. "And it won't be the last."

*   *   *

Liza stared at the television with a sense of disbelief. The local news was on. The headline story was a three-alarm, apartment-building fire in the Brentwood area of western Los Angeles. *Her* apartment building.

A thick plume of black smoke billowed from the roof into the smoggy sky. The news cameras captured the near chaos on the street level where apartment tenants, clinging to cherished possessions and pets, poured from the blazing building onto the cluttered sidewalk. Emergency equipment lined the street. The network reporter covering the story stood in the foreground, clutching her microphone in white-knuckled hands and reporting the details she'd gotten from the fire department.

But Liza was watching the scene that unfolded behind the reporter. As people streamed out of the building, two police officers were monitoring the crowd. To the casual observer, they appeared to be directing people to various shelters and temporary holding areas, but what caught Liza's attention was the deliberate way the two men sorted the crowd. Most tenants were sent to a cluster of ambulances and portable shelters up the street, but they sent one group to a second area where a lone ambulance sat apart from the other emergency equipment.

Had she been less observant, she might have assumed that the last group was in need of certain medical attention the EMTs on the scene weren't qualified to administer, but as Liza watched, a more sinister reason became crystal clear to her. Everyone in that group of tenants fit a single profile, shared a common look, had a similar physical description.

In fact, they all looked a bit like her.

The two officers were singling out women who matched her description. If she hadn't spent the last two days feeling certain that someone was tailing her, if Brad hadn't told her that her fears were not only reasonable but warranted, she might have been willing to dismiss her observation as premenstrual paranoia. But here, cooped up in this tiny hotel room waiting for Brad to call her with an escape plan, the idea that someone had deliberately set her apartment building on fire in order to get her out on the street seemed very real.

"These people could make you disappear." That's what Brad had told her when he'd asked her if she really wanted to be involved in this mess. At the time, her journalist's curiosity had brushed off the risk as a cheap price to pay for the opportunity to break a major story that tied upper-level administration officials to an illegal military plot and the murder of the White House press secretary. But as she watched the story of the fire play out in front of her now, she began to question the wisdom of her decision. What good was a Pulitzer prize if she wasn't alive to enjoy it? Shivering, she slid beneath the covers and wished she could call her dad.

He'd disappeared in the event Brad called the Rapture. Living for the last several years in a nursing facility near Los Angeles, he'd always been Liza's conscience and sounding board. A journalist himself, he had been the shoulder she'd always leaned on, the wise counsel she'd always turned to. Even though his health had declined in recent years, his mind had remained sharp and clear. And though they'd been friends to the end, there was one issue upon which they'd never agreed. He, like Brad, had been what Liza called a religious fanatic. He'd talked to her about the fate of her soul. He'd contended that she needed to get things right with God, that time was waning, and that she was facing eternal damnation if she didn't recognize her need for a Savior.

Liza had brushed off his arguments as generational. She'd dismissed his religious fanaticism as the ramblings of a weak and dying man. She'd always figured that, when he was stricken with incurable cancer, her father had turned to religious zeal for comfort. How could she blame him for that? He was entitled to his little fantasy.

But it didn't mean she agreed with him.

Now, as she watched her apartment building burning, she realized with an awful sinking sensation that most of what she possessed was gone. She couldn't use her credit cards, get to her bank account, or run back home to stock up on clothing. All she had available to her was the cash in her pocket, a cheap cell phone, a friend in Washington, and the makings of a story that could easily turn the Fitzhugh administration on its ear.

A year ago, all of that probably would have been enough, but the events of the last few weeks, the terror and fear she'd seen on the faces of her colleagues and coworkers who'd lost friends and loved ones, gave her the unmistakable feeling that, for the first time in her life, she was caught up in something beyond her control. The feeling had begun to chip away at her usually formidable optimism.

Tonight she needed more than a pep talk and a pair of proverbial bootstraps to pull herself up with. Tonight she needed direction and answers for what had happened in her world. With a shake of her head, she jerked open the drawer of the nightstand. Inside was the one of the ubiquitous Bibles placed in hotels everywhere by an organization her dad had supported during his lifetime—Gideons International.

Liza pulled the book out of the drawer and studied its blue leather-look cover. She ran her fingers over the gold lettering. *Holy Bible.* Did it have the answers Brad promised? And if it did, could she trust it?

Her father had argued that the Bible was literally true, that everything "from Genesis to maps" was absolute, true, and real. Liza wasn't sure she could trust a book with stories about Noah's ark, talking donkeys, and a giant who fell victim to a shepherd's river rock as a reliable source for answers to the questions spinning through her mind.

But Brad trusted it, too. Despite his losses, despite the incredible pressures he now faced, Brad had seemed able to rely on the answers in this book. He seemed to have a peace and composure she could only wish for for herself. She knew several things about Brad Benton—both from her recent experiences with him and from their past association. He was smart. He was politically savvy. He was decent. He didn't suffer fools gladly. And he'd never been this comfortable in his own skin before, this sure that there was a plan for his life, not even when his life had been one golden moment after the next. It was like he'd had to lose everything to find his way somehow.

If Brad had found answers in this book, maybe she could too.

Liza slid deeper under the covers and cracked open the Bible. What was it Brad had told her the day they talked about his own recent religious conversion? He'd found his answers in the book of John.

It was where she'd start looking.

5

Brad paused in the corridor of the West Wing as two uniformed members of the coroner's office rolled by pushing a gurney with a body bag.

"Benton—"

Brad glanced up to find Harmon Drake approaching him. "I'm glad you're here. The D.C. crime scene investigators are demanding to get in the office. I've been holding them off by telling them there are classified and confidential documents you need to secure."

Brad nodded. He'd followed this procedure before. Twice when employees had been fired, and then again after the Rapture for missing members of the White House staff. But this was his first body bag. "Any idea yet on the cause of death?"

Drake frowned. "He blew his brains out," he said bluntly. "Suicide. Classic case."

"The police are still going to collect forensic evidence, aren't they?"

That won a harsh laugh. "If you want to call it that. One thing that's always made my job easier is the complete and utter incompetence of the D.C. police department. It's not overly difficult to protect your territory when your rivals aren't much of a threat."

Brad resisted the urge to point out that Drake's job was to protect the president, not to rule the White House with an iron fist. He moved toward Tetherton's door. The police officer who stood guard held up a hand. "I'll have to see ID," he said.

Drake swore beneath his breath. "He's the White House chief of staff. He's cleared."

"I have to see ID," the woman said more forcefully. She gave Drake a pointed look. "It's my job to make sure no one goes in who's not supposed to go in."

Drake took a menacing step toward her, but Brad moved quickly to intercept him. He was already pulling his wallet from his pocket. "It's all right, Harmon. The officer is doing her job. I appreciate her attention to detail."

Drake cursed again and turned to stalk down the hall. "You've got twenty minutes, Benton. Then I'm sending in my men."

The officer checked Brad's ID, returned it to him, and swung the door open.

"Thank you," Brad told her.

"I can't buy you any extra time," she said. "You'd better do what you got to do."

Frustrated, Brad shuffled through the drawers of Forrest's desk a second time. He'd already pulled all the files and data CDs he needed and dumped them into a box. Now he was looking for something—anything—George may have left behind when he occupied this office that would tell him where the key in his pocket belonged.

The desk yielded nothing. He shot a quick glance at the digital clock. Less than ten minutes left. *Where? Where?*

He moved to the row of file cabinets by the window. One at a time, he pulled open each drawer and checked beneath the files. Either George had left the office in pristine condition before he died, or Forrest had diligently purged it of any traces of his predecessor.

Brad raked a hand through his hair. *Lord, help me. Help me.* A sudden rap on the door's frosted-glass window startled him.

"You just about done, sir?" the guard called.

"Almost," Brad shot back. "A few more minutes."

"Eight," she said. "I can't give you any more than eight."

Brad slipped his hand in his pocket and removed the key. "Come on, George," he said quietly. "Give me something to work with."

He paced the confines of the room, checked behind the pictures, traced his fingers along the book bindings. One wall was lined with bookcases jammed with political references, congressional reports, and government documents—more than Forrest Tetherton would have been able to accumulate in the short time he'd occupied this office.

Another rap at the door. "Five more minutes, Mr. Benton."

"I understand."

Brad studied the bookcase. He stepped over the bloodstain on the carpet and made his way to it. He didn't have time to search it, yet something told him the answer he wanted was there. George had loved books, collected books. Among the staff, his knowledge of political trivia had been legendary. Each year when the *Almanac of American Politics* arrived, George would disappear into his office, where he'd sit for hours reading and digesting the four-inch tome. He'd emerge several days later announcing facts about which member of Congress had won the thirty-seventh precinct in Ohio, or whose daughter-in-law had recently passed the bar and was poised to run for office. Copies of the *Almanac* from years past lined several of the shelves in neat rows.

Brad ran his hands along the spines. "Come on, George," he said again. "Talk to me."

One shelf held reports from the Office of Management and Budget. Another had reports of former special prosecutors on political investigations from past administrations. A third was jammed with congressional budget reports. Brad ran his hands along each row. "Where is it?" he whispered.

"Two more minutes," came the voice from outside the door.

He skimmed over a shelf full of foreign-affairs journals and *Jane's World Armoured Fighting Vehicles*. There were bound editions of the *National Review*, binders with every copy of *Time* and *Newsweek* published since Gerald Fitzhugh had taken office. George had one shelf filled with political biographies and another with first editions of masterworks by political legends. Commentaries, constitutional reviews, and pictorial histories of the White House were arranged in neat rows.

"Mr. Benton?"

He looked at the door. "One more minute."

"The forensics unit is here."

"One more minute," Brad repeated, turning back to the bookshelf. "Come on. Come on." He examined the last shelf. He had no idea why he was so certain the answer was here—whether it was instinct or divine revelation. But he knew—*knew*—George had left behind information that explained the brass key. The same meticulous attention to detail that had documented the information in the files he'd given to Jane Lyons would have made George create a contingency plan. George had to have known when he talked to Fitzhugh that he was taking a tremendous chance. It explained why he'd given the files to Jane in the first place, and it suggested that he would have separated the information about the key from the key itself.

"Mr. Benton?"

Brad continued to search the shelves.

"Mr. Benton?" This time the policewoman rattled the doorknob.

"Something," Brad muttered, "give me *something*."

"Mr. Benton." The officer's voice had turned demanding.

Brad was looking again at the second-to-last shelf, where George had stored notebooks full of speeches and position papers he'd written throughout the campaign and into the Fitzhugh presidency. Each was dated and marked by location and the stage of the campaign or administration. *New Hampshire Primaries. Iowa Caucuses.*

"Mr. Benton? Are you all right?"

Convention. Super Tuesday. Inauguration. First 100 Days. The Fitzhugh Legacy. State of the— Brad froze, then went back to the notebook marked *The Fitzhugh Legacy.* It was smaller than the others, as if George hadn't anticipated needing very much space to contain whatever hallmark events he had planned to include.

"Mr. Benton?"

"One second," he yelled.

What was it Randal had overheard in the car that day with Rudd's associates? The day after his death, George had supposedly had a meeting scheduled with a well-known literary agent in New York. Speculation was that George had been ready to bail on the administration, too disillusioned by the president's lack of fortitude and commitment to the agenda that had gotten him elected.

If that was true, then George would have had notes,

outlines, information he planned to use in the book. Brad grabbed the notebook from the shelf.

"Benton!" It was Harmon Drake's voice. "We're coming in. There's a procedure here." Brad heard the rattle of keys in the lock.

He tossed the notebook into the file box with the other papers and files he'd removed from Forrest's desk. The procedure Drake spoke of wouldn't allow him to leave with any material on his person. He'd have to figure out later how to retrieve the notebook.

The door flew open. "What's going on in here, Benton?"

Brad shrugged as he put the top on the box. Drake was flanked by three police officers, a forensic investigator, and two Secret Service agents who were supposed to escort Brad to the evidence locker where Forrest's files would be stored until they were needed or the investigation into his death was completed.

"It just took a while. Tetherton wasn't an especially organized guy."

Drake narrowed his eyes. "You got what you needed?"

"I think so, yes," Brad said.

One of the agents moved to take the box. "This is ready for the locker?"

"Yes," Brad affirmed. "Let's go log it in."

Liza's ringing cell phone startled her awake. Drowsy from a mostly sleepless night, she fumbled for the phone on the hotel nightstand. "Hello?"

"Sorry I woke you." It was Brad. "Are you all right?"

She fell back against the pillows. "They burned down my apartment building last night."

"I know," he said. "I'm sorry."

"I've got nothing but the clothes on my back and the money in my pocket. Did you get the package I sent you?"

"Not yet. It's not even nine o'clock yet. Another hour."

Liza squinted at the digital clock. "Did Forrest Tetherton really commit suicide last night?" She'd seen it on the news in the small hours of the morning.

"I don't know," he confessed, "but Rudd was in the White House last night for that dinner. It's awfully coincidental that people keep turning up dead everywhere he goes."

"What are we going to do, Brad?"

"I think I have almost everything I need to break this story. If the evidence I found last night in Forrest's office turns out to be what I think it is, it'll lead us to whatever George was working on just before he was killed."

"What do you want me to do?"

"You need to come to Washington."

Liza drew a shaky breath. "I can't just—"

"We're transferring the new *Air Force One* from Seattle to Andrews Air Force Base later today. We're going to fly it out of Whidbey Island."

"In Seattle?"

"That plane's at the Boeing facility there. I've made arrangements for you to be a credentialed member of the press corps for the maiden flight."

"How am I supposed to get to Seattle?"

"There's a MAC flight going out of the Los Angeles Air Force Base in an hour. You're traveling under the name Maria Zephyr. Last week the president announced that he was bringing in a scientist from California to sit in the House gallery when he addresses the Joint Session before he leaves for Jerusalem. She's a chemist from UCLA who's been doing some analysis of the Rosenzweig formula. I spoke with her yesterday, and she's had to make an emergency trip out of the country on family business. So for today, anyway, you're going to be Dr. Maria Zephyr. It'll get you out of LA on a military flight without arousing any suspicion since they were already expecting Dr. Zephyr to fly with them."

"I don't have ID."

"I'm going to give you a name and address in LA county where I want you to go as soon as you leave the hotel. They've got papers and a wardrobe waiting for you."

"Are you serious?"

"Liza, these people burned down your building last night. They weren't trying to get you out on the street just to ask you a few questions."

She shuddered. "I'm having a little trouble believing all this," she confessed. Her gaze fell on the Bible on the nightstand. She wanted to talk to Brad about what she'd read, wanted to ask him the thousand questions buzzing in her brain, but for now, she knew the urgency behind what he was telling her overrode any other consideration.

"I know, but it's almost over. Just a few more days."

"Where do you want me to go?"

"Get a pencil," he told her. "I'll give you everything."

★   ★   ★

Brad looked at the papers on his desk with a slight frown, then met Charley Swelder's gaze. "And we're okay with this?"

Swelder shrugged. "We knew we had to hire a new pilot for *Air Force One*. Clayton wasn't qualified on that type of jet."

Brad rubbed his thumb over the crest on the Global Community stationery Charley had handed him. Nicolae evidently already assumed that his plan to rename the

United Nations Global Community was a foregone conclusion. He'd printed his own stationery with a crest that looked suspiciously ostentatious for a man who claimed he had no aspirations of power. "I know," Brad said, "but I thought we'd agreed on Roger Destrin."

"Well, Pan Con sent us a new list. Destrin asked to have his name taken off the list of candidates. I'm guessing he wasn't thrilled about having to fly Carpathia around."

"So we're going to take Carpathia's suggestion and hire this—" Brad checked the name— "this Rayford Steele, sight unseen. Do we know anything about him?"

"Pan Con says his flight record is flawless. He aced his qualification trials on the new jet, and Carpathia seems to like him."

Always a plus, Brad thought cynically. "What about security?"

Charley shrugged. "It's not as if he's going to be flying POTUS, at least not at first. What do we care if the guy's a closet terrorist? Maybe he'll crash the plane over the Atlantic and put Nicolae Carpathia out of our misery."

Brad sighed heavily. "Do you have any idea—"

"Look," Charley said, his patience obviously beginning to wane, "we're up to our eyeballs dealing with Tetherton this morning. I figure we have about another ten minutes or so before the wild stuff breaks loose around here. The media's already got the story, because the Metro police leaked it. My phone is ringing off the hook. The least of my worries today is who flies the new self-proclaimed holy Roman emperor to Israel. Clayton's going to fly us, and that's all I care about. So just sign the stupid paper and let's move on."

Brad hesitated a moment longer, then reached for his pen. "For the record," he told Charley, "I would at least have liked to meet the man before I made him a permanent member of our staff."

"So noted." Swelder grabbed the paper, examined Brad's signature, then folded it with quick dispatch. "We're going to meet in the Oval in fifteen minutes for a briefing on Tetherton. The guy picked a great time to pull this."

"We don't know that it was suicide," Brad said.

Charley's expression turned angry. "Of course we do."

"I talked to the coroner. He's not so sure."

Charley Swelder leaned over Brad's desk and gave him a hard look. "Listen to me, Benton. We're releasing a statement this morning that says the president was deeply grieved to hear that his press secretary committed suicide last night following the state dinner. Tetherton had been depressed and experiencing considerable stress dealing with the demands of his job after George Ramiro's disappearance, but none of us had any indication that he was that desperate. We think the prescription meds he was taking may have had something to do with it. That's what the statement says. And that's our story."

"It's not just the coroner's concerns. I have some concerns, too. There's no note," Brad pointed out.

"There will be by noon today."

It took a moment for Brad to realize what Charley was saying. "You're going to manufacture a suicide note? That's wrong! What about his family? They deserve answers."

"I serve at the pleasure of the president of the United States," Charley said. "My job is to protect Gerald Fitzhugh—I frankly don't give a rip about Forrest Tetherton's family."

"Your *job* is to serve the people of this country who elected Gerald Fitzhugh. Do you think that manufacturing evidence is the way to do that? I don't. And what if Forrest was murdered? Don't we need to know who's responsible?"

"He wasn't murdered. Do I need to give you a script? So, no, we don't need to know who is responsible." Charley pushed away from the desk and stomped toward the door. "Look, all we need to know is that this matter is over. Forrest was obviously into something he shouldn't have been. That's a surefire way to get yourself in trouble around here, Benton." He jerked open the door. "I'd advise you to remember that."

Before Brad could respond, an intern stuck her head in the door. "There's a delivery for you, Mr. Benton. FedEx."

★ ★ ★

"I need to see some identification, ma'am."

Liza reached into the oversized purse that held the clothes she'd worn this morning, a copy of the material she'd sent Brad, and the few personal possessions she'd scavenged from her car. With trembling hands, she handed over a driver's license.

The freshly laminated ID had been waiting for her when she'd arrived at the address Brad had given her, on her way to the Los Angeles Air Force Base. She hadn't bothered to ask where they'd gotten her picture, nor how they had managed to alter it to match the blonde wig and heavy glasses she now wore. Though she knew the ID was less than four hours old, it had been aged appropriately—even had a convincing bend in the corner.

The airman gave the ID a perfunctory look. "So you're that chemistry professor headed for the White House?" the airman said.

Liza nodded. "That's me."

He shook his head with a slight laugh. "I gotta tell you, ma'am, when they told me we were giving a lift to a chemistry professor, I was thinking it would be some Einstein-looking guy."

Liza shrugged. "Sorry to disappoint you."

"I'm not disappointed," he told her. "Just a little surprised, that's all." He motioned Liza to a waiting area near
the door. "Just have a seat over there, ma'am. They're fuel-
ing the plane now. As soon as we're ready, I'll come to escort you aboard."

"Thank you." Liza headed for the hard plastic chairs,
grateful for a chance to sit down. Since Brad's call this
morning, she'd felt hunted and on the run. She'd left the
hotel so hastily she hadn't even bothered to check out. Her
car was still parked in the downtown lot where she'd left it
yesterday, so she'd picked it up, fought the morning traffic,
and found the address he'd given her to pick up her new ID
and the baggy clothes and wig they'd provided for her. Liza
didn't know the names of the people who'd handed over
the ID and she hadn't asked. She didn't know how or why
Brad knew them, or what their connection was to the White
House, but when they'd told her to clear whatever she
wanted to keep out of her car, she hadn't asked questions.
She'd just done it.

And she knew now why they'd asked her to clean out
the car.

With less than forty minutes to make it to the base, one
of the men had led her down a set of back stairs to a subter-
ranean garage where he'd instructed her to lay down on the
backseat of a nondescript beige sedan. As they'd driven out
of the parking deck, the sound of an explosion had ripped
through the early morning air. Liza had lifted her head just
enough to see her car, still parked in front of the building,
engulfed in flames.

Stifling a sob, she'd laid her head back down on the seat
as the driver merged into the city traffic.

He'd been on the interstate before he gave her permission to sit up. "What happened to my car?" she'd asked as
she emerged from her sprawl across the backseat.

"Not your problem. We can't leave a trail," he said. "It served its purpose today. You'll be provided with a new vehicle when you get back to Los Angeles."

The chances of that ever happening, she'd thought darkly, were looking bleaker by the moment.

Once on the base, she'd managed to negotiate her way through the security checkpoints with a minimum of hassle. Brad's people had been very thorough.

She'd finally made it to the hangar ten minutes before her scheduled flight to the base on Whidbey Island.

Liza reached into the oversized bag and rubbed her fingers over the grainy cover of the Gideon Bible she'd taken from the hotel room. She hadn't bothered to ask herself why it had seemed so important to her, nor why she'd felt the need to pack it with the few personal items she now possessed. But something about having it gave her a sense of peace—as if Brad's God, the same God her father had claimed to know so well, would get her safely to Washington if she planned to make good on the promise she'd made her father to at least consider the possibility that God was in control of her circumstances. At the moment, with the mental image of her burning apartment building, her charred vehicle, and the strange feel of the wig and glasses against her skin, it made her feel a little less panicked to think that God might be running the show.

"Ready for me to spring you?" Brad asked Randal later that morning. He tossed a small duffel bag onto the hospital bed.

"Are you kidding?" Randal reached for the bag. "I'm going nuts." He hit the button on his remote control to turn off the TV. "There hasn't been any new news on Tetherton since early this morning."

"That's the way Swelder wants it."

"Did he really kill himself?" Randal grabbed the duffel bag and began pulling the clothes out.

"I doubt it," Brad said. "I expected to find your mom here."

"Marcus dragged her off to the airport already. They're both going to New York today."

"He talked her into it?" Brad asked.

"That's one way to put it." Randal tossed the sheets aside and began to pull on his jeans. He shot Brad a dry look. "Bullied her is more like it. He just basically told her that if she'd really decided that God was using these circumstances to widen her circle of influence, then who was she to tell Him He didn't know what He was doing."

Brad let out a low whistle. "I'll bet that went over well."

"Nobody can get away with stuff like that except Marcus."

"Yeah."

"Wish I had the touch," Randal said, wincing slightly as his head pounded like a high-school-band drum, but he ignored it as he reached for the sport shirt on the bed. "Well, she went anyway. That was the important thing."

"You're sure you're okay?"

"My head hurts," he admitted as he pulled on the shirt. "Big deal. The doctor said it was going to hurt whether I lie around or run the marathon. He also said I was fine. I've got a bottle of headache medicine, so I'm good to go."

"If you feel up to it, I've got a job I need you to do."

"Anything. Just get me out of here."

"Do you still know that intern in the White House security office?"

"Bryce McIntosh? Sure."

"Good. Finish getting dressed and I'll tell you what I need you to do."

★ ★ ★

"I can't believe I let you talk me into this," Mariette told Marcus as the plane reached a cruising altitude.

"You did the right thing. Randal would have resented you. Not only that, he'd have been furious with you if you'd let this opportunity pass you by because you wanted to baby him."

"I'm his *mother*. It's my right to baby him. I still wonder if he has a coat when it's cold outside. It's like a reflex or something."

Marcus laughed. "Some things don't change, I guess. At least he's got Brad looking out for him."

"*That's* comforting. My son is in the hands of a man whose idea of a square meal is pork rinds and ravioli. A man with a target on his back, a magnet for enemy fire."

"They'll be fine." Marcus squeezed her hand. "They're in God's hands, Mariette. Brad may be in the crosshairs of the enemy, but he's made it unharmed this far. I believe that God has a plan for him. Just like God has a plan for us."

"Yeah, well—" she shook her head slightly—"I know you're going to tell me this is stupid, but sometimes, I just wish He'd ask my advice on how He should handle things."

"It's not stupid. It's normal. Being willing to surrender control of our lives and our circumstances to Jesus is the hardest thing any of us have to do. It's not in our nature. That's the same thing that keeps people from turning to the Lord in the first place. Maybe they're willing to believe in God, but they're not willing to trust Him. It takes humility. You have to realize that you can't be good enough, or do enough, or succeed enough to measure up to His standards.

You can only surrender all that you have. There is no halfway commitment."

"I know that," she insisted. "I believe that, but I feel like I'm getting sucked in over my head. This commission—" Mariette glanced around, then lowered her voice a notch— "in my wildest dreams I never imagined working for Nicolae Carpathia."

"God's all about proving that our wildest dreams aren't always wild enough, Mariette. He has something for you to do. Everything that seems to be standing in the way of that right now is just the enemy trying to keep you from living out God's will for your life."

She sank back into her seat. "Is it always going to be this hard?" she asked him.

"No." Marcus paused for a moment, then gave her a look filled with sympathy. "I'm afraid it's going to be harder."

★ ★ ★

"Hi, Bryce," Randal said as he casually approached the basement storage area the Secret Service referred to as the evidence locker. Here, all sensitive papers and information were stored pending criminal and civil investigations of any wrongdoing at the White House. Though most public documents were stored at the Library of Congress, any confidential information that posed potential security risks or even political hazards for U.S presidents and their staff was kept here in the Old Executive Office Building.

And here was where boxes of confidential information were held until a determination could be made about jurisdiction over a certain case—like the box Brad had removed from Forrest Tetherton's office earlier this morning.

"Randal!" Bryce McIntosh gave him a surprised look.

"You're the last person I expected to see today. How are you, man?"

"Head's killing me," Randal confessed. He shoved his hands into his back jeans pockets.

"I still can't believe all this. I mean, the limo explosion, Tetherton's death. It's kind of unreal, you know."

"A little more than you bargained for when you came to work here, huh?"

"Yeah, you could say that." Bryce looked over Randal's casual clothes. "So, um, you're obviously not driving today."

"I've been given a paid leave of absence for a few days. Nobody wants a driver with a possible concussion."

"Least they could do," Bryce quipped. "I mean, saving the president's life and all. You'd think you'd get some kind of medal for that."

"Right now, I'll just settle for the leave." Randal eased closer to the desk. "Listen, Bryce, I kind of need a favor."

"Sure. What's up?"

Randal glanced over his shoulder, then gave Bryce a slightly sheepish look. "Well, I don't know if you heard, but part of why the whole thing with the car happened yesterday is because I forgot to file my log sheet when I got back from running that errand for Brad."

Bryce nodded. "That's why you had the Service pull the limo. Fortuitous, that's for sure."

Randal pulled a folded piece of paper from his pocket. "Well, after everything got so crazy, I never did give it to Dispatch. Now, they've pulled all the records for the investigation and stored 'em in here. But I've still got the log sheet."

Bryce took the piece of paper and studied it. "It's supposed to be in the evidence record."

"I know. I know. I just—they took me to the infirmary

and then the hospital, and I totally forgot it was still in my pocket until this morning."

"They're going to need this."

"Yeah. I know," Randal said, "and I figured I would just give it to Mr. Benton and let him take care of it, but then with this whole Tetherton mess, well, the last thing he needs to worry about right now is some stupid log sheet that says I drove the car out to Sterling to drop off a book for Emma Pettit."

"You got a point there."

"So—" Randal glanced behind his shoulder again, then lowered his voice—"I know it's not exactly regulation procedure, but do you think I could just slip inside the locker for like two minutes and shove this in the box?"

Bryce appeared to hesitate. "I don't know, Randal."

"I won't even open the box," Randal promised him. "I can slide it under the top without breaking the seal."

Bryce exhaled a long breath. "I'd like to help you out."

"Come on. It'll be quick, and I really don't want to bother Mr. Benton with this. It's not like it's some crucial piece of evidence."

Bryce paused a moment longer, then handed Randal the paper. He reached behind him and pressed the button that caused the heavy door to swing open. "The security cameras inside the vault take new stills every two and a half minutes," Bryce told him. "They just cycled, so that's all the time you have before someone sees you on camera."

"Thanks," Randal told him. "I owe you one."

6

Mariette and Marcus made their way through the Marine Air Terminal at LaGuardia toward the ground transportation area. Though Marcus had finally persuaded her to make this trip, Mariette couldn't shake the unease that had haunted her since she'd seen that limousine explode yesterday morning at the White House.

When her cell phone rang, she pulled it quickly from her pocket. "It's probably Daniel," she told Marcus. Daniel Berger, the New York City mayor who had been working with Mariette for the past few weeks on solving some of the disastrous supply problems New York had faced following the Rapture, had promised to arrange limousine transportation for both of them. Mariette would head straight to the UN, where her meetings were set to commence within the hour, while Marcus would go to the mayor's office where he and Daniel had arranged to meet this afternoon. The international council of religious leaders' summit he was to attend was scheduled for the next morning.

Mariette glanced at the caller ID and felt her heart clench. It was Max. Her ex-husband had only two reasons to call her: he needed a favor, or something had happened to Randal.

Marcus gave her a curious look as she continued to stare at the ringing phone. "Mariette?"

"It's Max. Or Max's office." She took a deep breath and pushed the button to receive. "Mariette."

"It's Max."

Her fingers tightened on the phone as she met Marcus's concerned gaze. "Is something wrong?"

"You could say that." Max dropped his voice a decibel. "I'm assuming you've talked to Randal."

"Not in the last few hours. What's going on, Max?"

"Don't jerk me around," Max ground out. "You know what I mean."

"No, actually, I don't. I talked to Randal this morning before I left, if that's what you—"

"Left? You're not in Washington?"

Why did she hear an indictment in the question? "I'm in New York."

"New York—" Max swore softly. "The UN Relief Commission—or what is it called now, Global Community?"

She ignored his acerbic tone. "What about Randal?"

He paused a few seconds. When he spoke again, his voice sounded hushed. "Randal called me yesterday morning before the explosion."

Her heartbeat kicked up a notch. "Why?"

"He wanted information on Major Nuñez. I'm fairly certain he thought Major Nuñez was a military officer."

"He's not?"

"Not exactly." Max paused. "The boy's in way over his head, Mariette. I wasn't so sure yesterday, but after that explosion—"

"Did you *know* something about that?" she asked in horror.

"Randal really hasn't talked to you, has he?"

"No. He's been sleeping off getting bounced across the White House lawn. Tell me what's going on, Max."

Marcus seemed to sense her growing distress and guided her to one of the large windows of the terminal where they were somewhat secluded from the crowd. Mariette dug in her pocket for a small notepad and pen. While Max told her about Randal's phone call the previous morning, she scrawled *Max—he knew about assassination attempt* on the paper and shoved it into Marcus's hand.

"Here's the thing, Mariette," Max was saying. "I have no idea where Randal got his information about Major Nuñez, but I think he assumed that Nuñez is a person."

"You said he's not."

"There once was a person by that name. But that's not what got Randal into trouble. These days, Major Nuñez is the code name for a covert operation being run out of the upper level of the Pentagon."

"How upper level?"

"As high as you can imagine. There are two phases of this operation. The minor phase was completed about a month ago, just before the disappearances. The major phase is in effect now."

"And it involves *assassinating* the president?" she demanded.

"It involves," Max said harshly, "protecting the national security and interests of the United States."

"Max, someone planted a bomb in the president's limousine. Are you telling me you knew something about that?"

"Don't be so naïve," he bit out. "It's not that simple."

"But you did know about it?"

"I found out when Randal called to ask me about Nuñez."

"And you dragged him into it."

"No."

"But you warned him about the bomb."

"I told him that under no circumstances could he allow the president to ride in the lead limousine in the motorcade. Under the circumstances, it was the best I could do."

She clenched a hand at her throat as she realized the ramifications of what Max was telling her. "Are you telling me that you *involved* Randal in this?"

"Give me some credit, will you, Mariette? I have no idea how he got information on Nuñez. What else was I supposed to do?"

"Who else knows about this?"

"The Secret Service is investigating, obviously. They're demanding information from us."

"Is it going to implicate Randal?"

"They know he asked about Nuñez. They know that when he asked me about Nuñez, I was able to procure information that helped the White House avoid the assassination. They're going to want to know where Randal got the name."

"I can't believe this."

"Look. I tried to call him, but I haven't been able to get through to him. Maybe he just won't take my phone calls. I don't know, but he needs to know that this is way bigger than he thinks."

"I'm sure he gets that," Mariette shot back. "He got a concussion saving the president and the secretary-general of the United Nations from an assassin. I'm pretty sure he's aware of the scope of things by now."

"This is no time for sarcasm."

"No, I don't suppose it is. I merely got our son a government job. You've managed to suck him into a criminal and treasonous plot, something that could potentially land him in jail—or worse, get him killed."

She heard the creak of Max's chair and could picture him leaning back with that same tight-lipped, disapproving look on his face he'd had every time he'd lectured her during the latter part of their marriage.

"Look," he said. "The key here is that Randal needs to be alerted to what's going on. Once he has the information he needs, he'll be in a better position to protect himself."

"Or you," she shot back. "I'm not an idiot, Max. I know what you're doing. You're covering your back, just like you always do."

"Thank you for your faith in me," he said bitterly. "I don't suppose it occurred to you that I might be concerned for Randal?"

"In my experience, you aren't generally concerned about anyone but yourself, Max."

The moment she said the angry words, she felt Marcus's gaze on her. She refused to meet it. Her statement had come from the deep reservoir of hurt and resentment she still felt about her ex-husband. Where that lined up with Jesus' commandments to forgive, she couldn't say, and she wasn't ready to face Marcus's indictment of her behavior, no matter how gently it might be delivered to her.

"I guess I deserved that," Max said quietly.

Mariette drew a calming breath. "I'll call Randal," she said. "I'll tell him to talk to you ASAP. And, Max?"

"Yes."

"If he suffers because of this, I'll never forgive you."

"I didn't expect you to forgive me anyway."

★   ★   ★

Randal waited for the heavy door to swing shut behind him. Bryce had given him the shelf location and file number for the evidence box that contained the White House reports on the previous day's limousine explosion.

But he had to find the box Brad had taken from Forrest Tetherton's office. He was banking on the evidence boxes being sorted by date. If that was the case, the box he wanted should be near the evidence from the explosion. Randal checked the slip of paper and hurried through the rows until he found the proper section. He easily located the box from the explosion and began searching the shelves next to it. Harmon Drake had logged an extraordinary amount of evidence. There were easily twenty boxes stacked on the ceiling-high shelves. Finally, he found a box marked *Tetherton Death* on the second shelf from the top. Down the row about thirty feet, he saw one of the wheeled ladders the evidence clerks used to file and retrieve the boxes.

He shoved the ladder into place and climbed up to retrieve the box. Using the small metal tool Brad had given him, Randal pried open the seal on the box. The notebook Brad had described still rested on top of the other files.

Randal grabbed it, then thrust it inside his shirt and resealed the box. He looked quickly over his shoulder at the clock on the wall. He had about a minute and a half before the camera's next cycle. He clambered down the ladder and moved it out of proximity to the Tetherton file. Moving quickly back along the row, he located the limousine files again. He pulled the folded paper from his back pocket and slipped it into the box marked *Dispatch Logs*. He figured he had time to make it out of the evidence locker, no sweat.

He was headed for the door when another box arrested his attention. Stacked with the other limousine files was a box labeled *Max Arnold*. It had to be the records of Randal's call to his father in the minutes before the explosion. Heart now pumping, he glanced at the clock again. He still had over a minute. Though Brad had asked him to get the notebook and get out of the vault as quickly as possible, Randal couldn't let this opportunity pass. He still had no idea how his father had learned of the bomb in time to warn him— nor what connection the mysterious, and as yet unidentified, Major Nuñez had to the situation. Randal made a quick decision and pulled the box down.

There were several items in the box: a copy of the call log from his phone call to Max; a log of calls to and from Max's office that day; copies of the White House security pictures that showed Brad handing Randal the yellow slip of paper with Nuñez's name; a copy of Max's appointment log for the last six months; and, most chilling, a file folder containing various pictures of Max meeting with different military officers in a range of locations in and around the D.C. area.

Randal examined the pictures with a frown. None of them appeared to be the usual journalistic photos taken by news photographers and archived for posterity. These had a definite clandestine feeling. Some had been taken through a car window. Others had the blurry foreground images that indicated a high-power zoom lens had been used to take the photos from a distance.

Randal shot another glance at the clock on the wall. He had less than twenty seconds to make it out of the vault. He heard the door open. "Arnold?" Bryce called. "Everything okay?"

Randal quickly stuffed the photos into his shirt with the notebook. "Finished," he called to Bryce. "I'll be right there."

He slid the top back on the box and resealed it, then jammed it onto the shelf. Five seconds. He zipped his Windbreaker to disguise the bulge beneath his shirt as he approached Bryce. He slipped through the open door just as he heard the buzzer that indicated the cycling of the security cameras.

Bryce gave him a curious look. "Cut that a little close, didn't you?"

"Yeah, I guess." Randal's heart was thundering in his ears.

"Did you get lost or something?"

"I don't know." Randal crossed his arms over his chest, conscious of the bulge beneath his coat. "I guess I'm still a little groggy from all that medication they gave me last night. I had to stop for a second and get my bearings."

That made Bryce laugh. "I wouldn't be surprised. I had knee surgery last year and I was whacked for like a month."

Randal nodded. "Anyway, I found the file and added my log sheet. I really appreciate this."

Bryce shrugged. "No harm done. You got out before the cameras cycled, so no one knows but us."

"Thank the Lord," Randal said. He wiped a hand over his forehead where sweat had beaded at his hairline.

"You look a little flushed, by the way. You sure you're feeling okay?"

"I'm a little beat," Randal told him. "I guess I need to go home and get some rest after all."

"Not a bad idea, dude. Mr. Benton seems like the kind of guy who will cut you some slack until you're feeling better."

"He's the best," Randal agreed.

★　★　★

Randal cast a final look over his shoulder, then slipped into the car at the corner of Pennsylvania Avenue and Twelfth Street.

"Did you get it?" Nero asked him.

Randal leaned weakly back in the passenger seat. "I think so." He pulled the notebook out of his jacket, careful to leave the strange pictures of Max behind. He wasn't sure

yet what he wanted to do with them—wasn't even sure if he
wanted to tell Brad about them. If only his head would stop
hurting long enough to allow him to concentrate, maybe
he could come up with a solution. The ringing of his cell
phone arrested his attention. He glanced at the LCD dis-
play where his mother's number blinked insistently.
Randal sighed and hit the mute button. He wasn't up to another lecture about zipping up his jacket and not going outside with wet hair.

"You need to get that?" Nero asked.

"I'll call back."

Nero threw the car into gear and merged into traffic.
"Mr. Benton is waiting for us at the FEC. He said to tell you
the reporter should be here in a couple of hours. You ready
to go?"

"Yes."

"You sure?" Nero gave him a narrow look. "You look
kind of pale."

"Just a little winded." He managed a halfhearted grin.
"Maybe I'm sicker than I thought."

"You need a doctor or something?"

Randal shook his head. He pressed the photos against
his stomach and begged God for wisdom. "No, I'm fine.
Really. Let's go meet Brad."

★   ★   ★

Randal found Brad seated at one of the small worktables
poring over an Federal Election Commission report. He
slipped into the cubicle next to him and handed him the
notebook. He'd left the pictures of Max in a sealed brown
envelope in the car with Nero. "Is that the right one?"

"Yes." Brad gave Randal a searching look. "Any problems?"

"No. I made it in and out before the cameras cycled. As long as Bryce doesn't rat me out, I think we got away with it."

"You still trust him?"

"Yeah, I guess. As long as he believes that all I did was add my driver's log to the limo box, everything's okay. If he finds out I tampered with evidence, he won't cover for me."

"I wouldn't expect him to," Brad said. He tore a sheet of paper off the large stack of printouts he'd been studying, then tucked the notebook under his arm. "Where's Nero?"

"Outside with the car. The parking's terrible here."

"Then let's walk," Brad said.

He led Randal through the sterile-looking government building out onto the street. Taking a careful look around, he handed him the torn printout before flipping open the notebook. "I hope this has what I'm looking for."

Brad had told Randal about his suspicion that the notebook would contain some indication of where the key Jane Lyons had found in George's file belonged. Both men knew the chance was slim, but at the moment, it was the only lead they had. "Did you have a chance to look over Liza's package?" Randal asked.

Brad glanced over his shoulder and studied the crowd for a moment. Nero was parked in a delivery zone half a block away. "Basically, it had exactly what she described to you. The evidence that links Kostankis and Rudd is another piece in the puzzle, but I still don't have the one answer I need."

"Who sent the pictures?" Randal supplied.

Brad continued to flip through the notebook. "Yeah. And why. I have to believe that if George was really about to break open this story, he had an inside source, someone who was feeding him information."

"And you think his source sent the photos, and maybe knows where the key belongs?"

"Yes." Brad studied a page of the book, flipped forward three pages, then back another. He cast another quick look over his shoulder. "I don't know why I was so sure it would be here."

"What are you looking for?"

"A name. A place, something. I don't know." He kept flipping the pages.

Randal walked along the street with Brad, his mind turning over questions of his own. He couldn't shake the feeling that someone was watching them. The pictures of Max had disturbed him in many ways—but most especially because they had clearly been taken without Max's knowledge. As the son of a prominent U.S. senator, Randal had learned to expect public scrutiny. Being photographed at public events, at family gatherings, and on all the occasions the press considered fodder for public consumption was perfectly normal, but the pictures he'd taken from that evidence box had broken the boundaries of safety that Randal had learned to rely on. No matter how intense the scrutiny, no matter how difficult the public demands had become, his mother had always found a way to carve out safe zones for them, places where he could be assured of a secure haven from the prying eyes of reporters and cameras. In a few brief moments in a locked room where he wasn't supposed to be, that safe little world had been shattered.

How had his father known about Major Nuñez? And did those pictures somehow implicate Max in the plot to assassinate the president? And if so, was his father also implicated in whatever illegal activities Brad was about to reveal to the world?

"Randal? Did you hear me?"

He glanced guiltily at Brad. "What?"

"Are you feeling all right?"

"Yeah, why?"

"You seem a little distant. I promised your mom I'd take care of you."

"Yeah, yeah, I'm fine." Randal thrust his hands into his jeans pockets. "So what did you find?"

Brad studied him a moment longer, then pointed to a place on the page. "There are copies in here of George's appointment logs for the six weeks before he died. On the Tuesday afternoon before the coroner placed the time of death, he has a one-hour block of time marked off with the initials MEP and the number 1436." Brad flipped back several pages. "Here it is again. One week before. When I spoke to Fitz last night at the dinner, he indicated that George had told him he had certain suspicions the day before he died." Brad tapped a page of the book. "That would have been here, and George has the same indication marked that morning." He flipped forward. "This is three days before the Rapture. His last entry shows a meeting with Jane Lyons. That had to be when he passed her the files."

"You think all this has something to do with the key?"

"What if George had a regular contact, someone else in the White House who was aware of his circumstances, someone else who knew what was going on. They met to exchange information while they each collected information independently, then George stored evidence in a safe-deposit box—"

"Box 1436?"

"Or a box located at street number 1436."

"MEP?" Randal mused. "Could that identify the box?"

"Possibly. Maybe George set it up so both his signature and that of his contact were needed in order to access the evidence. Or some kind of safeguard like that."

Randal frowned. "But how would they transfer information to the box if neither one could get to the box without the other's involvement?"

"I don't know," Brad said. "Could be George just set it up and his contact has never actually seen the evidence. Maybe they used a secure courier so even George never accessed the box."

"The same way the pictures were delivered." Randal nodded. "That makes sense."

"Especially if the same person that used the courier service to transfer evidence to the safe-deposit box also used it to send me those photos."

"But the security office never could determine which company had delivered them. They have no record of the delivery of the photos."

Brad thumped the book. "And I let them stop looking," he said. "I think that's the problem. Conner Trellis told me he couldn't determine who sent the photos because the envelope was unmarked and the guard at the gate hadn't logged the arrival. I took that at face value."

Randal frowned. "The chief of security? Brad, you don't think—"

"Hear me out." Brad tucked the notebook under his arm. "What if they couldn't determine where the package came from because the package didn't come from outside?"

"You mean—"

"There's no way that, given the security situation at the White House in the days following the Rapture, any security guard would have failed to log an outside package. Maybe under normal circumstances, but not during all that."

Randal nodded. "I'd have to say that's true. Everything has been so tight and by the book lately. Not even a rookie would have made that mistake."

"But if the package came from inside—"

"Then how did it get to the gate?"

"The person who delivered it was well-known and trusted enough to drop it off unobtrusively. It went unnoticed until they realized my name was on it."

Randal thought that over. "Which suggests that George's contact was a White House insider."

"And probably someone who is still inside the White House."

"But who?"

Brad indicated a small landscaping wall in front of one of the buildings where they could sit. "Someone with access to George."

"And who has access to classified or secret documents."

"Someone who trusted me to do the right thing with those photos."

Randal pursed his lips. "Or someone who wanted to set you up by sending you those photos."

Brad rubbed the back of his neck. He glanced up and down the street again. "Maybe. Certainly someone who knew George was murdered."

"When and where George was murdered," Randal mused. "They had to know when to take those pictures."

"Or they had to hire someone to take those pictures."

"With the intention of giving them to you." Randal shook his head. "But who would have the motivation to do that?"

Brad studied the notebook again. "That's the question, isn't it?" When his phone rang, he pulled it from his pocket to take the call. "It's your mother," he told Randal.

"Tell her I took my vitamins," he muttered.

While Brad took the call, Randal glanced down the street to where Nero still sat parked in the delivery zone. He knew Brad intended to head straight for Andrews Air Force

Base where Liza would arrive this afternoon on the new plane, but Randal couldn't get his mind off those pictures.

"Mariette," Brad was saying, "are you sure? Does Marcus know?"

Randal looked at him sharply, belatedly remembering the call from his mother he'd ignored earlier. "What's going on?"

"I'll tell him. You okay?" He waited for her response. "Everything's going to be all right," Brad assured her. "It's almost over." He slapped the phone shut and stuck it in his pocket.

Randal stood abruptly. "Something's wrong, isn't it?"

Brad looked down the street and signaled for Nero. "We've got to get out of here."

"Is Mom okay?"

"Yes." Brad glanced both ways, then headed for the approaching car. "She's fine. She heard from Max."

Randal's heart leaped. "What's up?"

Brad slipped a hand under his arm and hurried him toward the car. "Let's go. We'll talk in the car."

7

Liza made her way past the rows of reporters and journalists who'd been invited to make the maiden journey on the new *Air Force One*. Since Fitzhugh had promised the plane's official maiden voyage to Carpathia for the treaty signing in Jerusalem, Liza supposed that anger over being cheated out of the first flight had prompted the president to allow the media to make this transport flight.

Tradition had always given the president the right to make the maiden voyage on an upgraded *Air Force One*. Generally, the trip was made with no media aboard. It gave the president, his staff, and his guests the opportunity to explore the new plane at leisure without any pressure.

Liza grabbed a pillow covered with an *Air Force One* pillowcase and found a seat near the rear of the press-corps area. She'd cleared security with no problems, but what Brad hadn't counted on was the natural curiosity and scrutiny she'd have to endure on board. Already, the press-corps camaraderie had colleagues and old friends swapping jokes about the president and the administration. Newcomers were vetted for their credentials and contacts.

If anyone on board doubted Fitzhugh's pride and obsession with the plane, those doubts had been put to rest when they'd received their briefing packets. Liza had scanned the high points of the packet, using the ornate package as a shield to avoid making eye contact.

The new plane had an opulent presidential bedroom suite complete with a shower in the nose of the aircraft. A full-size replica of the Oval office was next door to the suite with a flanking wood-paneled conference room with high-speed Internet access and state-of-the-art communications facilities. A lap pool with adjustable flow speeds had been installed so Fitzhugh could keep up his exercise routine. Liza wondered how the pool would cope with turbulence. The plane also had a satellite-television system so Fitzhugh could watch his favorite teams play while in flight.

With over four thousand square feet of interior floor space, standing over five stories tall and as long as a city block, the flying conference center had more than one hundred and twenty telephones, fifteen bathrooms, and an emergency-surgery bay with a pullout operating table.

With hundreds of stored meals and the capability of being refueled in midair, the new plane could stay aloft for over two weeks. Its state-of-the-art engines could fly the president and his entourage halfway around the world and carry up to ten thousand pounds of baggage.

Then there were the ubiquitous *Air Force One*–marked boxes of candies and snacks, pillowcases, fleece blankets, cocktail napkins, and the much-coveted bars of soap with the presidential seal embossed on the top. While her colleagues admired the vaunted new amenities on the plane, Liza eased into the corner and pulled a pair of head-phones out of her large bag, which she'd salvaged from her car. She didn't have anything to plug them into, but she hoped they'd serve as a deterrent to any would-be conversationalists.

She wedged the pillow against the window, put the headphones on, and closed her eyes. After the mostly sleepless night she'd spent, she should have no trouble sleeping on the flight to Andrews Air Force Base despite the allure of the upcoming blockbuster movie premier for the flight's guests, accompanied by unlimited gourmet popcorn.

Sure smells good, she thought, but then sleep shook even that thought out of her head. She was so tired she didn't even dream.

Brad slowly examined the photos Randal had given him as Nero negotiated the midday downtown traffic. After Mariette's phone call, he'd made the decision to take Randal and head directly for Andrews Air Force Base. There was a part of him that believed that if he could simply get all the people he'd dragged into this mess under one roof at the same time, he could protect them from the fallout. Another part of him feared that he was merely creating a target-rich environment for his enemies as he brought his friends together.

Brad had not heard from Liza since she'd arrived at Whidbey Island. He had to assume that was good news. If she'd been denied boarding, he would have been called. His last check with the White House indicated that the plane was in the air and that all of the expected passengers had checked in and boarded on time.

He'd hurried Randal into the backseat of the vehicle and given instructions to Nero to head for the Beltway. Randal had produced the pictures and explained where he got them.

As Brad studied them, he began to see certain patterns.

Each had a date-and-time stamp. The earlier photos showed Max Arnold with different high-ranking military officials—including Dave Marsden from the Joint Chiefs of Staff—in a range of public settings. A fund-raiser. A restaurant. On the steps of the Capitol.

But the later photos were in more private settings like the Mall, near the Lincoln Memorial, and on some undisclosed street corner after dark. For the most part, he recognized the people in the photos. Occasionally he did not.

"Is my father in trouble?" Randal asked.

Brad studied a picture of Max accepting a large envelope from an unidentified army lieutenant. "I'm not sure."

"Drake had to have put those photos of my dad in the evidence boxes from the assassination attempt because he knows Dad tipped me about Nuñez."

"I'm sure he did. Your mom said that Max indicated to her that he might know a good bit more about Nuñez than we thought. She said she wasn't free to give me the details, but she wants me to call your father."

"Why doesn't she want me to call him? I'm the one who talked to him."

Brad slanted him a knowing look. "She does—but not for official information. She wants you to call him because you're his kid. I'm the chief of staff at the White House. And apparently I may be a target."

Randal muttered beneath his breath, then looked at Brad, pain in his eyes. "I just want to know if Max is doing something illegal. The guy is my father. I know he's no angel, but this makes no sense to me. I mean, do you think he could have known about this Nuñez guy because he's involved in whatever happened yesterday?"

"I don't know." Brad stuffed the photos back into the envelope. "All we can do is ask him."

"You know what I think?" Nero said.

Surprised, Brad looked at the squarish profile of the young man who'd come recently into their circle of brothers in Christ. In his experience, the young man spoke rarely and offered his personal opinions even less frequently. "I'd like to know what you think," Brad told him.

"I think that, whatever's going on, there's a whole mess of people doing the devil's work. Kind of makes me wonder if they know they're doing the devil's work, or if they just got sucked into the whole thing."

"Nobody works for the devil by accident," Randal said.

"No?" Nero met Randal's gaze in the rearview mirror. "You never screwed something up so bad you didn't know how to get back out again? You never made a mistake so big you thought nobody could forgive you?"

"Maybe. But I didn't work for the devil," Randal answered.

"It's like Marcus always says: 'If you're not for God, you're against Him. There's no middle ground.'"

Randal folded his arms and leaned back in the seat. His resentment of his father, Brad knew, ran deep, and despite the fact that God appeared to be at work in his life, the young man still held past events—admittedly traumatic ones—against Max.

Forgiveness, Brad knew, could be hard.

"Yeah, well," Randal said, "I think some people are beyond redemption."

"You think Jesus was thinking that when He died on that cross?" Nero said.

Randal look stunned, but didn't reply.

"Nope." Nero shook his head. "I don't think He was. I think He forgave us all. And then He died for our sins. And He's still redeeming us. 'Cause a whole lot of people gave up on me a long time ago. It took someone like Marcus to show me that it's not too late for anybody. Grace is forever, you know."

Randal didn't say anything, just turned to look out the window. Brad thought about pressing him, but decided against it. Getting Randal to forgive his father was a long-term project Brad intended to see through to fruition, but for the moment, he merely wanted to keep everyone alive.

Brad settled into his seat and began to examine George's notebook again. There had to be answers here somewhere.

★　★　★

Nicolae Carpathia's entrance into the conference room at the United Nations headquarters had the impact of a coronation parade. Immediately after he appeared in the door, twenty-three members of his hand-chosen Commission for Global Compassion and Wellness, as Mariette had learned he planned to call his new international relief agency, stood and burst into applause. As the twenty-fourth member, she managed to busy herself straightening the enormous briefing packet she'd received when she arrived.

"Please," Carpathia told them, holding up both his hands in a regal gesture, "please, this is not necessary."

A young woman Mariette recognized as a member of the board of the International Committee of the Red Cross moved toward the secretary-general. "Oh, but it is." She indicated the room with a sweep of her arm. "I think I speak for everyone here when I say that this has been a dream of ours for years. No one could ever muster enough political clout to bring us all together like this. Together, we can do so much more than we ever could do apart."

Carpathia accepted the compliment with his usual humility and aplomb. Mariette felt the hair on her arms stand up as she saw the way every other person in the room seemed to tumble so easily into this man's charming web of deceit.

"We are indeed blessed with a unique window of opportunity," he said. He accepted a leather-bound portfolio from the attractive young woman who'd entered the room with him. "And I am the one who should be grateful. I know you all made tremendous personal sacrifices to be here. With everything that has happened recently, your agencies and organizations are tapped out, but I selected each of you because of your unique qualifications and expertise." He glanced at his companion. "Ms. Durham, would you please pass out the agendas?"

The woman hurried to do his bidding. Nicolae turned back to the group. "As you all know, I personally requested that each of you attend this meeting. When I was growing up in Romania, I had no idea what kind of horrors and pain poverty and war could impose on the world. I was from a small village. When someone was in need, we shared what we had."

He gave a self-deprecating smile that made Mariette shudder. "Until I was old enough to leave home, my idea of a natural disaster was the year we had a drought and the man on the neighboring farm lost his wheat crop. I wish things were still so simple."

That won nods and collective mutters of agreement. "But now," Carpathia continued, "we face a disaster of unimagined proportions. We are in a world that has been devastated economically, spiritually, and emotionally. People are hurting, and though I am excited about the opportunities we now have for peace, I cannot ignore that all the peace treaties in the world are worthless if the people have no bread to eat."

Again, the crowd expressed its collective agreement. Mariette accepted an agenda from Ms. Durham and wondered how she might have reacted to this speech a few months ago. He was certainly hitting all the high points, every button guaranteed to win the undying loyalty of the group.

"And in organizing this commission," Carpathia said, "I turned to people with a proven expertise in their field. Each of you was selected because of your achievements and creative problem solving." He began to move through the room as he continued speaking. He laid a hand on Peter Dugan's shoulder. "My friend Mr. Dugan is here on behalf of the Red Crescent." He squeezed Dugan's shoulder lightly, then moved on. "Captain Sidell is here from Army Emergency Relief."

He introduced three other attendees, then stopped at Mariette's chair. "Ms. Arnold," he said, greeting her with a warm smile that made her feel slightly queasy, "I trust your son is much improved today?"

"I wouldn't be here if he weren't," she said.

Carpathia nodded. "I am certain you would not be." He turned to the group. "Many of you may not know this, but I am here today only because Mariette Arnold's son saved my life yesterday in Washington. If you saw the news report, he is the young man who was almost killed when he prevented the president and myself from boarding the limousine with the bomb."

The room reacted appropriately. Nicolae held out a hand to Mariette, a hand that she had no choice but to accept.

"I was overwhelmed when I learned that the young hero who had saved my life was Ms. Arnold's son." He indicated the chair at the head of the oval conference table where no one had dared to sit and placed a persuasive hand at the small of her back. "You see, I had already decided to ask Ms. Arnold to chair this commission. I had no idea her son would soon play such an important role in my life."

Mariette cringed inside, but accepted the head chair he pulled out for her. "Now," he said. "I have a treaty signing in Israel to arrange. I look forward to hearing what you all propose over the next few days. We all have a lot to do. I am depending on you all."

As his assistant finished handing out the agendas, Carpathia took the opportunity to introduce her. "This is my able and talented personal assistant, Ms. Hattie Durham. If you need anything at all, please let her know. I have instructed her to take care of you."

Mariette searched the young woman's face for any sign that she found his condescending tone irritating. She saw nothing but adoration in the blonde's eyes.

"Ms. Arnold," Carpathia said, "I trust you can proceed without me?"

Little does he know, Mariette thought. "We'll be fine, Mr. Secretary-General."

That won a slight smile from him. "I find that title so cumbersome and awkward. Until we think of something less ostentatious and easier to say, please call me Nicolae."

Mariette swallowed. Now she was on a first-name basis with the Antichrist.

Great. Just great.

Mayor Daniel Berger greeted Marcus warmly. "I'm so pleased to finally meet you," he said as he ushered Marcus into his elegantly appointed office. "Mariette has wonderful things to say about you."

"The feeling is mutual," Marcus assured him. Mariette had met the dynamic young mayor of New York on her last trip to the city. With its massive population, transportation challenges, and enormous logistical needs, FEMA had faced unique difficulties in helping the city recover from the Rapture.

Mariette had found an unexpected ally in Daniel Berger, both in her mission and in her spiritual journey. Berger had been elected mayor just five short months before the Rapture had devastated his life and his city. Through the remembered counsel of an old friend who'd been swept away in the Rapture, Daniel had turned to the God of Israel for answers. The Jewish mayor had found the answers he was seeking in Scripture, and had asked Jesus to come into his life. But he had been an isolated new Christian until he'd met Mariette.

She'd been trying for a week to arrange a meeting between Daniel and Marcus. Not only did she think the men could become fast friends, but she also recognized the potential advantage of Daniel's connections to Marcus's God-given vision for the future.

Marcus had told his small circle of friends that he felt God calling them to use the money his ministry was about to inherit to build a shelter that would protect believers from the coming disasters the Bible predicted during the Tribulation. He also felt called to play a key role in helping believers escape Carpathia's eventual persecution by organizing a new underground railroad that would help smuggle targeted believers out of harm's way, even out of the country. With his connections and control of New York's gateway to the world, Daniel Berger could prove to be invaluable in this cause.

Daniel handed Marcus a glass of ice water, then indicated the two chairs across from his desk. "I'm eager to talk to you," he said. "Mariette has given me only a few details, but I feel that this may have been what God has been preparing me for. I have so much to learn."

Marcus settled into the chair with a slight smile. "We all do."

"Tell me. How is Randal?"

"He'll be fine."

"I was a bit surprised that Mariette still made the trip to New York today."

"So was I. She almost didn't."

"You must have been very persuasive to get her to leave her son at home."

"He's with Brad Benton. She trusts Brad to take care of him."

Daniel glanced at the clock. "I suppose they're meeting even now at the UN."

Marcus nodded. "They should be."

"And what about Benton?" Daniel leaned closer to Marcus and lowered his voice as if, even here in the security of his office, he recognized the gravity of the situation and sought to protect it. "I saw the news reports on that explosion yesterday. Wasn't Brad supposed to be in that car?"

"From what I understand, it was just the president and the secretary-general who were supposed to be in the lead vehicle. It's hard to say who the assassin was after."

Daniel's expression was grim. "I have to tell you, Reverend, the more I learn and the more I see, the more I shudder to think what would have happened to me if my friend hadn't—" He broke off, clearly emotional. After a moment, Daniel settled back into his chair and crossed his long legs. "We have the afternoon, Marcus. I cleared my calendar, so please, tell me what you envision and how I can help."

★ ★ ★

"Mr. Benton?" A young airman approached Brad, Randal, and Nero where they waited inside the security gate at

Andrews Air Force Base. "We're expecting *Air Force One* in about ten minutes. Can I get you gentlemen something while you wait?"

Brad shook his head. "We're fine. Have you confirmed coordinates on the plane?"

"Yes sir. Fifteen minutes ago."

"Good." Brad indicated a waiting area on the far side of a couple of bookshelves. "We'll wait there."

Nero and Randal followed him to the small area and took a seat. Each reached for a magazine. Brad rubbed his eyes with his thumb and forefinger and tried to sort through the information he'd seen that morning in George Ramiro's notebook. There had to be something he was missing, something that would unravel the mystery of MEP and 1436 and tell him where the key that was burning a hole in his pocket belonged.

Try as he might, though, nothing came to him. Without the identity of George's contact in the White House, he would probably never know. The only choice left was to bluff their way through. If he and Liza leaked parts of the story to the press, there'd be a feeding frenzy in Washington. Rudd and whoever else was involved in the operation had no way of knowing that Brad didn't already have all the evidence he needed. With a little divine intervention, he might be able to bluff them into tipping their hand. He sure hoped so—if the leaks didn't shake something loose, he wasn't sure what he'd do next.

"Confirmed," he heard the woman at the reception desk say into the phone. She looked at Brad. "*Air Force One* has entered our airspace. They'll be on the ground in about five minutes. You're welcome to wait on the tarmac."

"We will," Brad said, standing. "I still have to swear in the new pilot before he's officially on our payroll."

The tarmac was alive with activity. Technicians and

ground crew moved the various barricades and directional blocks into place. A small truck approached, dragging the metal exit stairs for placement at the plane door.

Brad showed Randal and Nero a roped area with a red carpet. "We can all wait here," he said. "It should be a few minutes."

Nero was looking around with avid interest. "I got to tell you, Mr. Benton, this is kind of unreal. I never expected I'd be standing on a runway waiting for *Air Force One* to land."

Brad could well imagine. Like many of the District of Columbia's residents, he had lived in the shadow of the White House but had never seen beyond that shadow to the world inside until the last few years. "Wait until you see the plane," he said.

"It's massive," Randal told him. "I always forget how big it is. This new one is supposed to be even bigger than the old one."

"Do we get to go on board?" Nero asked.

"I've got some clout," Brad assured him. "I think I can arrange it." In the distance, he heard the approach of the plane. Activity on the tarmac picked up. They were soon joined by several air force officers and a contingency of enlisted men and women Brad knew would bear responsibility for escorting the media safely down the stairs and off the base.

Nero nervously stuffed his hands into his pockets. "I'm nervous. I don't know why I'm nervous. I mean, the president isn't even on board, is he?"

"No," Brad confirmed. "Just the media contingent that we're flying in to cover the trip to Jerusalem on Monday."

"Good," Nero said. "I don't think I could handle meeting the president."

Randal laughed. "Believe me, he puts his pants on just like the rest of us."

"Yeah, but he's got his own jet, his own boat, his own limousine, and his own seal on his bathrobe. I never met anybody who had a seal on their bathrobe."

"He's got monogrammed soap too." Brad smiled.

Randal shot Brad a dry look. "Do you think anybody will notice if a couple of the fleece blankets disappear after the press disembarks?"

"Happens every time they take it up." Brad shook his head. "Reporters, you know. Carpathia's making the first flight on the plane anyway. If someone checks the inventory, we'll charge 'em to the UN."

★   ★   ★

Liza shoved her headphones into her bag and prepared to exit the plane. The moment it landed, she wanted off. She'd managed to avoid questions by sleeping through the greater part of the trip.

In the last twenty minutes as they'd prepared to land, the pilot had turned the plane over to his copilot and come back and introduced himself as Rayford Steele. Liza wasn't sure what it was about that man she found so arresting, but he'd had a certain bearing that reminded her of Brad—as if he had the same trustworthy nature and inner decency that could be counted on in a crisis. He'd made a few brief remarks, thanked them all for joining him on his first flight of the aircraft, then returned to the cockpit. With everyone fully aware that the plane was nearing the base, people began moving around and collecting their gear—and, Liza noted cynically—their *Air Force One* souvenirs.

Apparently the organizers of the flight had anticipated that very phenomenon. A member of the *Air Force One* crew walked down the aisle of the plane, handing out souvenir blankets in sleek wrappers that proclaimed "Inaugu-

ral Flight of *Air Force One*," along with the date, in big gold
letters. When the crewman reached her, she took the blanket he handed her with a polite word of thanks, thinking
that now most of the passengers on this plane had a
matched set.

The rumble of the landing gear signaled their final de-
scent. Liza busied herself rearranging the contents of her
bag, ostensibly to pack in her blanket, but actually so she
could avoid making eye contact with anyone.

She found the Bible she'd taken from the hotel room.
Her hands froze on it. Though the fly page of the book indicated that she was welcome to take it, she still felt like a
thief. What kind of desperate person steals a Bible? she
wondered. And would Brad be able to answer her questions? Acutely aware that she could easily be facing serious
peril in the next few hours, her grip tightened on the Bible.
If You're there, Lord, she prayed, *then whatever happens, please
protect Brad. I may not deserve Your attention, but he does.*

She heard the thump of the wheels on the runway as the
pilot eased the plane into a butter-smooth landing. The
press corps burst into applause. The maiden voyage of *Air
Force One* was officially complete.

Brad saw the plane land and something inside him began
to uncoil. Liza was safe on the ground. He'd feel better
when he actually saw her, although, he thought wryly, if his
contacts in Los Angeles had done their usual excellent job,
he'd have a hard time recognizing her in the disguise they'd
provided.

"This is it," Randal told him.

Brad nodded. They moved toward the plane along with
the rest of the military contingent. Most of the enlisted men

and women had placards with the names of their assigned members of the press corps.

"Who we looking for?" Nero asked.

Brad had to laugh. "To be perfectly honest, I'm not sure." He ignored the strange look the younger man gave him. "It's a woman. About ten years older than you. A blonde. She should have glasses."

Nero scanned the crowd. "Who are all these people?"

Brad explained the protocol to him as the reporters began to disembark. One by one, they were escorted to the holding area, where their credentials were checked again and they were assigned a military escort.

Brad saw Liza at the top of the stairs. She was searching the crowd. He made a slight wave of his hand to attract her attention. Her look of relief when she saw him was unmistakable.

"That's her?" Randal asked.

"Yes," Brad said as relief rushed through him. At least this part of his plan was coming together. He began to shoulder his way through the crowd until he reached her. Now, if he could just get her off the base and somewhere that they could go over George's notebook, perhaps Liza could shed some insight on the information it contained.

Liza had carefully descended the metal stairs. They exchanged relieved greetings and Brad escorted her away from the stairs. He was about to offer to take her bag when he heard a slight commotion to his left. The crowd began to react to the disturbance before Brad could discern what had caused it. "Clear," Nero yelled before he planted a wide shoulder in the middle of Brad's back, pushing Brad and Liza to the ground.

There were screams and cries of panic as a shot rang out through the crowd. Then another and another. Chaos ensued.

Brad was buried beneath Nero's weight and was squash-
ing Liza into the tarmac. He squirmed clear of them both as
airmen began running across the pavement. He glanced
down at a terrified Liza.

"You all right?" Randal asked her, beside them on the
tarmac.

She gasped for air and sighed with relief when her lungs
inflated. She moved her arms and legs tentatively, rubbed
her head, then sat up. "I'm fine," she said shakily. "Just
bruised and winded."

"Good, I was afraid I'd flattened you," Brad said.

"Thank heaven," Randal said. He gave Nero's shoulder a
push. "You can get up now, hero." Three military police
had wrestled an airman to the ground and pulled a .45-
caliber weapon from his hand.

Liza got to her feet. "Sir? Sir, are you all right?" She
touched Nero's shoulder in some concern.

"Yes, Nero. Thanks for the push. But now we have to get
out of here," Brad said.

Randal gave Nero another shove. "Nero, what's the
deal, man? Everything's okay. Get up."

This time, Nero rolled onto his back. That's when the
friends saw the spreading red stain on Nero's chest.

Liza gasped in horror and covered her mouth. "Oh, my
. . ." Her stomach twisted as she saw the monstrously wide
puddle of blood begin to seep onto the pavement.

"We need a medic," Brad whispered, then yelled, "We
need a medic!" He scrambled to his knees and began un-
buttoning Nero's shirt. "Hang in there," he said, his voice
raw. "Help's on the way."

"There's an operating room on the plane." Randal's face
had turned sheet white. "I read about it." He looked
around, his eyes frantic. "Where's the medic?" he yelled.

An airman approached them at a run. "On their way, sir. How is he?"

Brad had ripped open Nero's shirt to find that the bullet had entered the center of Nero's chest. The blood pumping out of the wound was bright red. It made Brad's gut tighten and his head pound as he realized what that meant—arterial bleeding. . . . *Oh, Nero,* he thought, feeling fear and grief tear at his heart, *I'm so sorry. Dear God, help us through this.* Even as he prayed, Brad wadded the torn shirt up and pressed it hard against the entry wound. Nero's breathing had already begun to turn shallow. Brad cradled the young man's head. "Just keep breathing, Nero," he said. "Hang on a few minutes. Help's coming."

Nero's eyes fluttered open. "Did they get him?" he whispered.

"Yeah. Yeah, they got him."

"Is the lady okay?"

"Yes." Liza dropped to her knees and slipped her folded sweatshirt under Nero's head. "The lady is fine. Don't try to talk. Just keep your eyes open and look at me."

Nero looked at Brad. "I sure did want one of those blankets, Mr. Benton. Isn't that silly? Here we are getting ready to get on the plane of the president of the United States, and all I can think about is scoring one of those blankets."

"We'll get you one," Brad promised.

Liza laid her hand on his arm. "I have one," she said. She pulled the fleece blanket from her bag and removed it from its protective plastic bag. Gingerly, she slipped it under Nero's arm.

He managed a slight grin and clutched it tightly. "My little baby girl sure is gonna love this blanket."

A military ambulance screeched to a halt a few feet from them. Two medics came running.

"Mr. Benton?" Nero asked.

"Yes?"

He coughed. "I never thought much about being a hero, you know. I just wanted to do something for God with my life before it was too late." He grimaced in pain. "You think He'll be okay with what I done when I get there?"

"You have nothing to worry about, Nero," Brad assured him.

Liza moved away to make room for the medics. They immediately moved Brad's hand away and applied pressure to Nero's chest wound and began taking his vital signs. Brad would have moved aside entirely, but Nero's grip tightened on his hand.

"I'm going to see the Lord," Nero said. "And my wife and little daughter." He gave Brad a probing look. "Can I tell 'em I turned out good after all?"

Brad nodded. "You won't have to tell them anything, Nero. You turned out good. And they'll know it."

8

A devastated and emotionally drained Liza, Brad, and Randal made a mostly silent trip back to the temporary residence hotel in Alexandria where Brad had been living. While Brad dealt with the inevitable barrage of phone calls from White House security, Liza paced to the window where she stared sightlessly out at the view of downtown Alexandria.

Randal took responsibility for calling Marcus and Mariette and delivering the news. He was unable to reach his mother, who was still tied up in meetings at the UN, but Marcus answered on the second ring of his cell phone.

"We didn't know if there was someone we should call," Randal told Marcus.

The paramedics had finally moved Nero into the ambulance and sped off toward the base hospital. While they'd worked on him, Brad had sent Randal to find out what he could about the man who'd been arrested for firing into the crowd. A flash of Brad's White House ID had given Randal access to the office, where the military police and base security were trying to piece together what had happened on the tarmac.

They still had no reasonable answers. The airman they were holding in the brig wasn't talking, and, for the moment at least, the primary goal of base security seemed to be covering their own rear ends. Nero had been the guest of an upper-level White House official. Lax security around *Air Force One* had allowed someone to put a bullet into that guest. *Nobody* wanted to claim responsibility for that.

Brad had called Randal away from the security-control center an hour later. The doctors had pronounced Nero dead on arrival at the hospital. It had taken over an hour to complete the necessary paperwork and make arrangements for his body to remain in storage at the base until they could decide what to do.

Now, Randal took some comfort from his pastor and friend's gentle words and merciful heart. Marcus shared his grief, but reminded him that Nero was now with Jesus—a place they all aspired to be one day. Nero had been spared the horrors to come in the Tribulation, and God had chosen to take him home where his eternal life had begun even if his earthly life had ended. The loss for them, Marcus told Randal, was made bearable when they accepted that Nero was now living in glory.

Marcus was right. Secure in that thought, Randal smiled as he pictured Nero walking up to the throne of grace carrying the *Air Force One* fleece blanket he planned to give to his daughter. Though Randal knew, of course, that the blanket wasn't really going to make it past Nero's grave, that mental image gave him a strange comfort.

"Nero has no living family that I know of," Marcus was saying. "His people were taken in the Rapture. The church was all he had."

"Brad wants to know the feasibility of holding a memorial service for Nero before this Sunday when he has to leave for Jerusalem. Do you think you'll be back by then?"

"Yes," Marcus said without hesitation. "I don't expect these meetings to take long. Carpathia's got the deck stacked in his favor. It's all a matter of formality now."

"What about Mom?"

"That's harder to say, but if I know your mother, she'll make it happen. Call Velma Watkins at my office and let her know we need to make arrangements to have the service on Saturday morning. She'll take care of the rest."

Randal hesitated. He didn't think he could explain it to Marcus, but there was a part of him that wasn't willing to simply pass the matter off to someone else—no matter how capable she might be. He felt a sense of responsibility—a kinship to the young man who'd become his brother in Christ, and, arguably, one of his best friends in the past few weeks. "I'll handle it," he told Marcus. "We'll set it up for Saturday."

"Good. How's everyone doing, Randal?"

Randal glanced at Brad and Liza. Liza still stood by the window, her expression distant and immutable. Brad was on the phone with someone who was obviously irritating him. "Okay," Randal assured Marcus. "Could be better, but it could be a lot worse. Pray for us."

"All the time."

★   ★   ★

"I think we're agreed, then," Mariette told the group, "that we're going to establish regional directors and a coordinated international agency?" The people around the table nodded in agreement.

The battle had been hard-won, with territorial agendas playing a prominent role in the negotiations. So far, Mariette suspected, very few of the delegates had accepted the reality of Carpathia's plan: that soon, their individual agencies

would cease to exist. Everyone would work for his new so-
called Global Community. It seemed to be a foreign concept
to those present. But after an hour and a half, they'd finally
hammered out an agreement that would let them continue
without too much dissent. "Good," Mariette concluded.
"Then I recommend we break for dinner."

"Are we coming back again tonight?" someone asked.

Hattie Durham had slipped into the room a few moments earlier. Now she leaned over Mariette's shoulder and
handed her a pink phone message. Mariette's heart lurched
when she scanned it, and she began to quickly gather her
files. "After dinner we'll resume our deliberations at the
appointed time."

The others in the room gathered up their things, leaving
Mariette standing next to Carpathia's assistant.

"I'm sorry, Ms. Arnold," Hattie Durham said. "The call
just came through. Were you very close to him?"

Mariette stuffed her belongings into her briefcase. "Yes,"
she managed to whisper, "I was."

"Well, you'll be glad to know that Secretary-General
Carpathia would like you to join him for dinner," Hattie
said. "I'm sure you won't want to be alone." She said it as if
the invitation would automatically override whatever feelings of grief the news of Nero's death might have caused
Mariette.

Incredulous, Mariette stood and looked at the younger
woman. "I need to make some phone calls," she said
through gritted teeth. As the committee began to disperse,
several approached her.

"What time do you want us back again?" one asked.

"Eight-thirty," Mariette told him. "As we discussed earlier. That will give everyone enough time for dinner."

"I thought we covered a lot of ground today," another
said.

Mariette nodded. "I'd like us to knock out a few more items before we break for the night."

"Do you have dinner plans?" a third, a woman from the Red Cross Mariette had known for years, asked.

Hattie Durham touched Mariette's arm and said to the delegate, "Ms. Arnold will be dining with the secretary-general."

Clearly surprised, the committee member raised her eyebrows. "I see."

Mariette extracted her arm from Hattie's grasp. "Actually," she told the woman, "I've just gotten some news from home. I'll probably just grab something in my room and make some phone calls."

"Oh." The woman's brow creased in concern. Whatever territorial and philosophical differences separated the members of the group, Mariette knew one common denominator united them all: They were in the relief business because they all possessed a strong sense of empathy and compassion. "Is everything all right?"

"A friend of the family died today," Mariette said. "I just found out."

"Oh. Oh, Mariette, I'm so sorry."

Mariette fought back tears. "Me, too."

"Let us know if we can do anything," the woman said.

"Of course. I'll see you back here at eight-thirty."

A few more questions followed. Hattie stood by and waited patiently while Mariette addressed them. More than anything else, Mariette wanted to cancel the evening's session, but she knew that would be folly. They were barely a quarter of the way through Nicolae's agenda, and taking the evening off would simply slow them down. Her primary goal was to get out of New York and back to Washington as quickly as possible.

When the last committee member left the room,

Mariette turned back to Nicolae's assistant. "Please thank Mr. Carpathia for the invitation—" she indicated the pink message in her hand—"but ask him to give me a rain check. I've really got to take this time to call my son and find out what's happening."

Hattie looked dumbfounded. "But he's got a reservation at the best restaurant in town," she insisted, as if the lure of a five-star restaurant should be salve enough for Mariette's grief.

Mariette stuffed the message slip in her suit pocket and reached for her briefcase. "Then hopefully," she said, "he can cancel it or enjoy it with someone else."

★   ★   ★

"Then call me as soon as you know something," Brad told Harmon Drake. He wiped a hand through his hair as he ended the call and tossed his cell phone onto the bed. Both Liza and Randal were watching him. Brad exhaled a long breath. The afternoon had taken its toll on them all. "Did you reach your mom?" Brad asked Randal.

"She just called. They took a break for dinner. She's at her hotel."

"How are things going?"

"I didn't ask. She wants to be here."

Brad could well imagine. "What about Velma?"

"I left a message," Randal told him. "She wasn't home."

Liza, who was seated at the desk surrounded by the files of evidence Brad had accumulated in the last week, slid George's notebook aside and slumped in the chair. "This is unbelievable." Her voice was slightly shaky. "I just never imagined—"

Brad frowned in concern. In the hours since the shooting at the base and Nero's death, he'd been so preoccupied

with getting them to safety and dealing with the implications of Nero's death, that he'd forgotten the stress Liza had
been under for the last few days. The fire at her apartment
had destroyed virtually everything she owned. Brad wished
he could have avoided pulling her into the same web of
danger that had been tightening around him for the past
several weeks. Her life was as much at risk as his, but she
lacked the cloak of protection his high-profile life and security-
intense profession offered. She looked shaken, edgy, and
terrified.

Randal looked drained. Brad wasn't sure how much of
his bleak expression came from sheer physical fatigue of
fighting the lingering symptoms of his concussion and
how much came from the stress of the day, but both were
cause for alarm.

He wished Marcus were here. Marcus would know in-
stinctively what to do. For his part, Brad had no experience
with this. "Do not depend on your own understanding"
had been the biblical text of Marcus's last sermon. *God*,
Brad prayed, *we need You so much. I need You to speak through
me. I need You to show me how to comfort them.* "Okay," he
said, crossing the room and pulling a chair up to the desk
opposite Liza.

Randal was in the armchair near the window. He turned
to join them.

Brad placed his hands, palms up, on the desk and
looked from one to the other. "I think we need to pray.
Liza—" he glanced at her—"I know this isn't necessarily as
comfortable for you—"

She shook her head and slid her hands into his. Her fingers were cold and a little shaky. "I'd like that."

Randal took their hands and completed the circle. "Me
too."

With a slight nod, Brad bowed his head. "Lord, we're kind of shaken up here. I feel over my head. I'm scared."

"Me too," Randal added.

"We miss Nero," Brad continued, "but I know he's with You. I know You're looking out for us. I know You have a plan, but I'm not sure I'm strong enough to see this through. I know I'm not strong enough to see this through without You. We need Your wisdom." He fell silent.

"God," Randal said after a few seconds of contemplative silence, "God, I'm so scared. I thought I was ready for all this. Marcus has been warning us. I really felt like I was close to You. But I don't know, Father, I just gotta confess— after this . . . after today . . . God, what are You doing? Please show us what You're doing. Take care of my mom. Take care of Marcus. Show us what You want us to do."

Brad waited several moments, then closed the prayer. "Thank You for loving us, God."

"Yes," Randal whispered.

"Thank You for being our Savior. Thank You for watching over us. Thank You for our friend Nero. Thank You for restoring him to Your bountiful presence."

"Thank You, Lord," Randal added.

"Help us to be faithful. Amen." Brad squeezed Liza's and Randal's hands before letting go. When their gazes met, Randal looked slightly teary. Liza looked terrified. Brad put a reassuring hand on her shoulder. "Everything's going to be all right."

She studied him a moment. "How can you say that?" She indicated the pile of evidence with a sweep of her hand. "We've got all *this*. We know Rudd is behind the plot to move the gold out of South Range and ship it through Kostankis's contacts, but we still have no proof. We don't know who his contacts are at the White House or at the Pentagon. We don't know who's been covering for him.

And, except for whatever cryptic notes are in Ramiro's note-book, we don't know how to find it. You're fairly sure that key Jane Lyons sent you opens a safe-deposit box where George stashed the evidence. And you're fairly sure that this Major Nuñez is the answer to the situation at the Penta-gon."

"Nuñez isn't a person," Brad clarified. Not that they knew much more than that. All Mariette had been able to tell him about her conversation with Max Arnold was that the mysterious Major Nuñez was not a military officer and that Brad would have to get additional clarification from the senator.

"He's not?"

Randal shook his head. "That's the one thing we did find out from my father. Nuñez is the name of a covert op-eration. It had a minor and a major phase. The minor phase is completed. The major phase is in full swing. We think my dad is involved somehow."

"Okay." Liza nodded, thoughtful. "You have some pho-tos that suggest someone's been following your father and secretly photographing him, one phone call, and this infor-mation about Nuñez that suggests the senator may be in this up to his eyeballs. In the words of my friends at the prosecutor's office, we've got motive and opportunity, but no smoking gun." Liza shook her head. "Without that last piece of evidence, we can't go public with this, and if we do, it'll probably get us killed. Today proved that. There are some very important people who want this to go away."

Brad nodded. "I know. Believe me, nobody knows better than I do why we have to unravel George's notebook. I've been living with this kind of pressure for weeks."

Her face registered concern. "I didn't mean to suggest—"

"It's all right, Liza," he told her. "I understand. I just wanted you to know that I feel the same stress you do. I had hoped we'd have enough by now to at least bluff Rudd into thinking we have it all—but without knowing who his contact was at the Pentagon . . ."

"Maybe," Randal said, "we can find that out from Max." He tipped his head toward the pictures. "I have a feeling he's not going to like finding out that the White House was keeping covert pictures of him in an evidence box about an assassination attempt on the president."

"You think he'll meet with us?" Liza asked.

Randal looked at Brad. "You talked to Mom about him today. What do you think?"

Brad thought that over. "Your mother seemed to think he was eager to talk to you. If he thinks someone in the administration is going to take a fall, he's probably not willing to cover for them simply because he knows more than he should."

"You've got that right." Randal rubbed his palms on his thighs. "Look, I know you guys need to talk about this, and I know you want this resolved before you leave for Israel—" he looked at Brad—"but tonight I need to take care of Nero."

Brad raised his eyebrows. "Randal—"

Randal held up a hand. "I know it's just a body. I mean, he's not really there, not anymore, and that his soul is at peace, but with everything that's been going on, how sure are you that his body is really going to get transferred from the base to the funeral home tonight?"

"I don't think Nero was the target," Brad said gently.

"I know that." Randal rubbed a hand over his face, "But still, I just don't feel like I can leave him in the hands of strangers. I kind of owe him, you know? He stayed in that hospital all night and watched out for me. He watched out for my mom. I just—I want to stay with him until I know he's in a safe place. I want to make sure his body gets to the funeral home okay."

Brad saw the anguish and grief in the young man's eyes, and his heart twisted as he remembered his own son who'd had the same deep empathy and compassion Randal possessed. He nodded solemnly. "I understand."

"You don't think I'm weird?"

Brad shook his head and reached for his phone. "I think you're a remarkable young man, Randal. Let me make one call and I'll make the arrangements for you to accompany the body."

Randal sagged in his chair in relief. "Thanks."

Liza rubbed the grit from her eyes and struggled to focus on George Ramiro's notebook. For the past two hours, she and Brad had pored over every piece of evidence, every e-mail message, every file and reference they'd collected as they'd tried to extract the truth from the illusions. After Brad had arranged for Randal to ride with the funeral director to retrieve Nero's body, he'd suggested they move Liza to her hotel. For reasons ranging from security to appearances, he'd decided she shouldn't stay in the same hotel where he'd recently relocated. Part of his survival strategy since the bomb that had destroyed his apartment several weeks ago had been to relocate on a weekly basis. The Homestead Hotel had been one of several places where Brad had been living out of his suitcase.

The implications had made Liza shudder. She couldn't live like that. She needed roots, connections, a place to shelve books and hang laundry. It was beginning to seem as though they'd never be free of the mess they'd uncovered when they'd started asking questions about George Ramiro.

Brad was right, she knew. Until they were able to break

the story and bring everything out in the open, they were both at serious risk. She had to face the fact that the shooter at the base this morning had been gunning for her. Though the military police had not yet released any information from their investigation, the coincidence was unsettling. She was now as firmly caught in this snare as Brad.

But, maddeningly, the more she studied the evidence, the more obvious it became that they did not yet have all the pieces. "I know we're missing something."

Brad studied the pictures Randal had taken from the White House evidence box. "I've been telling myself that for a week."

She glanced at the clock. "Do you think we'll hear from Randal soon?"

"I hope so. The guy at the funeral home told me he planned to get the body at eight. By the time they finish clearing the paperwork—" he shrugged—"they should be back in the District at anytime, I think."

Liza dropped her pencil on the desk and sank back in her chair. "He was really shaken up." The lights from the city cast long, eerie shadows into her sterile hotel room. "It still seems almost unreal to me."

"I feel responsible," Brad admitted. "Randal wasn't fit to drive today, and I didn't want to mess with having to park the car when I was down at the FEC." He wiped his hands over his face with a weary sigh.

"I thought it was sweet that he wanted to do this."

"Randal and Nero may have known each other only a couple of weeks, but they'd become fairly good friends."

"They seem like an unlikely pair."

That won a small smile. "I can see why you'd think that, but that's one of the things God has been teaching me. There's a verse in the book of Matthew where Jesus is explaining salvation to the disciples. He has just told a rich young ruler that if he wishes to follow Jesus, he has to sell everything he owns first. No one understands why Jesus says it has to be so difficult, and when they ask Him, Jesus says, 'Humanly speaking, it is impossible. But with God everything is possible.' "

Brad had finally opened the door Liza had been waiting for since she'd picked up that Gideon Bible this morning and left the hotel with it. She'd thought about discussing it with him earlier, but with Nero's death fresh in all their minds, she hadn't felt comfortable. "Um, Brad . . ."

He held up a hand. "Don't worry. I'm not going to try and shove my faith down your throat. But you've got to know by now that it's a part of me. It's not something I can turn on and off just because it makes some people uncomfortable."

"I'm not—"

Brad rose and began to pace. "We've talked about this before, and I know you asked me to respect your privacy, but after what happened today—" he raked a hand through his hair—"well, what kind of friend would I be if I didn't try and persuade you that you need to deal with the future of your soul? I mean, if I really believe that faith in Christ is the only course to salvation—and I do—then I have to tell you about it. If I care about you at all, I have to do everything in my power to convince you to see the truth." He turned to look at her. "I'm sorry if this makes you angry, Liza, but don't you think that when Nero started his day, he had no idea it was going to be his last? We're both in danger here. You're in danger because I dragged you into this."

"Brad!" Her abrupt tone finally captured his attention. "Will you shut up for a second?"

His eyes widened. "Liza—"

"Sit down." She indicated the chair across from her. "I realize you don't want to talk about this."

"Actually, this is *exactly* what I want to talk about," she assured him.

"It is?"

"Yes." Liza reached for her bag and pulled out the Gideon Bible. "I couldn't sleep last night, especially not after I saw my apartment going up in flames. I was a little wired." She shoved the Bible across the desk at him. "Dad always used to say there are two things in every hotel room in America: CNN and the Gideon Bible."

Brad picked up the Bible and thumbed through it. "It's a King James version. Did you read it?"

"The book of John—like you told me to. Though you could have given me clearer instructions. It took me a while to figure out which book of John you meant with all that 1 John, 2 John, 3 John in the back."

"Just John."

She nodded. "Just John. That's the one I tackled."

"Reach any conclusions?"

"Maybe a few. I have some questions."

"I don't know if I'm the best person to answer them, but I can try."

Liza turned her gaze to the window, where she could see boat lights bobbing on the nearby Potomac. "Here's the thing, Brad. My dad called himself a Christian. He used to talk a lot about salvation and sin and redemption and all that stuff. He seemed like a regular guy, you know, not a nut." She looked at him. "Not a zealot."

"You mean like me?"

She shrugged. "I wouldn't say that exactly. I mean, he was always telling me I had to get 'right with God' before it was too late. I just chalked it up to a different generation and his need to have some hope while he was living in a nursing home."

"But?"

"But then all this happened." She propped her elbows on the desk. "I was sitting in the Staples Center when all those people just vanished. I saw it. I lived it."

"You told me that. I really can't imagine what it must have been like to be in the middle of it all."

"If you never believed that the world could come to an end before, then living through something like that would make you believe it now; I'll tell you that much."

Brad nodded, thoughtful. "I guess you could say it had that effect on most of us. If I'd believed it before it happened, I might have accepted the truth a long time ago, and if I had, I wouldn't be here."

Liza frowned. That was the very thing she was having the most trouble with. "But see, that's just it. It doesn't add up for me. I mean, John talks about God's loving the world, about His wanting to give us all eternal life. John paints a picture of this God who is light and life and truth and love and all the things that seem in total contrast to what we're living through. How could a loving God—"

Brad held up his hand. "Hold it. That's just what the trouble is, Liza. You think that God *caused* all this to happen."

"Didn't He? Isn't that what you've been telling me?"

"No. God's plan from the beginning of time was for us to have fellowship with Him. He created us to live in His will and in His presence. When man chose to sin, that's when we brought judgment on ourselves. The Bible says that God is love, but it also says that God is holy and just and must punish sin. Sin is what keeps us from enjoying fellowship with a perfect God. When Adam sinned in the Garden, the clock started to tick until God would judge the world. He told us about it. He warned us about it. He gave us every chance to get a VIP pass out of judgment by accepting the salvation He provided, but He gave us choice. When it came to redemption, we could take it or leave it.

"When the time was right, He gathered His believers and left the rest of us here to face the consequences," Brad finished.

"So there's no hope?"

Brad shook his head, a slight smile on his lips. "That's the amazing part. God's grace is limitless. He hasn't pulled His hand away even from us. We can still choose to serve Him during the time we have left. We can make our lives count for something. We can still accept Jesus' redemption. The choice is ours."

Liza picked up a pen and twirled it between her fingers. "Why?"

"Why what?"

"Why would God do that? I mean, if we're all so bad, why not just wipe us out and be done with it?"

"Go back to the first question you asked me."

"Huh?"

"About God and how John says He loves us. Love and grace go hand in hand. I'm not going to tell you I understand it, Liza. To be perfectly honest, the whole idea of God's grace blows my mind. I mean, we sin, we betray Him, we reject Him, but even though He knows all that, He offers us Jesus as the price for redemption. He promises He forgives us completely when we repent. It's mind-boggling."

"And hard to believe."

"By human standards, yes. After all, in Jesus' day, the idea was so radical and so appalling that the religious leaders killed Him because of it. They didn't like the concept either."

She tapped the end of the pen on the desk in an uneasy rhythm. "I really don't think I could believe it at all if it weren't for people like you."

"How do you mean?"

"It makes a difference in your life," she said. "It matters to you."

"It's everything to me," Brad assured her. "My faith and my trust in God are the only reasons I've been able to live through this. I know my family is secure in heaven, that I'll be with them again."

"Do you think my dad is there?"

"If he had a personal relationship with Christ, then yes, he's there."

Liza glanced at the window again. This seemed so foreign, so completely alien to the open-minded culture she'd learned to embrace in college and in her career. "But Dad always said there was only one way to heaven."

"Jesus said the same thing," Brad told her. " 'I am the way, the truth and the life. No one can come to the Father except through Me.' "

"Don't you think that's kind of restrictive? I mean, if God wants us all there so badly, how come He makes it so difficult?"

Brad scooted his chair closer to the desk. "Liza, one of the greatest lies the devil tells is that all roads lead to heaven. He wants us to believe that if you're a good person or a devout person, that it's all going to be okay. But God knew the only hope for us was to sacrifice His own Son to make us holy enough to be in His presence. Can't you see how He would *require* that we accept the reality that we can't get there on our own?"

"I suppose."

"The bottom line is this: God calls each of us to choose whether we'll serve Him or live in the world. For a long time, I made the wrong choice. It took something as catastrophic as the Rapture for God to get my attention."

"And now what?"

"Now I know that whatever happens, I'm going to be in

the center of His will for me. I've learned a lot about what the Bible says about this period in history. Marcus has taught me so much, but I've still got a lot to learn. The truth is, though, even if I didn't know that the end was coming and that God was unleashing His judgment on the earth, even if I didn't *know* that my faith in Christ assures me eternal life in heaven, I'd still want to have the relationship with God that I have now. I wouldn't want to face any of this without Him."

Liza reached across the desk and took the Bible. "I don't know, Brad. I'm going to have to think about it some more."

He looked disappointed, but didn't press her. "I understand. I wish you could feel what I feel, though."

"I just don't think I'm ready to make a decision like that."

"Be careful not to leave it till it's too late." Brad exhaled a long breath. "I put it off once," he said quietly, "and look where it got me."

"Brad—"

He held up both his hands in surrender. "I'll drop it for now. But please promise that you'll come to me if you have any more questions. Okay?"

Liza agreed. "Okay."

He reached for a file. "All right, let's take a look at this again. The answer's got to be in here somewhere."

9

"It's me," Randal said into his cell phone. He glanced at the closed coffin of his friend Nero.

After nearly an hour of haggling with base security, he'd managed to get the body released to the funeral director. The coroner had already prepped the body for transport, but Randal had still insisted on identifying Nero before they'd placed him in the coffin. He had looked peaceful and content. Randal had been gratified to see that though they'd stripped the body, they'd packed the blanket inside the body bag. It was a silly thing, he knew. Nero wasn't there. The blanket really meant nothing, but somehow it made Randal feel better.

The trip to the downtown funeral home had been simple and quick by comparison. Randal had helped the funeral director transfer the body inside, then had pulled up a chair near the coffin where he intended to maintain his all-night vigil. It was important to him to know that no one violated the man who'd given his life protecting them. After calling Brad to let him know they'd successfully made the transfer, Randal had pulled his Bible from his backpack and settled in for the night.

He'd read for a while, but had continued to be pestered by Marcus's revelation that Nero had no family. His wife, baby daughter, mother, and sisters had all been caught up in the Rapture. Nero was completely alone in the world.

Randal never remembered being alone. During his parents' tumultuous marriage, he'd had friends and family around him at all times. Many people had wanted to be close to Max Arnold's rising star, and Randal had caught the overflow of attention—both positive and negative. He couldn't imagine lying in a coffin while his handful of friends struggled to figure out whom to call. In Washington, people flocked to high-profile funerals. Guest lists usually had to be managed.

But he hadn't been any richer than Nero because of it, he realized. All the attention and public adoration had gained him a rotten relationship with his father and an enormous chip on his shoulder at his father's betrayal of his mother.

Just last week he and Nero had met for prayer and Nero had gotten on his case about calling his dad. Randal had told no one.

Nero's own father had left his mother alone and pregnant with Nero—their third child. He'd never known the man who'd fathered him but he'd been able to look Randal in the eye and swear he didn't resent the man. Unlike Randal, who found his father's behavior detestable, Nero had long since forgiven his father for his weakness. "The way I see it," Nero had told him, "he's the one who lost out." He'd grinned so broadly at Randal that his gold tooth had glinted in the sunlight. "I mean, not every stiff gets to have a guy like me as a son, you know."

Randal had been ready to dismiss Nero's outlook as

naïve until Nero had pointed out that Jesus' doctrine had been one of forgiveness and grace. Randal was still haunted by Nero's reminder that Jesus had even forgiven the Roman soldiers at the foot of His cross. Nothing Max Arnold had done to Randal or Mariette compared to that.

Feeling petty and immature, Randal had changed the subject.

But tonight, alone with the casket, Nero's words haunted him. What if he had been the one to take that bullet today? Was he ready to go to his grave without resolving his relationship with his father? More important, was he prepared to let any opportunity pass to tell him that he needed the Lord in his life? *And what better way*, a haunting voice asked, *to show your father what grace has done for you than to exhibit that grace yourself?*

After struggling with his conscience for over an hour, Randal had finally dialed his father's number.

"It's me," he said again when his father didn't respond.

"Randal?" Wherever Max was, Randal could hear a lot of noise in the background. He recognized that noise, since his father had called him from a lot of political events over the years.

"Yeah. Look, if this is a bad time—"

"No," Max said. "No. It's not a bad time. Just hang on a second. I'm going to go somewhere quieter."

Randal waited while his father made his way through the crowd. He heard him greet several supporters with the usual political small talk before the noise suddenly stopped. "Okay," he finally said, "I'm alone."

"Mom said you wanted to talk to me."

"How are you?" his father asked.

"So-so. Head is killing me."

"Your mother said you have a concussion."

"Slight. I'll survive."

"I couldn't reach you this morning."

"I was tied up." This was not going well. Randal wondered just what he thought he'd accomplish with this call. After ten years of tension, he doubted either of them was ready to start an intimate conversation.

"I understand," his dad said. "Thanks for calling me back. I appreciate it, and I know it wasn't easy for you. Are you somewhere you can talk?"

"Yes."

"You're sure that you can't be overheard?"

Randal shot a quick look at Nero's coffin. "Yeah," he said. "I'm sure no one's listening."

"All right, then listen to me. I know things haven't been good between us, but this is important, Randal. You've got to believe me when I tell you this."

"Is this about Nuñez?"

"Yes. Your mother told you?"

"Actually, she talked to Brad. She told him. He told me."

"Then he's in danger, too."

"Dad, there's something you should know before you say anything else." Quickly, Randal told him about the pictures he'd taken from the White House evidence locker. "Someone's been following you," he added. "And whoever it is wants to implicate you in the assassination attempt on the president."

"That doesn't surprise me."

Randal's feet hit the floor with a thump. "What do you mean by that?"

"You know how this town works," his father said dismissively. "If your party's in, the other party is trying to get you out. If your party's out, you're trying to get in. It's the name of the game."

"Someone tried to *kill* the president of the United

States," Randal said. "That's a little more than a filibuster to kill a bill. Wouldn't you say?"

"Don't be trite," his father snapped.

"Don't be—look. I'm not sure you really have an idea how serious this is."

That won a harsh laugh. "I assure you, there's probably no one in this town who's got a better understanding of how serious this is."

Randal reached for his patience. He'd intended for this call to be an olive branch between him and his father, not a cause for further tension. "Tell me about Nuñez," he said. "Isn't that why you wanted me to call?"

"Yes. What do you already know?"

"Only that the name popped up on a computer and Brad asked me to check it out." He deliberately avoided mentioning Grayson Wells or Brad's investigation into the C-5 mishap that was supposed to have killed him. "I called you. You told me not to let the president get into the lead limo. I complied, and now the Secret Service wants to know what you knew, what I know, and who else is involved."

"All right. All right." His father's voice dropped to a near whisper. "This is what I can tell you. It's no secret that Fitzhugh has been at odds with some of the Joint Chiefs of Staff since his inauguration. Dave Marsden, especially, has said the president is weak on defense."

"It's gotten worse since the Rapture."

"The what?" His dad caught himself. "Oh. Your mother told me you'd had some kind of religious experience or something."

Randal stifled a sigh. This was not going well. "I became a Christian," he told his father. "I accepted Jesus as my Savior."

"Well, whatever works for you, I guess. Anyway, since the disappearances, the tensions between the Pentagon and the White House have only gotten worse. There are upper-level Pentagon officials who think Nicolae Carpathia is the next Nikita Khrushchev when it comes to U.S. security."

"I'm sure there are."

"And even before all this happened, the president was under pressure. Depending on who you listen to, the president did or didn't authorize a certain covert deal with rebel forces in Abkhazia who were trying to recapture control of Sukhumi from the Hizb ut-Tahrir al-Islami."

"I heard the rumors. But there *is* a covert operation, right? Regardless of whether Fitzhugh authorized it or not?"

"There is."

"And it's illegal."

"It is."

"Who knows about this?"

"For sure? The perpetrators, you, Brad, and probably a handful of upper-level staff at the White House. Look, Randal, don't be naïve. This kind of thing goes on all the time. It only causes trouble when it's exposed."

"But someone got killed over this. Someone was desperate enough to cover it up to try and kill the president. Why?"

His father was silent for several seconds. "I'm not sure."

"You're not sure—or you won't tell me."

"I'm not sure. There are civilians involved."

"Civilians?"

"I think. I don't have any proof."

"What do you mean?"

"There wasn't enough money to finance this. That's how I was brought into the picture. The Senate Armed Services Committee was approached about diverting funds from the war in Turkey."

"And did you?"

"No chance. Since 9/11, it's all too public. I told them they had to find the money another way."

"So they turned to Victor Rudd."

"You know about Rudd?" his father asked, clearly shocked.

"Yeah." Randal wiped a hand through his hair. "We know about Rudd. And Kostankis."

His father swore. "I had no idea it had gone this far."

"But you knew about Nuñez."

"I knew that when they approached me about the funding, they were calling the operation Nuñez after some Special Forces officer who'd died in the region several months ago. I suspected they planned to turn to Rudd for the funding. It made sense. I have no evidence or knowledge that they actually did."

"There are pictures of you meeting with Pentagon officials."

"I'm chairman of the Senate Armed Services Committee. It's perfectly reasonable for me to meet with top brass from the Pentagon."

"Someone killed George Ramiro to keep this from going public. Do you realize that?"

"I understand that's what Benton thinks. Maybe it's true."

"It is true."

"And now he's dragged you into it. I don't think you know what you're messing with here, Randal."

"Oh, I know," he said. "And Brad didn't drag me into anything. He's my friend. If anything, I dragged him."

"If he thinks he's going to take down Victor Rudd, he's a fool. Lesser men have tried and failed. Rudd's not going to be exposed as a criminal. This is worse. If this comes out, it's treason."

"It's going to come out."

"Then Benton had better play his cards very carefully.

He'd better have ironclad proof, and he'd better make sure Rudd can't get to him."

"He will," Randal said, though he knew that all Brad had linking Rudd to the crime were the circumstantial ties of Rudd's political activities to Kostankis's nonprofit donations. They had no names from the Pentagon, no signed papers authorizing the operation, not even the exact details of the operation itself. But he was hardly going to admit that to Max. "Brad's got George Ramiro's notes. He has the same evidence that got George killed."

His father's laugh was harsh. "Is that what he thinks?"

Randal's eyes narrowed. "Why are you laughing?"

"Because I had a meeting with George Ramiro two days before the disappearances. He wanted to know what I knew about Nuñez. I told him exactly what I told you. I offered him immunity if he'd testify before the Armed Services Committee."

That didn't surprise Randal. His father would have seized on the opportunity to protect himself and capture the publicity of embarrassing the Fitzhugh administration. "He didn't take you up on it?"

"He said he had to talk it over with his partner. Ramiro had an inside source. Someone in the White House was helping him gather this information. If Brad doesn't know who Ramiro's contact was, then he has nothing. Ramiro told me that both he and his partner had ensured that neither of them could access the evidence on their own. That's the way they protected each other."

"Brad has more evidence than George had," Randal countered. "He can prove the link between Kostankis and Rudd. He can document the trail of paper at the Pentagon. He's got a reporter who has been working on this with him."

"Maybe," his father said. "It might be enough. For his sake I hope so. But it could simply widen the range of the splatter zone when Rudd takes him down. Ramiro did tell me that whoever he was working with would make sure that Brad didn't get taken down if the Fitzhugh administration fell over this. Ramiro liked Benton. I think he didn't want to see him hurt. Evidently, neither did his partner."

"Evidently," Randal said. "Is there anything else?"

"No. That's everything I know." He paused. "Randal, you're in over your head. I know you think your mother is trying to baby you—"

"She is."

"Maybe. But she's right this time. This is bigger than you. George is already dead over it. I've lost count of how many times Benton has been targeted. I don't understand why he's still breathing. He's like a cat with nine lives, I guess."

"Maybe."

"Is it true that someone took a shot at him today at Andrews?"

Randal glanced at the casket. "Yeah. It's true. They missed Brad, though."

"It's just a matter of time before they get him. These are powerful men."

Randal wavered for a moment, wondering about the wisdom of telling his father that whatever happened, Brad was trusting God to take care of him. Max, he figured, would not react well. *God*, he prayed, *I think You want me to talk to him. I know You want me to be honest with him, but I don't know how to handle this.*

"Randal? Did I lose you?"

"Oh. Sorry. I'm here."

"Believe it or not, I like Brad Benton. Given what your mother has told me about the situation you're in, I'd probably even bet I like him better than she does."

"Mom likes Brad just fine," Randal countered. "She just

doesn't like seeing me get my brains rattled on the White House driveway on CNN."

"Can you blame her?"

"I guess not."

"So here's the thing," his father said. "Benton's playing with fire. He may be in too deep to drop this, but if he is, then he'd better act fast. His luck won't hold forever."

"He knows that."

"Yeah, but the question is, does he know who Ramiro's contact in the White House was?"

"Brad's not going to let up on this until he knows who killed George Ramiro. That's the bottom line."

"Then I hope Ramiro's contact is watching Benton's back the way Ramiro figured."

"Yeah," Randal agreed. "I hope so too."

"Whatever you do, keep your head down. If you get killed, your mother might take Benton out herself."

Randal recognized the ill-placed attempt at humor as his father's way of trying to prove he had a sensitive side. It had never worked when Randal was a child, and it was even less effective now. "I'll remember that," he said, struggling to keep the bitterness out of his voice.

"Tell Benton I said the same thing. Maybe he'll finally knock Vic Rudd down a peg. The jerk could use it."

"Does that mean Brad can count on the Senate Armed Services Committee to conduct hearings after the story goes public?" Randal probed.

"Naturally. It will be my pleasure. I've got a presidential campaign to run."

"I'll let him know," Randal said. "Thanks for the heads-up on Nuñez."

"Sure. How about sending me a copy of those pictures you pulled out of evidence?"

"When I can, I'll get them to you."

"All right, Son. Be careful."

Randal glanced at Nero's coffin. "I will. I promise." He ended the call with his father and dropped his head into his hands. That had been a dismal failure. *God, I tried. I really tried. I just can't—I know You'd forgive him. I know You want me to forgive him. You've got to help me want to, Lord, 'cause to tell You the truth, I'm not really even sure I care what happens to him.*

Randal cringed as he realized the implications of that thought. Was that really true? Had his relationship with his father really disintegrated to the point where he didn't honestly care if the man spent eternity in hell?

He rubbed his hand along the polished wood of the casket. "You'd be ashamed of me, Nero," he said. "You'd tell me I was being too hardheaded and arrogant."

Frustrated, he surged to his feet and began pacing the small, cold room as he wrestled with his conscience. A part of him knew that his father wasn't an inherently bad person. Ambitious, self-absorbed, and notoriously ruthless when it came to protecting his territory, Max Arnold was an icon of American politics. As a child, Randal had idolized him. That's why the evidence of the man's philandering had wounded Randal so deeply. Though his mother had never put pressure on Randal to make choices, his loyalties had been torn between her, who loved and nurtured him, and the father whose approval he'd wanted so desperately.

The father, Randal thought, who needed to come face-to-face with the Lord.

He rubbed a hand over his face. He was so tired. His head was killing him. His entire body ached from the stress of the day and from the latent symptoms of the concussion and bruises he'd received in the blast. Even his brain felt tired—so tired, in fact, that he was having trouble deciding why his father's comments were still niggling him. There'd been something there, something in what his father had said tonight that had seemed important. It had contained a ring of truth that Randal felt he should have seized upon.

He sank into the chair next to the coffin and thought through all that his dad had told him and all that he'd learned today.

And in a sudden burst of insight, Randal sat upright and reached for his phone. Impossible though it seemed, he knew who George Ramiro's contact at the White House was.

★   ★   ★

"What are you talking about?" Brad asked. Randal had called to tell him about his conversation with his father.

"I figured it out. I called my dad to ask him about Nuñez and I figured it out."

"What did he say about Nuñez?"

"It's what you think. George had the evidence. To get the evidence you need his contact from the White House."

"All right, slow down." Brad walked across the room to the window. Liza had been so exhausted, she'd nearly fallen asleep midsentence. He'd left her in her hotel room with written instructions to call him when she woke. He'd double-checked the security he'd posted at her hotel, then returned to the Homestead Hotel to go over George Ramiro's notes yet again. He hadn't been able to sleep.

His ringing cell phone had seemed unnaturally loud in the stillness of his temporary residence. "Just slow down," he told Randal again. "Are you still at the funeral home?"

"Yes. I called my father to talk to him about Nuñez, to see what he knew. Brad, he met with Ramiro just before the murder."

"What did George say?"

"Ramiro claimed he had evidence that implicated Rudd along with the Pentagon officials behind the covert operation. He probably had evidence implicating White House officials too. Dad wasn't sure, but it was what he said about George's contact at the White House that made me figure it out. He said that George was sure his contact would make sure you didn't take the fall if this took down the Fitzhugh administration. He was really sure that George and his contact meant to protect you."

"George Ramiro brought me to the White House. I'm not surprised."

"But his contact—" Randal broke off—"Brad, I know this is going to sound nuts, but I figured it out. I know who George's contact was inside the White House."

"What do you mean you figured it out?"

"MEP. George's contact MEP. It can only be one person, Brad. There's only one person that makes sense."

Brad's fingers tightened on the phone. "Who?"

"Like I said, I thought it was nuts, so I called the switchboard and double-checked her name." He paused. "It's Emma, Brad. Emma's name is Marion Emma Pettit. She was the one helping George get to the bottom of the Nuñez operation. She was the one covering your back. She's the one George entrusted with everything from the safe-deposit-box number to all the suspicious information he had."

"Emma? Randal, that's crazy."

"Is it? Think about it. Who else in the Fitzhugh White House was likely to make sure you didn't take the fall for this? Who else would have trusted you enough to send you those pictures of Ramiro's body? Who else was in a position to keep Rudd's accomplices from getting to you? Who knew your schedule well enough to divert them?"

"But Emma couldn't have taken those pictures."

"No," Randal agreed, "but if the person who murdered George wanted George's accomplice to cease and desist, what better way to scare her into silence than by sending her those pictures?"

"Which she sent to me because she knew I'd investigate," Brad mused. He rubbed his eyes. "But why wouldn't she tell me?"

"To protect you." Randal paused. "To protect herself. We all just assumed that the sniper in the White House garage was after you. But he hit Emma and then stopped firing. What if he wasn't after you at all? What if it really *was* Emma he was aiming at?"

The truth of that hit Brad with the force of a freight train. Emma had not yet returned to work despite her doctor's permission to begin a light schedule. She'd stayed cocooned in her home, keeping in touch with Brad only through an occasional phone call or note. She'd rarely asked him about the situation at the White House, and Brad had reasoned that she was not yet ready to deal with the pressures that had nearly gotten her killed.

But now that he thought about it, that wasn't like Emma at all. Had the signs he'd interpreted as concern for him and a lingering anxiety from her accident really been signs of terror and fear for her own safety?

"Brad," Randal continued, "I read the report of the sniper incident today while we were looking through all that evidence. Emma came out to the car to bring you some reports you'd asked for on Carpathia. Do you remember?"

"Yes."

"Did you tell her you needed those reports that night? Was there any reason why she had to bring them to you in the garage? Wouldn't that type of thing have normally waited until the next morning?"

"Yes," Brad agreed.

"Did you ever actually *see* those reports?"

"No," Brad admitted. "After the accident, I met with

security, then headed to Marcus's house in Georgetown. I forgot about the reports."

"Were they in a standard, manila, interoffice envelope?"

Brad struggled to remember. "I think so, yes."

"Like the one delivered to you at the gate the next morning?"

Brad's eyes widened. "Yes. They were."

"So what if Emma had really been bringing you those pictures? What if she dropped them when she was shot, and in the confusion, they got picked up and left in the security office? Wouldn't the envelope have had your name on it?"

"Yes," Brad agreed. "And it would have been an untraceable delivery if they'd found it the next morning in the security office."

"Which explains why there was no log sheet—even with the tighter security," Randal added.

"Dear Lord," Brad said, "I can't believe—"

"What are you going to do?"

"I've got to contact Emma."

"You can't let them know you figured it out, Brad. She's pretty much defenseless."

"I know." Brad began to pace in front of the window. "I know. I can't imagine what she's been through."

"Me, either. But I think I know why her sister seemed so protective now."

"Emma's not just recovering; she's terrified."

"And so is Pearl."

Brad thought it over a moment. "All right, Randal, you've made me a believer. And this is what we're going to do."

10

Liza fought the urge to look over her shoulder as she walked up the picturesque suburban sidewalk to deliver an arrangement of flowers. Brad had called her last night and apprised her of the situation. If he was right, the only way for them to get the information they needed from George Ramiro's safe-deposit box was to get the name of the bank from Emma. Randal and Brad had agreed that Liza was probably the only person who could go to Emma's home without arousing suspicion. As the net on Rudd and his accomplices continued to close, the chances were good that Emma's house was being watched.

Brad had made a couple of phone calls to a trusted friend and managed to arrange the cover of a flower delivery. Liza had no idea how they'd procured the delivery van or the flower arrangement on such short notice, but she'd agreed to make the trip.

As she approached the front door, she saw the flutter of a curtain from the corner of her eye. Someone was watching from the front window. She used a deliberately lazy pace as she approached the door, though her heart was thumping in her throat.

The door cracked open before she could use the brass knocker.

"May I help you?" It was an older woman. Brad had shown Liza a picture of Emma this morning. In the photo, Emma was seated with Brad's family at a family gathering. The woman at the door bore a resemblance, but her cap of white hair didn't match Brad's description of Emma's salt-and-pepper curls.

This, Liza guessed, must be Emma's sister, Pearl. "I have a delivery for—" she checked the card—"Marion Emma Pettit."

"I'll take it," the woman said.

Liza pulled the clipboard from under her arm and handed it to Pearl. "I have to have a signature."

Pearl accepted the clipboard, scanned the attached note, then stepped aside to let Liza into the house. "Thank God," she whispered as she pushed the door shut behind her. "Oh, thank God." She indicated the living room with a wave of her hand. "I don't think we could have taken this much longer. Emma's in here."

★　★　★

Marcus glanced around the room of global religious leaders gathered at the United Nations headquarters and suppressed a shudder.

Mariette had managed to get away from her meetings long enough to meet him and Daniel Berger for a quick dinner. As she'd reported the results of her afternoon, a sense of oppression had begun to bear down on Marcus.

Carpathia, he had known, could not be stopped. The Bible clearly foretold that the Antichrist's plans would enjoy apparent success during the eighteen months of peace preceding the Tribulation. During that period, his public-approval rating would reach unprecedented heights. His plans for global conquest would face no meaningful resistance. And person by person, family by family, neighborhood by neighborhood, nation by nation, he would seduce the world into following him.

What could his small band of friends possibly hope to do when faced with Carpathia's massive political machine? What meaningful impact could they have?

Mariette had told them that among the initiatives the new Global Community Compassion Agency had agreed on was the need for a worldwide registry of every person in every community on earth. This registry, they contended, would allow them to quickly identify victims and survivors in disaster areas. Families could more rapidly check on the well-being of their loved ones. Corporations could more easily assess their personnel losses.

Despite the apparently insurmountable challenge of developing this registry, Mariette's committee had voted to endorse the registry and allocate funds toward its development. No one, she'd told them, had even questioned the danger of such a tool. No one had seemed even remotely uncomfortable at the thought that a registry of that sort would put into Nicolae's hands detailed personal information about every living soul on the planet.

Now, as Marcus found himself surrounded by a group of men and women who were apparently ready to compromise the tenets of their faith for the sake of Carpathia's vision of "common good," that cloak of oppression returned with a vengeance. He closed his eyes in prayer. *Father, strengthen me. Give me clarity of mind. Give me wisdom, grace, and discernment. Protect me from evil.*

"Dumont?" Marcus glanced up to find Cardinal Peter

Mathews, dressed ostentatiously in his red cassock and robes, studying him with a calculated gleam. "I wouldn't have expected you here."

There was a wealth of meaning in that statement, Marcus mused. The cardinal was among the Catholic leaders scrambling for answers in the wake of the Rapture. The newly appointed pope had been among the raptured believers, along with thousands of nuns, monks, local priests, and missionaries, leaving church officials who'd been left behind struggling to piece together a cohesive and united answer for the apparently selective decimation of their leadership. Peter Mathews, the cardinal over the archdiocese of Chicago, had quickly emerged as the new leader of the powerful North American arm of the Catholic church.

No doubt the sight of an evangelical preacher at this meeting where, rumor had it, Mathews intended to get himself appointed leader of Carpathia's new global religious organization, surprised him on a number of levels. There were few evangelicals left—a fact that Mathews and his fellow church leaders had used to form a theory that the Rapture had actually been a "cleansing" of the church. God, they said, had winnowed the chaff from the wheat and left the wheat behind to rebuild His church. Many had challenged this theory, pointing to the disappearance of the pope himself. But Mathews had vigorously defended it as absolute truth and used it to promote his personal agenda to become the new pope of the Catholic church— an ambition second only to his vision of heading the global religion Carpathia had promised.

Marcus stood so he was eye level with the cardinal. "President Fitzhugh asked me to attend," he said. "I'm here to represent the Christian position."

Though Mathew's expression didn't change, Marcus sensed the tension rising in him. "I think you're missing the point, Dumont. This summit is about putting our differences behind us."

"I am who I am. I believe God is who God is. I've never apologized for that, and I'm not going to start now."

"That's an interesting position given what's happened to most of your colleagues."

"I've made my peace with God," Marcus said. "I won't fail Him again."

Mathews straightened his shoulders beneath the folds of his red robe. "I trust that if you can't be on board with our mission here that you'll have the grace to withdraw rather than cause division."

Marcus slid his hands into his pockets. "Just tell me this, Peter: Did you set your sights on the Vatican before or after the Rapture proved God's Word was true?"

A flush stained the cardinal's face. "How dare you—" He bit off his tirade a second before Marcus felt a hand land on his shoulder.

"Cardinal. Reverend. I trust everything is all right?" Nicolae Carpathia's voice was unmistakable.

Marcus had to fight the urge to brush the man's hand off his shoulder. Mathews gave Marcus a warning look, then turned a warm smile to Carpathia. "Naturally. I've known Reverend Dumont for years. We were renewing our acquaintance."

Nicolae squeezed Marcus's shoulder. "I was very sorry to hear about your young friend, Reverend," he said. "I just met the young man the other night at the hospital. Jefferson? Nero Jefferson, I believe?" Nicolae shook his head. "All this violence. How old was he? Twenty-one? Twenty-two?"

Marcus's heartbeat kicked up a notch. He had no idea how Nicolae had gotten word of Nero's death, but it didn't surprise him. "Twenty-four," Marcus confirmed.

"Did he leave a family behind?"

"His family is with the Lord," Marcus said.

He didn't think he imagined the way Nicolae's lips tightened and his beatific smile slipped. "I am glad his friends can find comfort in that," Carpathia conceded. He glanced at Peter Mathews. "Cardinal, I think we should get this meeting started. I would like you to do the honors."

Peter Mathews seemed to visibly puff up before Marcus's eyes. "I'd be delighted, Mr. Secretary-General."

Nicolae clucked his tongue. "We really must do something about that title." He slid an arm around the cardinal's shoulder. "It is so awkward."

"I don't know," Mathews said with a slight laugh. "In my experience, the more ostentatious the title, the more authority it conveys."

Marcus watched as Nicolae led the cardinal to the front of the room. His skin felt clammy. His heart pounded in his chest. His palms were damp. Even his knees felt weak. To his knowledge, he'd never watched a man seal a pact with the devil before, but Mathews's intentions were clear. By the end of the day, he intended to secure his position as the head of Nicolae's global religion.

Marcus shuddered and dropped back into his chair. *Lord, he prayed, I don't know why You have me here. Give me the strength to speak the truth. Give me the courage not to fail You. Watch over me. Watch over my brothers and sisters. Protect Your children. Forgive us when we fall short. Lead us through this valley of the shadow of death. Cover us in the shadow of Your wing.*

★   ★   ★

Liza took Emma's hand and gave it a slight squeeze. "It's going to be okay," she assured her.

Upon meeting Emma, Liza had handed her the clipboard with Brad's briefly jotted note on it and watched the

color drain from the older woman's face. Emma had fumbled quickly for the television remote and turned on the
morning news, boosting the volume until there was no
chance their conversation might be overheard.

"Is he all right?" she'd asked Liza. "I saw the report of
what happened at the air force base on the news."

Liza couldn't imagine the kind of terror this woman had
been living with for the past few weeks. "Shaken," Liza had
assured her, "but all right. If that safety-deposit box has
what we think, it'll be over soon."

Emma's face had fought a surge of tears. "I couldn't bear
it if—I only meant to protect him."

"He knows that," Liza had said before taking the
woman's hand and uttering her assurance.

Emma accepted the tissue her sister pressed into her
hand. "I'll have to go with him to open the box. George set
it up that way for security. I couldn't get to it without the
key. He couldn't open it unless I personally signed for it.
Brad may have the key, but I have to go to the bank and request the box."

"Emma," Pearl insisted, "you know we can't leave here."

Emma met Liza's gaze. "We've been prisoners here."

"I'm sure someone is watching the house," Pearl added.
She glanced at Emma. "Tell her about the phone call."

"Two days ago, Randal came to get the security code for
the internal computer system. Five minutes after he left,
my phone rang. The man on the other end mentioned that
Brad was having a string of bad luck, and that a sniper's
bullet might be the least of my problems if I continued to
help him."

Liza thought that over. "Do you think they know you
were George's contact, Emma?"

"I think the only reason they haven't killed me is because they hope to terrify me into keeping my mouth shut

until they find out how much evidence George Ramiro had. They know that I don't actually know anything except where the evidence is and that they murdered poor George to keep him from revealing it. If they thought I knew anything, I wouldn't be alive to tell it." She pressed her lips together as she fought a surge of tears. "Brad won't either."

"Have faith in him, Emma."

"I do. I always have. And I know Brad would tell me that God has His hand on him. He feels called to do what he's doing." She shook her head. "I think in a way, he feels he has to make up lost time to God."

Liza was certain from her conversations with Brad that that was true. He was wrestling with a sense of guilt over what he called his "lack of faith" preceding the disappearances.

Emma gently blew her nose before continuing. "And even though he'd tell me my faith is weak—and maybe it is—I'm not sure that even God can protect Brad from these people." She leaned closer to Liza and lowered her voice. "Tell Brad that whatever he's going to do, he'd better do it soon."

Liza gave Emma's hand a final squeeze before standing to leave. "I will." She tucked the clipboard beneath her arm. "I don't know how and I don't know when, but we'll be in touch. Brad'll figure it out somehow. He'll get you to that bank safely. I promise."

Brad looked at Gerald Fitzhugh in amazement. "You're kidding." Brad had arrived at the office that morning to find a summons on his desk to meet with the president and Charley Swelder.

The president scowled at him. He was in a foul mood

this morning. "Do I sound like I'm kidding, Benton?" He surged to his feet and stalked over to the window. "You explain it, Charley."

Charley drummed his fingers on the padded arm of the blue sofa. "It's a simple equation, Benton. We probably should have done this weeks ago, but we've been a little busy." His laugh was derogatory. "Planning a national prayer service hasn't been as big a priority as protecting the national security of the United States. Figure that."

Weary, Brad stroked his forehead. His day had started early. He and Liza had picked Randal up at the funeral home and returned to Brad's hotel. After his mostly sleepless night sitting with Nero's casket, the young man had fallen asleep before his head hit the pillow in Brad's hotel room. Brad had spent the next hour making arrangements for Liza to make the flower delivery to Emma Pettit's house—the plan they'd both agreed would arouse the least suspicion. If, indeed, Emma's house was under surveillance, Liza would be the least recognizable of the three of them. She could most easily discern if Emma possessed the information they needed.

Once Liza was on her way to Emma's, Brad had hurried to the office. The best way he knew to avoid suspicion was to stick to a routine. In his wildest imagination, however, he hadn't expected the surprise that awaited him in the president's office.

"I understand that," Brad said now, "but I have to tell you, sir, that I don't think Nero Jefferson's funeral is an appropriate forum for this."

He'd barely entered the Oval Office when the president had informed him that he wished to use Nero Jefferson's memorial service as a platform for a national prayer service.

Swelder glared at him. "You said yourself the kid had no family. So there's no one to make noise about it. We need to make a concession to public appeal, and after last night's media storm about the shooting, Nero Jefferson has become a national hero."

Fitzhugh turned from the window. "The public feels they have a right to participate in his memorial service. The phone's ringing off the hook in the legislative affairs office. Every senator and congressperson on the Hill wants to know how we're going to respond to this."

Brad mentally steadied himself. "It's a private matter, sir. I don't think—"

"Don't be naïve," Charley grated out. "You can't get shot while playing the hero in front of a hundred reporters and expect it to be a private matter."

"He deserves a dignified service," Brad insisted. "Not a political platform."

"Then he should have gotten himself killed in a routine drive-by shooting and not twenty-five feet from *Air Force One*. It's out of our hands."

"Whether we like it or not," the president added, "it's become a public issue. The press has taken control of the story, and we might as well turn it to our advantage."

Brad leaned back in his chair and briefly closed his eyes as he realized the futility of his argument. They were right. The story of the shooting had played in every major news market in the country. Nothing Brad could do would prevent the media storm that would ensue at Nero's memorial service. "Tell me what you have in mind."

"Is your preacher friend doing the service?" Swelder asked.

"Marcus Dumont?" Brad nodded. "Yes. Nero attended his church."

"Fine." Fitzhugh folded his arms over his chest. "We'll move the memorial service to the National Cathedral, and Dumont can conduct it there."

"He won't do it," Brad said.

Charley looked outraged. "What do you mean, he won't do it?"

"I don't believe Marcus will agree to that."

"Then get him to," Fitzhugh stated bluntly. He gave Brad a narrow look. "If you recall from our conversation the other night, these are very uncertain times. You want the support of this administration, Benton, then prove yourself to be a team player. Am I making myself clear?"

Brad ignored the sharp look that Charley Swelder shot at the president. The warning was unmistakable. "Perfectly," he told him. "Perfectly."

★   ★   ★

Liza avoided looking up from her book until Brad sat down next to her on the bench. She'd been waiting for him for nearly half an hour. By mutual consent, they'd agreed that her visit with Emma was best discussed in person out in the open. Now that Brad knew Emma was at risk, his concerns about security had risen to a new level. "Sorry I'm late," he told her. He kept his gaze focused on the Washington Monument.

"Everything okay?" She turned a page of her book.

"You wouldn't believe it if I told you. How is she?"

"Scared, but fine."

Brad released a long breath. "Thank the Lord."

"The good news is, she does know where the safe-deposit box is."

"And the bad news?"

"It's set up so that neither of them could access it without the other. George had the only key, but she's the only name and signature on the card. You'll have to have her or a power of attorney with her notarized signature to open it."

"So that's how George set it up. Pretty clever." Brad tipped his head back. "But I can't risk asking Emma to do that."

"There's no other way. She wants to help you, but she's terrified."

"The house is being watched?"

"Yes. After Randal's visit, she was threatened."

"Oh no." Brad dropped his head into his hands. "What have I done?"

Liza waited silently while he gathered his composure. Beside her, she heard him whispering a prayer beneath his breath. She marveled at the faith that drove him to turn to God when every shred of evidence indicated that evil was about to triumph.

When Brad sat up again, he looked slightly haggard. "All right," he said. "I'll think of something."

"If whoever's behind this sees her with you, they'll kill you both," Liza warned. "I'm sure of it."

"I'll think of something," Brad said again. "Go back to your hotel and wait for me. I've got to spend some time praying about this, and then I'll let you know what I've decided."

Liza shut her book and stood to go. She thrust her hands into her jacket pockets. "Whatever we do, we'd better do it soon. I have this feeling that if we're right about all this, then Rudd and his accomplices aren't very thrilled about the treaty with Israel. I think if we don't break this story before you leave for Jerusalem on Saturday, we might be out of time."

Brad nodded. "I'm afraid you're right. Rudd's got too much invested to let that treaty get signed without a fight. If he really has control of the uranium at Sukhumi, he won't hesitate to use it as a bargaining chip to prevent the Arabs from coming to the treaty table."

"I'm not sure even Nicolae Carpathia is prepared to deal with the consequences of Rudd turning that uranium over to Hizb ut-Tahrir al-Islami."

"You'd be surprised," Brad told her. He looked up and met her gaze. "Check on Randal for me, will you? I'm worried about him."

"Sure."

Brad stood with a brief nod. "All right. I'll be in touch."

★   ★   ★

Marcus glanced down the long, mostly empty corridor as he listened to Brad's explanation.

He'd welcomed the vibration of his cell phone's silent ring as an excuse to step out of the meeting that was making his stomach churn. Once he'd made his position clear—that he was there to represent the Word of the Lord, and that under no circumstances would he allow the group of religious leaders to claim unanimity when they announced their heretical position to the public this afternoon, he'd become persona non grata in the room. Mathews made a point of belittling him and his position, which they'd labeled as unenlightened and narrow-minded, and though the labels didn't bother Marcus, their rhetoric appalled him.

Now came the news of Nero's memorial service and the president's intention of turning it into a political platform. "I don't know, Brad," he admitted. "That's a tough call."

"I told him you wouldn't do it."

Marcus managed a slight laugh. "I'd rather not."

"It's not a command performance," Brad assured him. "You can say no. But they have a point. Nothing we can do is going to keep this from turning into a media circus."

"That's true enough. In his wildest imagination, I'm sure Nero wouldn't have dreamed of this."

"He deserved better," Brad said, his voice breaking slightly. "He saved my life, Marcus."

"And Liza's." Marcus stroked his silk tie with his thumb and forefinger. "There's only one way I'd consider doing it. . . ."

"You're going to consider it?" Brad was clearly taken aback. "Marcus—"

"Hear me out," Marcus said calmly. "I was sitting in this meeting this morning—"

"How's it going?"

"You don't want to know. I've been listening to the rhetoric and it turns my stomach. I've made a lot of mistakes and I've refused to surrender to the Lord, but I'd like to believe I wouldn't have participated in this heresy because it was politically expedient." He paused. "Unfortunately, I'm not sure I *can* believe that."

"It's in the past, Marcus," Brad told him. "God's forgiven you. It's time to forgive yourself."

"Have you succeeded in forgiving yourself?" Marcus asked. Brad didn't respond. Marcus nodded. "I didn't think so."

"Tell me what you're thinking about Nero," Brad told him. "The president wants an answer."

"The other reality is, if I don't agree to do the service, the White House will get someone else to do it. Isn't that right?"

"They can't get Nero's body, I don't think. Although, with no family to claim it, I'm not sure what the legalities are, but yes, they'll hold a service whether you conduct it or not."

"So it's safe to say that if we want Nero's memorial service to accurately reflect his commitment to the Lord, I'll have to do it myself."

Brad hesitated. "Yes. That's true."

Marcus stared sightlessly at a piece of modern art as he considered the implications. "When do they want to do this?"

"Saturday morning. The White House contingent is leaving for Israel on Saturday afternoon. The treaty signing will take place on Sunday, but Fitz wants to fly in the night before."

"Any particular reason?"

"With everything that's happened here, the Secret Service feels they can better protect him if they don't have to fight the rest of the international traffic coming in on Sunday."

"Hmm. True enough, I suppose. When's Carpathia supposed to fly in?"

"I swore in the new pilot yesterday afternoon. He told me Carpathia wants to fly on Sunday." Brad paused. "Marcus, has there been any talk there today about the two prophets at the Wailing Wall in Jerusalem?"

Marcus frowned. "No. Why?"

"It was something I saw today—an interoffice thing. I think Fitzhugh is flying in early because he wants to try and talk to those two."

"What on earth for?"

"During his meetings with the president, Carpathia indicated that he's furious with the Israelis for not dispensing with them."

"There's not much Israeli security can do," Marcus pointed out. The two prophets at the Wailing Wall, just as the Bible foretold, were apparently supernaturally protected. Already, eight civilians and three Israeli soldiers had died trying to drive them away. Eyewitness reports of the men spewing flames from their mouth or bodies spontaneously combusting had piqued international interest.

"Carpathia evidently doesn't buy that. I think Fitz plans to use his security detail to get close to them."

"That could be dangerous."

"I'm not sure what to do, Marcus. I don't know if I should try to warn the president or keep my mouth shut."

"What's the status of the other issue?" Marcus asked. He knew Brad would understand the veiled question about George Ramiro's murder.

"Big developments. I can't talk about it right now."

"I understand. Do you think you've got what you need?"

"Soon. I have a plan. I think I can make everything happen before I leave for Jerusalem."

"I hope so."

"That's another reason I feel I have to try and warn the president about the situation in Israel." Brad had told Marcus about his conversation with Fitzhugh, in which the president indicated that Ramiro had confided in him before his death. The president seemed to know more about Rudd's possible criminal activities than he let on. Brad felt that given Rudd's vehement opposition to the treaty, Fitzhugh could possibly be in danger during his trip to Jerusalem. "But if the warning comes from me," Brad continued, "I'll get dismissed as a religious fanatic."

Marcus sighed. "I know the feeling."

"It's rough up there?"

"It hurts my heart, Brad. That's probably the hardest thing about all of this. I'm ashamed to admit it, but I never really cared enough about whether people were going to hell. The caring hurts."

"I know. It's harder."

"But I've been sitting here praying that God would give me a forum, a place to speak the truth to all these people who are blindly following Carpathia. I thought I'd find that forum here."

"It hasn't worked out that way?"

"No. And I'm beginning to wonder if God didn't send me here to rekindle my fire for preaching His Word."

"Has it been waning?" Brad sounded concerned.

Marcus struggled to explain himself. "I'm fulfilled with what's happening at church on Sundays, Brad. People are hearing and listening and understanding, and it's enough for me."

"But?"

"But," Marcus conceded, "I have continued to feel God's call on my life to reach a broader audience—to at least speak the truth where no one else will."

"A place like Nero Jefferson's memorial service."

"The president of the United States, most of Congress, and an enormous contingent of media will be there. The service will be televised. I don't think I could ask for a larger platform."

Brad let out a low whistle. "I'm really sure the president isn't expecting you to hurl fire and brimstone."

"I'm sure too. But I wouldn't consider doing the service any other way. It feels like an answer to prayer."

"I'm not sure what the political fallout will be, Marcus. With the lawsuit pending—"

"I'm not worried about it. Sanura has it well under control. I just spoke with her about it."

"You don't think a high-profile appearance like this would fuel Theo Carter's case?"

"I think it definitely will. I think it will garner me some powerful enemies." Marcus thought of Peter Mathews presiding over the meeting in his cardinal's robes and could well imagine what would be said about him. "In an environment where the most powerful and popular man in the world is pushing for a single world religion and throwing

around words like *tolerance* and *unity*, I think it's safe to say
that the doctrine of grace is going to offend a lot of people."

"People don't like it, Marcus. They crucified Jesus for it,
you know?"

Marcus laughed softly. "So I shouldn't expect any less?
Is that what you're saying?"

"I'm saying that if you're determined to do this, then
we'd better all start praying about it right now. It could get
ugly."

Marcus glanced through the window in the door at Peter
Mathews. "I'm almost counting on it," he told Brad.

★   ★   ★

With a sick feeling in his stomach, Brad watched Cardinal
Peter Mathews at the press conference announcing the results of the religious summit.

Marcus, not surprisingly, was not on the dais with
Carpathia and Mathews. While the two men glowed about
this "great new stride toward global peace," Marcus was already on a shuttle flight back to D.C., preparing his sermon
for Nero Jefferson's funeral. Liza had agreed to pick him up
at the airport so Brad could finish arranging the details of
the wake and memorial service.

Sometime after his conversation with Liza on the Ellipse, Brad had devised a plan that he prayed would get
Emma safely out of her house and to the First Federal Bank
of the District of Columbia, where George Ramiro had secured the evidence that would break the story of Rudd's
criminal activities wide open. The plan would require split-
second timing, scrupulous detailing, and the hand of God
if it were to succeed.

Brad switched off the television. He couldn't take any
more. He pulled open his desk drawer and removed the

Bible he kept there. He placed it flat on his desk and propped his elbows on it. Dropping his forehead to his folded hands, he turned to the Lord for strength and wisdom.

God, he prayed, *I'm scared. I'm scared for my friends. I'm scared for Emma and for Liza. Liza needs You. I think she knows that, but she's so confused. I feel completely inadequate to talk to her about You. Why should she listen to me when I've never given her any reason to trust my faith? Please give Marcus an opportunity this afternoon, Lord. He'll know what to say. And, God, watch over him as he prepares for Saturday. He's a brave man. A good servant. He's so worthy of Your protection. Guide him as he writes his sermon. Keep his thoughts clear. Give him wisdom. Lord, please watch over Randal and Mariette. I'm worried about Mariette in those meetings. You alone know how much evil surrounds her. Protect her. Lord, I want to be the man You've called me to be. I want to do everything for You that You've asked me to do, but I need Your help. I'm in over my head, Lord. Please help me. Please help us all.*

Brad swallowed a long sip of his club soda and glanced across the room at Liza. She was engaged in conversation with Mariette, who'd flown in after completing her first round of meetings at the UN.

Mariette, Brad noted, looked exhausted. He wasn't surprised. According to Marcus, the tension and atmosphere at the UN had been worse than they could have imagined. Though the public saw a Nicolae Carpathia who seemed dedicated to peace and international goodwill, at the UN the signs of his absolute control were obvious.

Emma's house was teeming with reporters, politicians, and curiosity seekers who'd seen Nero Jefferson's death announcement in the papers and had come to pay their condolences to his friends. Only a handful of people had questioned why the young man's wake was being held at Emma Pettit's house. Brad had told them that Nero had no surviving family, and that he'd met Emma through Brad. Recently out of work, Brad had recommended Nero to Emma, who was still recovering from the sniper attack, as a driver and general handyman. She'd been fond of the young man, and had offered to hold the wake in her home where well-wishers who'd been unable to get VIP passes to the memorial service could come and pay their respects.

The story was plausible and easy to accept once people met Emma and experienced her warm, gracious hospitality.

"Brad—"

He tore his gaze from Mariette to look at Edward Leyton, the secretary of defense, who'd approached him from behind. "Ed. Thanks for coming."

Ed Leyton sighed heavily. "I'm really torn up about this. I feel like it happened on my watch, you know?"

"Have the authorities at Andrews discovered anything new?" Brad asked.

Leyton shook his head. "Nothing yet. The shooter still claims he was trying to make a political statement, that nobody hired him to do the shooting."

"You don't believe it?"

"We looked into his financials. He's an enlisted man. Makes a base salary of $38,000. Two weeks ago, he made a quarter-of-a-million-dollar deposit in a savings account in his home state of Texas."

"I see."

"Thing of it is," Leyton told him, "the bank can't find any record of the deposit other than the fact that the funds are in his account. They've got no check and no record of a cash transaction on file."

"Wired funds?"

"Had to be, or else there'd be a paper trail." Leyton studied him for a moment. "Do you think this was another attempt on you, Brad?"

Brad shrugged. "I don't know. I just know I lost a good friend as a result of it."

Leyton leaned closer to him. "Level with me, Brad. What's really going on?"

"Someone wants me dead," Brad said with a slight shrug. "And the Service and White House security and the FBI can't seem to figure out who it is."

"Do *you* know who it is?" Leyton asked.

"Don't you think if I knew that, I'd have had the guy arrested by now?"

"Not if the people after you are powerful enough to anonymously wire a quarter million into a bank account and violate base security to try and get you killed." Leyton looped his fingers beneath Brad's arm and pulled him to the side. "Look, Brad, I'm going to tell you something I probably shouldn't because I trust you. Of everybody in the White House, I think I can trust you."

"Ed—"

Shaking his head, Leyton cast a quick glance over his shoulder before looking at Brad again. "I know about Nuñez," he said.

Brad's eyes widened. "Ed—"

"I don't have much information. Just a few sketchy facts. But I know there's something going on at the Pentagon that shouldn't be. The name Nuñez keeps surfacing. I've got some people asking questions."

Brad's breathing turned shallow. He silently prayed for wisdom. He liked Ed Leyton, always had, and knew that the secretary was paying an enormous personal and political price for the White House's assertions that the disappearances had been the result of a global attack. With a war already in progress on the Turkish-Syrian border, the Defense Department was now under fire to provide answers for why American military intelligence and technology had not foreseen the attack. Max Arnold had been among the first to hurl accusations about cover-ups and incompetence. Ed Leyton, common wisdom currently agreed, would probably not survive the political firestorm.

"Listen to me, Ed," Brad said quietly. "You have no idea what you're dealing with. It's all going to come out. Soon, it's going to come out, but you've got to trust me and let this lie until the story breaks."

"My sources indicate that Nuñez could have had something to do with the assassination attempt on POTUS."

Brad gave the secretary a hard look. "You're going to have to trust me," he said again. "Just let it lie a little while longer."

Leyton studied him a moment. "Not everyone in this administration is corrupt, Brad. I got into politics because I believed in an agenda and a mission. I want to do the right thing. Please—tell me how I can help."

Brad glanced over at Liza again. She was sitting with Emma now. He quickly scanned the room to make sure Randal was in place. As an idea began to form in his mind, he told the secretary, "You may get your chance. Sooner than you think."

★   ★   ★

Randal leaned back against the doorway to Emma's kitchen and continued to scan the crowd. It was mostly comprised of church members and Nero's friends who didn't rate tickets to the memorial service. The more he thought about it, the angrier it made him. Because of a political ploy, his friend's Christian brothers and sisters would not be able to mourn together at the service. While Fitzhugh was grandstanding to gather votes, those who'd been closest to Nero were going to have to watch via remote broadcast at Marcus's downtown church.

Randal almost wished he hadn't given up alcohol when he'd given his life to Christ. This would have been a good time for a beer. Instead, he nursed a soda and tried not to grind his teeth in frustration. He knew exactly why he resented this so much. This was the kind of stunt his own father would have pulled. He wouldn't have cared about Nero or Nero's life or Nero's friends. The chance to turn the memorial service into a publicity stunt would have been too good to pass up. Randal fully expected to see his father at the service on Saturday. He hadn't decided yet what he'd say to him—especially not after the conversation they'd had on the phone.

A dull headache had begun to pound his temples. Randal closed his eyes tight and fought it. It had plagued him since the explosion at the White House—the lingering effects of his concussion. He had a job to do tonight, and no time to give in to the pain. He and Brad had spent most of the day setting this up. They'd had to make half a dozen phone calls to arrange for the right vehicles. Liza had pulled every journalistic string she had to ensure maximum exposure for the news of the wake.

The large crowd played in their favor.

This was their only chance to get Emma out of the house and to a secure location until they could go to the bank tomorrow and retrieve the safe-deposit box. Brad had orchestrated it all. Parked outside were the ubiquitous black White House sedans and security vehicles.

Randal glanced across the room and noted that Brad's conversation with Ed Leyton was still intense but subdued. Liza, he saw, had made her way through the heavy crowd and was seated next to Emma on the sofa. His mother was near the patio door. Marcus was in the front hall offering comfort to a group of church members who'd recently arrived. Pearl was in the back bedroom as planned.

Randal slid his hand into his pocket and wrapped his fingers around the key ring to ensure it was still there. All he needed now was a signal from Brad.

It came two minutes later. Secretary Leyton made his way through the crowd to say a final good-bye to Emma. She greeted him warmly, clasping his hand in both of hers. Randal watched the exchange closely. Leyton passed a white handkerchief with Brad's monogram on it to Emma. She tucked it into her sleeve and stood to walk the secretary to the door. Leyton summoned his driver who was waiting near the fireplace. The young man began to make his way toward the door.

Liza rose from the couch, collected the glasses off the table, and headed for the kitchen. Mariette, dressed all in black as Emma was, saw the movement and exited through the patio doors in the rear of the house. Randal moved quickly to follow her. Outside, he joined Mariette, and they moved quickly toward the front of the house.

Randal slid behind the wheel of one of the black sedans. Mariette slipped in and lay down on the backseat. In his peripheral vision, Randal saw Liza enter another vehicle. Leyton's driver slipped into a third. Randal started the car and negotiated his way through the traffic and parked cars.

The trickiest part of the plan would be getting Emma down the short walk that led to the street. Marcus, Randal noted, had succeeded in ushering his large group outside. Twenty or thirty people now cluttered the front walk.

Randal pulled up to the curb. Leyton's driver parked next to him, effectively blocking the view on the driver's side of Randal's car. Liza closed in just behind them. Randal saw Brad come out of the house and join Emma and Leyton on the front stoop. Leyton's driver stepped out of his vehicle and signaled the secretary.

Leyton acknowledged the signal, then turned to shake Brad's hand. Together with Emma, the two of them moved toward the curb where the three cars waited. They were two steps from the curb when Emma twisted her ankle and began to fall toward Leyton.

He caught her by the arm. Brad steadied her shoulders. The two men guided her toward the car as Leyton's driver rushed forward to help. Randal dared a glance at his mother in the backseat of the vehicle. Her eyes were closed. Her lips were moving in silent prayer.

He pulled open the door and reached a hand toward Emma.

"Let me just sit for a moment," she said. "I'm still not as strong as I'd like to be."

Leyton and Brad helped her sit on the edge of the backseat.

"Now," Randal heard Brad tell Emma.

The older woman lay down on the backseat. Mariette slipped past her and perched on the edge of the seat, shielded from the house by Leyton and Brad. Marcus hurried down the walk and got into Liza's vehicle. She eased carefully into the street traffic.

Mariette, wearing a black veil like Emma's, sat on the edge of the seat. Leyton helped her out and wrapped an arm around her shoulders. He waved his driver aside as he began to walk with Mariette toward the house. Brad slid into the backseat of the car next to Emma. Randal scrambled behind the wheel and resisted the urge to roar away from the house. *Smoothly*, he reminded himself. *Smoothly. God, help us,* he prayed as he merged into the traffic.

"Don't look back," Brad warned. "Just drive."

"Anyone following us?"

"Leyton's car is still blocking the street."

Randal dared a glance in the rearview mirror. He caught a glimpse of the secretary helping Mariette into the house. He made his way down the street with excruciatingly slow progress.

"Brad?" Emma's voice sounded shaky.

"Almost," Brad told her. "Just hold on a minute longer. Are you okay?" Randal knew she was lying down on the passenger seat next to Brad. The position had to be cramped and uncomfortable.

"I haven't felt this good in years," she told him.

Brad chuckled softly. "If I didn't know better, I'd think you were enjoying yourself."

"If I wasn't so scared, I might be."

Brad met Randal's gaze in the rearview mirror. "Anyone following us?"

"There's some street traffic, but no, I don't think anyone's behind us. I think we made it." He studied the scene in the mirror as he eased to a stop at the corner. "Leyton's getting in his car."

"Good. Perfect."

"How much did you tell him?" Randal asked.

"I didn't tell him anything. He'd heard about Nuñez. He doesn't know much, but he knows enough to be sure there's something going on that shouldn't be. He asked me how he could help. I told him I needed to get Emma out of the house without anyone knowing."

"Do you think that was safe?" Randal asked. "Can we trust him?" He turned into the intersection, where he spotted Liza's car ahead on the side of the road. As he eased past, she pulled in behind him. She'd cover their back in case they picked up a tail.

"I think he knew he was putting his life in my hands by mentioning Nuñez," Brad said. "I have to admit, he was an answer to prayer. We could have done this without him, but it would have been more difficult. Since he walked Mariette back to the house, it made the switch more convincing." Brad glanced over his shoulder. "Okay, Emma. You can sit up."

After he helped her up, she pulled the black veil from her head. "Are we safe?"

"I don't think we'll be safe until Victor Rudd and his accomplices are behind bars," Brad said.

"But did they see us leave?"

"It was dark. There was a large crowd outside. I think it worked. We'll know soon enough."

She exhaled a long, exhausted sigh. "I'm so sorry, Brad. I never meant to drag all of you into this. Until I got those pictures of George . . ." Her voice broke.

Brad slipped a comforting arm around her shoulders. "It's all right. I know you were trying to protect me. God is protecting us now. Everything will be all right."

"Everyone keeps saying that." She pulled Brad's handkerchief from the cuff of her sleeve. "Liza. Your friend Marcus. You. You all seem so sure."

"I *am* sure," Brad said. "Liza's going with you to the bank. Once we have the contents of that box, I think we'll have everything we need to put the whole matter to rest."

Randal wished he shared Brad's confidence.

Liza pulled Brad's baseball cap down lower over her ears before pushing Emma's wheelchair through the elevator doors into the lobby of the First Federal Bank the next morning. Neither spoke as Liza made her way through the impressive marble lobby. Emma sat hunched in the chair, with a scarf around her head and her handbag clutched in her lap. Driving Marcus's car, Randal had brought them to the bank just as it opened. They'd all spent a mostly sleepless night waiting for daylight and, hopefully, the evidence that would finally bring George Ramiro's murderer to justice.

Liza wheeled the chair over to the bank clerk's desk.

"May I help you?" the young woman asked.

"My mother needs to access her safe-deposit box," Liza said.

The woman glanced at Emma, then nodded briefly as she turned to her computer. "Sure. Let me just log on, and we'll access your account." She indicated the chair next to her desk. "Would you like to have a seat?" she asked Liza.

Liza dropped into the chair.

Excruciatingly long seconds passed while the clerk waited for her computer to finish booting. Liza nervously watched the customers entering and exiting the bank. Even the tall marble pillars seemed to have prying eyes. As people moved about in the bank's foyer, Liza concentrated on breathing normally—a task made difficult by the sense that they were being watched.

"Here we go," the woman finally said. "What's your box number, ma'am?"

"Fourteen thirty-six," Emma told her.

The woman entered the number. "Oh," she said, glancing at Liza. "Do you happen to know how long it's been since you've checked this box?"

"I've never checked it," Emma told her. "My attorney opened it for me."

The woman nodded. "That's probably what it is, then."

"Is there a problem?" Liza asked.

"No, no. I don't think it's a problem. There's just a security notice here that says your mother's signature has to be authenticated by a notary public before we can allow her to access the box. It's not unusual for these types of situations. It's one of our high-security boxes, and if your attorney opened it, he would have added the provision as an extra safeguard."

"What do we need to do?" Liza pressed.

"We have a notary here on staff. If you'll just give me a minute, I'll go get my boss."

"Take your time, dear," Emma said.

The woman walked way, her high heels clicking on the marble floor. Liza gripped the edges of her chair and fought the urge to watch her walk off. "Did you expect this?" she asked Emma quietly.

"No, but it doesn't surprise me. George was very cautious."

Liza could believe it. Last night, Emma had told them how George Ramiro had first approached her. He'd stumbled on information about the Nuñez operation while following up on a tip from a reporter. The reporter had been mysteriously killed a few days later. George had evidently understood almost immediately the explosiveness of the evidence he'd begun to find.

Within days, it had become obvious that whoever was behind the operation inside the White House was setting up Brad to take the fall. Given the unusual circumstances of Brad's position at the White House, that wasn't surprising. He had few friends in the Fitzhugh administration, and if he was implicated in an illegal covert action, few would probe any deeper. Brad, everyone knew, was not likely to have strong enough allies to be coordinating the operation with anyone else.

George had initially come to Emma on a fishing expedition. He'd been unsure what Brad's involvement might have been, but Emma had soon persuaded him that Brad had no knowledge of the scandal. George had then asked Emma to partner with him in uncovering the truth. As Brad's assistant, she had virtually unlimited access to employment records and background checks. All interoffice communications passed her desk before reaching Brad's. George had told her little, except to keep her posted on his progress. He'd sworn he was protecting her by keeping his discoveries to himself.

Three days before his death, however, he'd come to Emma early in the morning, before most of the White House staff had arrived. He indicated that he'd obtained key evidence while examining computer records Emma had given him. The files were copies of confidential documents Brad had pulled from the office of a departing clerk in the military attaché's office. She'd copied the files and passed them to George before archiving them in the White House vault.

That was when George had indicated the need for the safe-deposit box. He'd given Emma the name of the bank, brought her a signature card, and told her he'd set the account up so that only she could access it. He would keep the only key. That way, neither of them had exclusive access to the evidence. He had scheduled a meeting with a prominent New York attorney and journalist to leak the story to the press four days later.

And then he'd been murdered.

Liza turned when she heard approaching footsteps. The bank clerk was returning with her manager.

"Mrs. Pettit?" the manager asked, addressing Emma.

"Yes?"

"I'm sorry for the inconvenience of this, but we're going to have to check your ID against our records."

Emma reached into her handbag and produced her driver's license. The bank manager studied it carefully. "Your date of birth?" he asked.

Emma told him.

"Social Security number?"

She quoted it from memory.

"Do you have the key to the box?"

Emma produced it from her purse.

Apparently satisfied, the bank manager returned her license to her. "Well, we're very glad you came in today."

"Why?" Liza asked.

"Unfortunately, someone tried to access your box illegally yesterday afternoon."

Liza felt her blood run cold. "Excuse me?"

The manager nodded. "A woman came in claiming to be Mrs. Pettit. I met with her in my office. She had an ID and knew your box number, but claimed she'd lost the key and wanted us to replace it for her. When I compared the signature, it didn't quite match." He accepted a pen from the bank clerk and handed Emma a signature card. "If you'll sign that for me, I'll compare it with our records."

Liza carefully considered the possible implications of this new information. "What did you do with her?" she asked.

"I didn't let her access the box," he said, "but I didn't really have any proof of wrongdoing either. We checked, and you hadn't filed an identity-theft complaint with the police. There really wasn't anything we could do." He took the card from Emma. "Do you have any idea how this woman might have procured your ID?"

"No," Emma said. "But I've been in the hospital recently."

The bank manager clucked his tongue. "We're seeing more and more of this lately. Identity theft has been rampant since the disappearances. I suppose the computer and security industries were as hard hit as the rest of us. I'm sorry to have to be the one to tell you this, Mrs. Pettit, but it seems someone has violated your personal security."

"We'll look into it," Liza assured him.

He nodded, then waved the card. "If you'll just give me a moment, I'll check this with the original signature card."

He hurried off, leaving them with the bank clerk. "It

won't take long," she told them. "Then I'll walk you to the vault. Lucky you came in today, wasn't it?"

"It certainly is," Emma said.

The woman shook her head. "I just don't know what we're going to do in this business about computer fraud and identity theft. You can't imagine how many of these cases we see in a given year."

They waited a few moments until the bank manager returned. "Everything's fine, Mrs. Pettit," he said. "Marjorie will show you to the vault."

"Thank you," Emma told him.

"Thank you for doing business with First Federal. I hope you don't have too much trouble with this identity fraud."

"I hope so too."

★ ★ ★

"Do you see them?" Brad asked.

Randal squinted in the morning sunlight and tried to see through the bank's plate-glass windows. "No. What's taking so long?"

"It's only been ten minutes."

"It feels like ten years." Randal shaded his eyes and stared at the bank's heavy bronze door, waiting for Liza and Emma to emerge. He and Brad were parked in a loading zone across the street and down a block. "Don't you think they should be out by now?"

"Not if the account had to be authenticated. That could take a while."

"I don't like this. I should have gone in with her."

"You could have been recognized. Liza was safer."

"What if someone gets to them while they're inside?"

"Believe me," Brad said, "Liza can take care of herself."

Randal continued to study the door. "Do you really think this is going to be the evidence that you need?"

"I hope so," Brad admitted. "I'm praying so."

"I don't know how many more near misses we have left." He turned to look at Brad. "I miss Nero."

"I know." Brad put his hand on Randal's shoulder. "I'm sorry, Randal. I know you two had gotten kind of close."

Randal struggled with a surge of emotions. "He shouldn't have died like that. He had so much to offer."

"It wasn't your fault," Brad told him. "It was his time."

"I know."

"But you feel guilty?"

"I don't know. I feel—unworthy."

"What do you mean?"

Randal looked at the door again, unable to hold Brad's gaze. "Nero was always pounding on me about my father and how I feel about him."

"Oh."

"I called him that night I spent at the funeral home."

"I see."

Randal shielded his eyes again. "He warned me about Nuñez."

"That's what your mother said." Brad paused. "Do you think he's going to be implicated in this, Randal?"

"I think he's going to figure out a way to use this to his political advantage and squirm out of the whole thing unscathed," Randal said bitterly. "Just like he always does."

"Randal—"

"I know it's wrong," Randal said. "I know I'm supposed to forgive him. I know I'm supposed to let it go. Turn the other cheek. Walk the extra mile." He shook his head slightly. "But I can't."

"Would it do any good for me to point out that you're hurting yourself more than you're hurting him?"

"Honestly?"

"Yes."

"Then, no. It'd just make me mad."

Brad smiled slightly. "Okay. I won't say it."

Randal gripped the steering wheel tightly with both hands. "I think I hate him, Brad. I think I want him to go to jail because I figure if he doesn't deserve it for this, he must deserve it for something. That's a terrible thing to think about your own father."

"I'm sorry."

"I can't even pray for him. I don't want to." He swallowed the hard knot of guilt in his throat. "I think I don't even really care if he dies and goes to hell, Brad." He made himself look at Brad again. "How rotten is that?"

Brad's eyes registered a wealth of compassion. "It's human, Randal. That's the carnal part of your human self at war with the presence of Christ in your life. The fact that you know those two things are at war is the first step in surrendering it to the Lord and letting it go."

"I don't know. I've despised him for so long, I can't imagine feeling any other way."

"Then start by asking God to make you *want* to forgive him. I promise to pray about that for you."

"It's worth trying. Thanks for the support." Randal glanced at the bank again. "Now, what is taking them so long?"

★   ★   ★

"If you ladies will have a seat over here," the bank clerk said, indicating a row of small cubicles outside the vault, "I'll get your box." She turned to enter a combination on the vault's digital keypad.

Liza was relieved to see they were alone. She pushed

Emma's wheelchair up to one of the cubicles. "This shouldn't take long," she said in a low whisper.

Emma waited until the bank clerk swung open the heavy vault door and went to retrieve the box. She leaned close to Liza. "Who do you think came here trying to get to the box yesterday?"

"I don't know. Who else could have known the box number besides you and George?"

Emma thought that over. "I can't imagine how anyone else could have known. I never told anyone, and neither did George—at least he said he didn't."

"Could anyone else have gotten access to the journal in Ramiro's office?"

"Forrest Tetherton," Emma said. "My goodness, do you think that's why he was killed?"

Liza glanced at the vault door where the bank clerk was emerging with a large safe-deposit box. "If it was, then we'd better hope that box has the evidence we need. I don't think we're going to get too many more chances."

The clerk set the box down in front of them. "Here we go. You can slide it in there—" she pointed to the single-use door next to the vault—"whenever you're done. If you need anything, just let me know."

"Thanks," Liza said.

As the clerk walked away, Emma handed Liza the key. With shaking fingers, Liza opened the box.

Inside were a thick manila envelope, two microcassettes, and a videotape. Liza quickly collected the material and shoved it into her tote bag.

"You're not going to look at it?" Emma asked.

"Not here," Liza said. She locked the box again and moved to place it in the depository. "We've got to get out of here. Whoever was after this evidence yesterday still wants it. If they have an inside source in the bank—"

She stopped short when a door at the end of the hall opened and another bank clerk came into the narrow seating area with a bank customer. Liza slammed the depository door shut and hurried back to Emma. Thrusting her bag into Emma's lap, she pulled the wheelchair back and headed toward the elevator. "We've got to get out of here."

12

Sanura Kyle shoved a cup of coffee into Marcus's hand as she pushed past him into the foyer of his town house. "Nice digs," she told him.

The knock on his door had found him on his knees in his living room, praying over his friends who were, probably even now, in serious danger. He'd hurried to the door with an uneasy feeling. A check through the view hole had revealed Sanura standing on his stoop. That uneasy feeling had given way to an entirely new one.

He paused before carefully shutting the door and turning to face her. Dressed in jeans and a T-shirt, she looked more casual than he'd ever seen her. She held a take-out bag in one hand and another cup of coffee in the other. "Thanks," he said. "It suits me."

Sanura held up the bag. "I brought breakfast. I figured if I fed you, you'd have to talk to me."

He winced. "I've been busy."

"I'm your lawyer, Marcus, not your mother. You don't have to explain yourself to me."

But he did, he thought. He'd been avoiding her and he

felt like a coward for it. Sanura was competent, intelligent, and attractive. She was also twenty years younger than he was. A capable attorney, she'd managed to guide him through the murkiest waters of the civil suit his former attorney had filed against him, and was rapidly closing in on a dismissal. He admired her as a lawyer. What bothered him was that he found himself drawn to her as a woman. The timing couldn't be worse, he told himself. He had no business even considering a relationship with Sanura Kyle when he knew what the future held. At most, they had seven years before Christ returned to the earth.

What's more, Sanura was not a Christian as far as he knew. He couldn't possibly consider drawing close to a nonbeliever. So, like a coward, he'd deftly avoided talking to her for the past couple of weeks while he'd waited for the tug of attraction to ebb. Looking at her now, he realized with a sinking feeling, it hadn't. "I'm sorry," he said. "I did get your messages. I should have called."

Sanura shrugged and waved the bag at him. "Let's eat, and you can make it up to me."

"This is not the best time," he told her.

Her bright expression slipped a notch. "Oh." She glanced around the quiet foyer. "Oh. Do you want me to leave?" She didn't budge, simply stood and waited for him to either ask her to leave or open himself to a conversation he didn't want to have.

He felt like a jerk, he realized with a rush of frustration. That was just one of the reasons he'd been avoiding her. She had a way of making him feel all the remembered emotions of his youth. The last time he'd felt tongue-tied and unsure of himself he'd been sitting in an English class in college trying to figure out how to ask his future wife on a date. The feeling hadn't seemed as embarrassing or annoying then. He exhaled a heavy sigh. "No," he said, "I don't want you to leave. I was just in the middle of something, and I'm not sure if I'll be very good company this morning."

"News for you, Marcus. You're hardly ever good company."

"Thanks."

Behind her wire-rimmed glasses, her eyes sparkled with amusement. "You got potential, though, kid," she assured him as she waved the fast-food sack at him. "Can we eat now?"

"The kitchen's this way," he said, moving past her to lead the way.

"Great." She followed him in silence.

That was just one of the things he liked about Sanura Kyle. She didn't have the need to fill up every silent space with chatter. She was content enough with herself and her place in the world that she could sit in silence and wait for the conversation to come to her.

Which was exactly, he admitted to himself, what he was afraid of. She wasn't the kind of woman to let him off the hook with a few signals. He was going to have to have a conversation with her. Unless his perception was completely awry, Sanura's interest in him went beyond a simple attorney-client relationship. He didn't think he'd imagined the spark of interest that had flared between them.

"Is this what I interrupted?" she asked, indicating the Bible and papers on his kitchen table. She placed the paper bag on the counter and began to remove the contents.

"No. That's from last night. I was going to get to it later this morning."

"What is it?"

"My sermon for Nero Jefferson's memorial service."

Her hand froze as she was pulling a paper wrapper back from a sausage-biscuit sandwich. "Your sermon?"

"Yes."

"Isn't the service supposed to be a national prayer service?"

"Yes."

"The president's going?"

"So he says."

"And most of the U.S. Congress?"

"I believe so."

She finished unwrapping the biscuit and handed it to him. "Is the president *expecting* you to preach a sermon? You want a plate?"

"No." He pulled out a chair with his foot.

"No, he's not expecting it, or no you don't want a plate?"

"Both."

She propped one hip against the counter as she pulled another breakfast sandwich from the bag. "But you're going to anyway." She joined him at the table.

"Um-hmm." He indicated the food with a wave of his hand. "I'll pray." A second before he closed his eyes, he saw her disgruntled expression. "God is great," he said softly. "God is good. And we thank Him for our food. Amen."

She was watching him through narrowed eyes.

"What?" he asked her.

"Are you mocking me?"

"No."

"Then what was that?"

"Grace," he said plainly. She still looked suspicious. "Isn't God great and good?"

She took a bite of her biscuit. Marcus followed suit.

After several long seconds of silence, Sanura stretched an arm across the back of her chair. With her other hand, she fingered her paper coffee cup on the table. She was studying the thermal wrapper with undue interest. "You know, at times I can't decide whether you're infuriating or charming."

"I have that effect on people."

She met his gaze. "What's the usual verdict?"

"Depends on the person, I guess. I'd say the majority come down on the side of infuriating."

"That doesn't surprise me. Have you always been this difficult?"

"Since birth."

She laughed lightly. "I'll bet you were a handful as a kid."

"My mother used to say her life would have been easier if she hadn't taught me to talk until I was ten."

Her lips turned into a smile. "Smart woman, your mother."

"Yes," Marcus said with an unfamiliar pang of loss. That was another of the many emotions he hadn't allowed himself to experience in years.

Sanura tilted her head toward the stack of papers at the edge of the table. "So what are you preaching on at the memorial service?"

"The truth," he said vaguely.

She frowned at him. "If you remember, my daddy was a preacher. I know preacher talk when I hear it."

"All right." He titled his chair back. "I'm going to preach on the love of Jesus."

"In this climate?" she prodded. "That'll make you popular."

"I'm not particularly interested in popularity."

"But you are interested in offending the most powerful people in the country?"

"The gospel's offensive," Marcus said with a shrug. "It's like Brad says, they crucified Jesus for it."

"Funny."

"Sanura, I'm sorry if this makes you uncomfortable, but it's who I am."

"I'm not uncomfortable."

"Aren't you the same woman who told me you didn't want to talk about Jesus?"

"I didn't say that."

He raised an eyebrow. "I think your exact words were 'I'm not ready to put any trust in a God who seems like a great cosmic bully unleashing His fury on the earth.'"

"That sounds like me," she conceded, "but I never said I didn't want to talk about it—just that I probably wasn't going to see things your way."

"Then you don't want to hear about my sermon," he assured her.

Sanura frowned at him. "I take it you're not going to give the topic some warm, gutless treatment that leaves everyone feeling comforted and secure."

He couldn't stop a slight smile. "That's not really my style, no."

"Do you think that's wise?"

"Do you?"

"As your attorney? No. Not with this lawsuit pending."

"Why not?"

"Because Theo Carter's entire case hinges on proving that you defrauded donors by persuading them that you believed the gospel you preached. Obviously, if you believed the gospel you preached, you wouldn't be here."

"I believed it," he told her carefully. "It's not enough to believe it. You have to accept it."

"You're splitting hairs."

"I can't believe that's my attorney speaking."

"You know what I mean. That service will be nationally televised. If you get up and tell the nation that they're all hell bound, it could play to Theo's favor."

"Maybe." Marcus cradled his coffee cup in both hands. "So now that I know your legal opinion, I'd like to know your personal opinion."

She hesitated before speaking. "People don't want to hear what you have to say."

"People? Or you?"

She frowned at him. "You're determined to make me talk about this, aren't you?"

"Sanura, what kind of friend would I be if I weren't worried about the fate of your soul?"

"My daddy used to say that," she told him. "It never worked for him either."

He studied her for a moment. "Have you always been this stubborn?"

"Always. It makes me a good lawyer. Good lawyers are persistent."

"And they like to argue."

"And they're good at it. So if you're not going to take my advice on this sermon, we might as well change the subject."

Marcus eased his notes aside so the table was clear between them. "What would you like to talk about?"

She took a deep breath and met his gaze. "Us."

"That's exactly what I was afraid of."

"Most men are."

"I'm not most men."

"I've noticed that. That's more or less what I wanted to discuss."

Marcus nodded. "I'm not surprised." He leaned back in his chair and studied her. "Sanura, I'm not going to lie to you. I admire you. I respect you." He paused. "I'm attracted to you. If things were different . . ."

"Is this about our age difference?"

"I'm twenty years your senior."

She shrugged. "It doesn't bother me if it doesn't bother you. I've generally dated older men."

He briefly closed his eyes. "That's not the only issue here, you know."

"I'm sure it's not. I may not have known you long, Marcus, but I think I know you well. You're not the kind of man who's afraid of a woman with a brain. You're not intimidated by me because I'm assertive." She narrowed her eyes. "In fact, unless my radar is completely off, you like it."

"You remind me of my late wife."

Her expression softened. "You loved her," she said.

He felt a familiar stab of pain. "Deeply. She was the joy of my life."

"You never had children."

"She couldn't." He tipped his head. "And, at the time, I didn't want to."

A myriad of emotions drifted across her expression. "Would you have changed your mind if you'd known she would die so young?"

"I don't know," he admitted. "I was a different man then."

"The young seldom have a grasp of their own mortality."

Marcus recognized the opening he'd been waiting for. "I was completely aware of my mortality, but I wanted control over it. I may be a minister, but then it was an occupation, not a calling."

The crease he'd come to associate with irritation appeared on her forehead. "Marcus—"

He held up a hand. "I'm sorry, Sanura, but you're going to have to hear me out. If you really want to discuss 'us,' then this is the root of it."

"You know, I've always heard that women fall for men just like their fathers. You're about to tell me that the only thing keeping you from caring about me is our religious differences, aren't you?"

"I care about you," he admitted sincerely. "In fact, that's probably part of my problem. It matters to me what you think, what you believe. It matters to me that your hope of eternity is secure." He paused. "It matters to me that you have a personal relationship with Jesus Christ."

Irritation registered on her expressive face. She exhaled a quick, frustrated breath that ruffled her bangs. "Look, Marcus, as a general rule, I like to live and let live when it comes to religion. What people choose to believe about God, as far as I'm concerned, is pretty much their business."

"But it's not," he countered quickly. Frustrated, he raked a hand through his hair. "Let me explain it to you like this: If I genuinely care about you, and I genuinely believe that unless you accept the Lord as your personal Savior that you're destined to spend eternity in hell, then I *must* tell you about it. If I didn't tell you, then I either don't really believe it, or I don't really care."

She frowned. "I argued with my father about this for years. Why does everything have to be so extreme? I mean, if God is the loving God my father said He is—"

Marcus shook his head. "Come on, Sanura. You're smarter than that."

"Smarter than what?" she asked, suspicious.

"You're smart enough to know that God is, indeed, a loving God, but He is also a just God and a holy God, and the only way any of us can hope to be acceptable to Him is through the blood of Christ. Without the blood of redemption, there's no hope."

She stroked the table in front of her. Marcus had had this conversation with enough people to fully recognize the signs of her discomfort. For a woman like Sanura, who was normally so composed and self-assured, the slight quiver of her fingers betrayed her. "I know you believe that," she said. "It's not like I haven't heard it all before. My father used to scream about it from the pulpit every Sunday morning."

He heard the underlying current of bitterness in her

tone and suppressed a sigh of regret. "Sanura, passion and anger aren't the same thing. Just because your father—"

"You weren't there," she said plainly.

"I wasn't," he admitted, but he felt he had some insight into the elder Mr. Kyle's frustration. "But I think if you'll give me the chance, I can help you understand why your father was so . . . adamant."

"Because he was a stubborn man who always had to have his own way."

"No, Sanura." He leaned forward. "It was because he cared. He cared about you. He cared about the people who heard his sermons, and—" he added with a sense of sadness—"he cared about their souls. That's one of the differences between your father and me."

"You care about people," she insisted.

"I do," he said carefully, mustering his courage, "and I care about you." He shook his head. "It's new to me."

"Caring about a woman?"

"Caring about anyone but myself."

At her frown, he shook his head again. "It's true. When I lost my wife—" he swallowed a wave of regret—"I didn't let myself care anymore. It was easier not to."

"I can understand that."

"But then we went through the Rapture." Marcus watched her closely. Her expression didn't change. "And God got my attention. I finally had to admit that I'd been too proud and too arrogant and too angry to listen to Him before."

"The Rapture," she said carefully. "You really believe that?"

"Vehemently."

Sanura pursed her lips. "I don't know, Marcus."

"All right, tell me what you believe."

"I don't know. I just know that it doesn't all add up for me. It's not . . . logical."

"It's not supposed to be."

"That's the part I find irritating and hard to swallow."

"That's why it takes faith, Sanura. God did all He could to reach us, but the final step is up to us."

She looked more frustrated than annoyed. He considered that a positive sign. "This would be a lot easier," she told him, "if I weren't attracted to you. Then I could just tell you to blow it out your ear."

He laughed softly. "To be honest, it would probably be easier if I didn't care about you either. Then it would still matter to me, but I probably wouldn't take it personally."

A playful smile tilted her lips. "Well, I could tell you that if you really wanted to convince me, you'd have to spend a lot more time with me."

He turned suddenly serious. "That's the other thing. Not only do I believe that we've experienced the Rapture, but I also believe we're living in the earth's last days. The way I read the Scriptures, we've got seven years left, and that's *if* we live to the end. The Bible clearly states that during this time, there will be martyrs of the faith. We're about to experience things we can't begin to imagine."

She frowned again. "Let's see, I think I remember Daddy's sermons on that. What are the four horsemen? Conquest, Pestilence . . ."

"War and Death," he added. "I don't know exactly what's coming, but I know it's unimaginable and horrifying. Frankly, I'm not sure I could face it if I didn't have the assurance from the Lord that I am His child."

"You don't think all that's literal," she countered.

"I think the Bible is completely infallible and utterly true. I may not fully understand it all, but I completely believe it."

Sanura shook her head. "I'm sorry, Marcus; there's just too much in there that doesn't match up with science."

"If you start trying to force an infinite and omnipotent God into the finite and limited confines of human understanding, you're going to hit a roadblock," he assured her. "It's inevitable."

"You are infuriating," she told him, but she seemed more intrigued than irritated. He took that as a positive sign.

Marcus wrestled with an unfamiliar feeling of uncertainty. She was clearly not ready to make a decision, and he struggled with a strong desire to argue with her. He drew a steadying breath. "The truth is, Sanura, that you matter to me."

"You matter to me too," she said softly.

"And because you matter, I can't just let this go."

"You're determined to save my soul, aren't you?"

"No," he said carefully. "But I'm determined to do whatever I can to convince you that it needs saving."

"Then what about us?"

He considered her for a moment. "I probably can't think of a worse idea than getting romantically involved with anyone at this time."

"But?"

"But my head doesn't seem to be having a lot of success persuading my heart. Against my better judgment, I'm already involved," he admitted.

"That explains why you've been avoiding my calls," she quipped.

"And because I'm involved, I'm going to keep trying to persuade you to see the light."

She seemed to consider that for a moment. "I guess I'm up to it if you are."

★   ★   ★

Brad put the videotape into the player as Liza dumped the contents of the envelope onto the desk in his new hotel suite. Randal and Emma were on their way to Mariette's home in Silver Spring, where she and Pearl were waiting. Late last night, well after Emma was safely away from the house, Brad had arranged for a private security detail to take Mariette and Pearl to Silver Spring.

Though Randal had argued, Brad and Liza both had felt that only they should see the evidence they'd procured at the bank. Until he was certain that neither Emma nor Randal could be held liable in any way, Brad was unwilling to expose them to the evidence. Ignorance, he'd insisted, wasn't merely bliss. In the world of criminal prosecution, it was immunity.

He'd also decided that it was time for him to relocate again. Since the bomb that had destroyed his apartment, he'd made a habit of moving from hotel to hotel, never staying for more than a few days. With Liza in town and the newly procured evidence in their possession, he could not afford to take any chances.

She'd watched nervously while he'd swept the living room for bugs before inviting her to enter. If he'd learned one thing recently it was that being visible to the public and being paranoid had kept him alive.

He hit the Play button and moved to sit next to Liza at the desk.

After a couple of seconds of leader, George Ramiro's image appeared on the screen as he adjusted the camera on its tripod. "Okay," he said to the camera. "I hope this is working. There's a reason why I stand in front of the camera and not behind it." George had made the tape in his office at the White House. The bookshelves Brad had searched were behind him.

Brad felt the sharp sting of sorrow as he watched his former friend shoot a wary look at the door.

"I don't know how much time I have," George was saying, "so I'll have to be quick about this. I would have done this at my apartment, but I'm sure it's bugged. My phone line is recorded here, but I asked the Service to sweep my office this morning so I think it's clean."

George took a deep breath, closed his eyes, and visibly collected his thoughts before looking at the camera again. "Okay. Whoever's watching this, there are only two reasons you have it. If I make it to New York the day after tomorrow, I'm taking all the stuff in that safe-deposit box to Matt Coles." Both Brad and Liza recognized the name of the *New York Times*'s veteran investigative reporter. "Conrad Dishun," George continued, "was going to set up an appointment for me."

"That explains the conversation Randal overheard between Rudd's people that day in the car," Brad told Liza.

"George wasn't writing a tell-all," she mused. "He was going to break the story."

"The other reason," George was saying, "is that I didn't make it to New York, and I got killed in the process." He wiped a hand through his hair. "If that's the case, then, Brad, I hope it's you watching this. If not, then you probably didn't make it either."

"Unbelievable," Brad muttered.

"I want you to know, I did everything I could to protect Emma. I was going to take this straight to you, but she wouldn't let me. She wanted to protect you from whatever fallout there might be over this. If there are hearings, you can honestly say you had no knowledge of what was happening. The only thing Emma knows is where this safe-deposit box is located. You can't get to it without her or her power of attorney. Other than that, I've never shown her any of the evidence. She may have to testify, but she's completely safe from prosecution."

"Wise man," Liza said.

George continued. "If you're not Brad, then I don't know why you're watching this, but for your sake, I hope Victor Rudd is in jail. If he's not, everything you need to know is in the envelope and the two cassettes I'm putting in the safe-deposit box. My advice is that you let the media break the story first, then take the evidence to the FBI." He leaned closer to the camera. "Don't trust anyone—not the FBI, not the Secret Service, not anyone. Matt Coles is expecting this evidence. If you contact him and tell him you're calling about the Nuñez affair, he'll see you. Whatever you do, don't tell anyone at the White House you have this."

George's expression saddened. "Against my better judgment, I'm going to talk to POTUS today. I still don't believe he's involved in this. My conscience won't let me keep the appointment with Coles until I warn the president. Brad, if this is you, don't make the same mistake."

The tape went black.

Liza and Brad sat in silence for several moments.

"Are you all right?" she finally asked him.

Brad nodded but didn't answer. He was struggling emotionally with the knowledge that George Ramiro, an honest, conscience-driven, honorable man had died and, in all likelihood, gone to hell at the hands of Victor Rudd and a betrayer in the White House. Brad had no reason to believe George had been a Christian. He'd never given any indication that his Catholicism meant more to him than a family legacy and an admirable lifestyle. Brad drew a shaky breath. "Do you know how to get in touch with Matt Coles?"

"Yes," Liza said.

"Are you willing to share the byline with him?"

She shot him a dry look. "Do you know that Matt Coles has won three Pulitzers? *Three?*"

"So?"

"So, I think the question is whether or not he's willing to share the byline with me."

"Liza, you've put your life on the line for this story. I'd say it'll fall right behind the Rapture and Nicolae Carpathia in the stories of the year—maybe the decade."

"Matt Coles may not see it that way."

"I don't think you understand," Brad said. "I'm not talking about who gets credit." He pressed a hand to his chest and gave her a searching look. "I'm a public figure. I'm protected by sheer nature of the fact that it'll be difficult to explain if I disappear. The Secret Service will have to protect me, whether they like it or not. Once the story breaks and arrests are made, the Justice Department's going to want me to testify. I've got the entire U.S. law-enforcement machine to make sure I stay alive to take the witness stand." He shook his head. "I can't protect you. I'm not sure anyone can protect you."

Liza looked scared. That, he thought, was probably a good thing. "I'm aware of that."

"But if your name is on the byline, the FBI will have to take responsibility for your safety. They'll offer you witness protection."

Her brow creased. "Will I have to enter the program?"

"For a while at least," he said. "It will be the easiest way to shield you from Rudd until after the trial."

"Then what?"

"They'll make an assessment about your safety. If they get the convictions they want, they'll probably offer you the chance to leave witness protection with a minimum security agreement."

"It could take years," she said.

"I know." Brad covered her hand and gave it a gentle squeeze. Guilt twisted his heart. "I'm sorry. I feel responsible for this."

She glanced at the evidence on the desk. "You know, when they burned my apartment, they destroyed all my stuff."

"I know."

"My dad is gone." She idly sifted the papers. "The only living relative I have is my brother—and we're not exactly close." She looked at him. "I didn't think it would come to this."

"I know. I'm sorry." It sounded inadequate, but Brad didn't know what else to say. "I can't advise you to take your chances without protection," he said. "It's too risky."

She picked up a pen and thumped it on the desk. "Do I have to decide right now?"

"No," he assured her. "If you want, they'll offer you pre-trial protection. You can make a decision when you're ready."

She was silent for a moment. "I've always wondered what it would be like," she finally said, "to hear my name and *Pulitzer prize* in the same sentence."

Brad waited, watching her. She was tapping the end of the pen on the desk in an uneasy rhythm. *God*, he prayed silently, *she needs You so much. I feel like this is my fault, and I don't want her to go through this without You. Help me show her that You can protect her and meet her needs. Help me reach her.*

Liza met his gaze again. "I'm not really going to have much of a choice, am I?"

"Not if you want to stay alive," he admitted.

"It's not fair." She didn't sound angry, merely resigned.

"No," he agreed, "it's not."

"Witness protection is for criminals, you know. People who got themselves in a mess by being crooks in the first place."

"In a fair and just world, we wouldn't need it at all."

"You have a point there."

"My first concern is for your safety," he assured her, "but I have to keep reminding myself that you remind me of my oldest daughter, but you're not. I don't have any control over your decision."

"Did you have any control over hers?" she quipped, a twinkle in her eyes.

"Not for the past ten years."

Liza nodded. "That's what I thought."

"But I'd be lying if I told you I didn't feel responsible for you. I got you into this."

"You didn't drag me into it kicking and screaming, you know."

"No," he conceded, "but you can't back out, either. They know you now. They might still be looking for you in California, but they know you're involved. For all I know, they recognized you the other night at Emma's house and again today at the bank. For that matter, the man who shot Nero could just as easily have been gunning for you or me. He hasn't confessed yet."

"I thought of that."

"So whatever we do, we need to do fast. I'm not comfortable leaving for Jerusalem until I know you're in a safe place—and I can't guarantee your safety as long as you're here."

She considered that for a moment. "Can you get me to New York unnoticed?"

"Mariette can help with that," he assured her. "She's got to go back as soon as Nero's memorial service is over. She's got contacts there. I think we can get you to the city and find a place for you to stay without anyone being able to trace you. You still haven't used your credit cards?"

"No. I'm living on cash. And I picked up a new prepaid

cell phone yesterday. As far as anyone knows, I left Liza Cannely in Los Angeles."

"Good. That makes it easier." Brad leaned back in his chair. "I think it would draw the least attention if you went today."

"Today?"

"Nero's memorial service is tomorrow. Anyone watching me will know I'll be here for that. I can slip you out on a shuttle flight late this afternoon without arousing suspicion."

"I can't fly without an ID. If the shooter at the base did know it was me, then Dr. Maria Zephyr is exposed. We don't have time to get a new ID before this afternoon." She tipped her head. "Or do we?"

Brad reached for his cell phone. "I'll tell you a secret about Washington," he said. "The president has two permanent box seats at every theater in town. He also has two tickets for nonessential White House personnel on every plane that leaves Reagan National. We can get you a seat, no ID required. You just have to know who to ask."

"Oh." She frowned. "Who do we ask?"

Brad punched a number on his cell phone. "Emma," he told her. "She knows how to make anything in this city happen on time and under budget, and she's got just about everyone wrapped around her finger."

"Well," she said, reaching for the phone on the desk, "then we'd better hope Matt Coles will take my call."

★   ★   ★

Marcus watched Sanura drive off before shutting his door and turning the lock. He leaned against the door, feeling oddly content and disquieted at the same time.

Sanura had a way of surprising him. Without guile or

embarrassment, she'd told him that she had indeed felt the same spark of attraction he had when they'd first met. She found him enlightened, interesting, compelling, and dynamic. She wasn't bothered by their age difference, but she did see his Christian zeal as a potential barricade between them.

Marcus had found it surprisingly easy to tell Sanura about his first wife and her death, about the events of his life that had hardened his heart against God, about why he'd found it so easy to use a pulpit to advance his career while never giving his life to Christ.

She'd empathized. She'd listened. And she'd questioned. Marcus had thoroughly enjoyed the exchange. Sanura challenged his mind and forced him to think. He hadn't realized how much he'd missed his wife's companionship until Sanura had entered his life and upended his carefully built defenses.

But she had not given any indication that she'd budged from her stubbornly held position that Jesus may have been real, He may have even been the Messiah, but that she didn't need Him or the salvation He offered.

Marcus knew many people like Sanura. He encountered them every day. They were willing, sometimes, to listen to him, but they refused to surrender their hearts. He hurt for those people. He prayed for those people. He never took it personally.

Until today.

He'd had to force himself not to argue with her. She seemed to have sensed his tension and had changed the subject to the pending lawsuit. They'd spent the rest of the afternoon poring over the details of the case, but while Sanura had discussed depositions and motions, Marcus had struggled with an unfamiliar feeling of inadequacy. Why, he wondered, had he been able to persuade so many people, and yet not this woman who was beginning to matter to him far more than she should?

By the time she'd risen to leave, he'd felt mentally drained. Sanura had given him a curious look. "Did I overwhelm you with too much legalese?" she'd asked him.

"No." Marcus rose to walk her to the door. "I've just got a lot on my mind."

"I wish you'd reconsider preaching that sermon tomorrow."

"I won't." When they'd reached the foyer, he'd given her a close look. "Are you coming to the memorial service?"

"Don't have a ticket. I don't know what Brad told you about my position at the White House, but believe me, I'm not the kind of employee who can score a pass to one of the most televised events of the year."

"I'm not sure I would have agreed to do the service if I'd known they were going to turn it into a circus."

That had won a slight laugh. "Welcome to the Fitzhugh administration," she'd said. "They can turn a trip to the supermarket into a global media event."

"Even without a press secretary?"

At the mention of Forrest Tetherton, her eyes had registered concern. "That's just awful, isn't it? No one knew he was so depressed. There was no indication—I guess there never really is. People are always saying that about suicide."

"So it has been ruled a suicide?" he asked.

"Last I heard." Limned in the sunlight that streamed through his foyer windows, she'd looked warm and alive and utterly charming.

Frustrated with himself, Marcus had closed his eyes and silently prayed for wisdom. "I'm sorry you'll miss it," he told her.

"I suppose if you're going to preach that sermon, I'd better listen to it on TV," she'd mused.

"Why?" He'd opened his eyes.

"Because you're my client. If you're going to kick up a storm, I'll need to be informed."

"And here I thought you were going to actually listen to what I had to say," he'd snapped.

She'd blinked, visibly baffled by the vehemence of his remark. "I didn't mean to hurt your feelings."

Frustrated, Marcus had shaken his head. What, he'd wondered, did she do to him? His composure was famously unflappable, but Sanura seemed to undo him with frightening ease. "It's me," he told her. "I'm just distracted. Don't take it personally."

"If you say so." She'd risen on tiptoe to drop a light kiss on his cheek before she'd left. The action had seemed natural and unpracticed, but it had left Marcus feeling shaken.

He had no idea how long he stood by the door reminding himself that he had absolutely no business getting involved with Sanura Kyle.

He finally gathered the strength to return to the kitchen, where his sermon was waiting for him. He took a moment to bow his head before digging back into the notes.

Lord, he prayed silently. *Thank You for protecting my friends. I know it's selfish, but they've come to mean so much to me. Please continue to watch over them all. Take care of Liza. Cloak her in Your protection so she's hidden from the men who want to harm her. Give Brad continued clarity and wisdom. I fear for him—especially as he prepares to leave for Israel. I don't know what he'll face there. And Mariette, Lord. She's under so much pressure.*

He paused for a moment and thought of Sanura. *I'm at a loss, Lord. I don't know what to do with this woman. Did You send her into my life to test me? Her heart is hardened toward You. I can't seem to reach her. I know that I closed myself off*

*after Lily died. I know that I used her death as an excuse to turn
even further from You.*

*Lord, if You brought Sanura into my life to show me that I
don't have to be alone, then I need a sign. I'm not sure I believe
that You would condone a romantic relationship of any kind during this Tribulation, but I do know that I can't be involved with a
woman who's not one of Your children. I need Your strength and
Your wisdom.*

*And tomorrow, Lord, I feel You are calling me to deliver this
sermon. You have given me such a powerful opportunity to share
Your love and Your truth with a hurting world, but You know the
opposition I will face. They may even try to stop me from—*

He paused. The temperature in his kitchen seemed to
have dropped suddenly. A draft of cold air gusted past his
legs, making him shiver. Had he forgotten to close the front
door? He thought he remembered locking it. A second gust
sent him to his feet. He strode quickly through the kitchen
to the front of the house, where he found the front door
securely shut.

A sense of unease filled him. He felt a presence in his
house, as if he were being watched. He switched on the
foyer light despite the ample sunlight. Chiding himself for
his foolishness, he nonetheless moved rapidly through the
ground floor, visually checking the rooms.

Once he'd assured himself that he was indeed alone, he
returned to the kitchen, where he sat at the table again.

The feeling of unease did not ebb. Determinedly,
Marcus closed his eyes and went back to the Lord in prayer.
The anxieties of the last few days had obviously taken their
toll on him.

He felt the gust of air again. This time it sent goose
bumps skittering over his flesh. He sat perfectly still, listening. The door that led from the living room to the kitchen

was slightly ajar. The setting sun streamed through the front windows and through the crack in the door.

As he watched, he saw a long shadow fall across the shaft of sunlight on the kitchen floor. His heartbeat accelerated. Through the door, he could hear the sound of the intruder's breathing. It was slightly labored and raspy. Marcus watched the shadow carefully. The door moved slightly as the shadow lengthened. The intruder was listening, Marcus realized, just as he was.

He reached behind him and switched on the radio on the counter. As music filled the room, the shadow shifted, but did not move closer.

Marcus gripped the edge of the table as he stood. Moving swiftly and quietly across the kitchen, he pulled a heavy meat mallet from the drawer. The kitchen door wavered again, swinging ever so slightly as if the intruder had pushed it farther ajar for a look inside. Marcus made his way silently toward the door. He glanced at the shadow. He thought he could make out a head and wide, thick shoulders on the opposite side of the door.

Lord, he prayed. *Lord, protect me.* Marcus held his breath as he slowly reached for the door, his heart pounding. His fingers closed on the cold knob and a bead of sweat slid down his spine. Mentally bracing himself, he raised the mallet and jerked the door open to confront the intruder.

The hallway was empty. Marcus sucked in a shaky breath and lowered the mallet. He wiped his hand over his face. His skin felt clammy. From the corner of his eye, he saw a curtain move in the living room and realized that the circulation fan was rustling the drapes. Evidently, the afternoon sun had sufficiently warmed the house to kick on the air conditioner. The floor ducts rustled the curtains, which must have caused the shadow.

Shaking his head, he leaned wearily against the

doorjamb and closed his eyes. He was feeling hypersensitive, he knew, after the two days he'd spent in New York surrounded by the delegates of Carpathia's religious summit. The event had drained him, spiritually and emotionally, but evidently it had affected him more seriously than he realized if he was seeing monsters behind the curtains.

Marcus set the meat mallet down on the counter and began to gather his Bible and his notes. He would move to his study to finish the sermon. Perhaps the change of scenery would help him concentrate. He had just tucked his notes into his Bible and reached for a stack of index cards when he heard the breathing again. He dismissed it this time, telling himself he had to remember to have his ducts checked. Perhaps some debris in them was causing the odd noise.

With his Bible and notes firmly in hand, he pushed open the kitchen door with his shoulder. What he saw reflected in the hall mirror sent his notes skittering to the floor and had him clutching his Bible to his chest. The shadow of a large figure appeared on the wall behind the door. The angle of the shadow indicated that the intruder stood just inside the opening to the stairs that led to the basement—blocked from Marcus's sight by the open kitchen door.

A chill shook him as a strong impression of evil weighed down on him. The sound of the figure's breathing was still the same labored breathing. Marcus watched the shadow rise up and down with each breath. *Lord,* he prayed silently, *darkness is on the other side of this door.* He knew—*knew*—that there was no physical intruder in his home. Instead, the shadow was cast by the presence of evil—an evil that wanted to deter him from preaching his sermon tomorrow. An evil that wanted to keep his lips sealed and cloak the truth. An evil that came from the depths of hell and had been sent to bear down on him as he prepared to answer God's call.

Marcus gripped his Bible to his chest like a shield and softly quoted, "'The Lord is my shepherd; I have everything I need.'" He kept his gaze focused on the shadow. "'He lets me rest in green meadows; He leads me beside peaceful streams. He renews my strength.'"

The shadow loomed larger. Marcus took a deep breath and continued more loudly, "'He guides me along right paths, bringing honor to His name. Even when I walk through the dark valley of death . . .'" Marcus moved into the hallway and clearly stated, "'I will not be afraid.'"

The shadow began to retreat. "'For You are close beside me. Your rod and Your staff protect and comfort me.'"

Marcus pushed the kitchen door shut and leaned against it. He could now see the stairway that led to the basement. There was nothing there, but he could still see the reflection of the shadow in the mirror. He stepped toward the stairway. "'You prepare a feast for me in the presence of my enemies. You welcome me as a guest, anointing my head with oil. My cup overflows with blessings.'"

The shadow began to break apart and fade. Marcus closed his eyes and continued quoting the psalm in a loud, clear voice: "Surely Your goodness and unfailing love will pursue me all the days of my life, and I will live in the house of the Lord forever.'"

When Marcus opened his eyes, the shadow was gone. He felt shaken and drained. He was drenched in sweat as if he'd just finished an hour-long sermon. Still gripping his Bible, he scooped up his sermon notes and headed for his study.

He was now certain of two things: Satan did not want him to preach the sermon he was preparing at tomorrow's service; and, under no circumstances, was he going to be deterred from delivering it.

13

Brad leaned against a tree and studied Marcus, who was headed slowly down the hill toward him. They'd been unable to meet here in Rock Creek Park for the past week, and Brad had missed the fellowship with his friend. "You don't look good," he told Marcus. His eyes were bloodshot, and his skin seemed sallow. "Are you feeling all right?"

"I'll be fine. Let's run."

"You're sure?"

"Yes." Marcus set a leisurely pace.

Brad fell easily into step. Since the day Marcus had led him to the Lord in this park, these early morning runs had become vitally important to Brad. Here he met with his pastor and friend. Here he shared his heart, his fears, his spiritual struggles. Here he talked openly with God and with the man who had become his best friend and his brother in Christ, without the constant worry of listening ears and prying eyes. "I talked to Liza this morning," Brad said. "Berger picked her up at LaGuardia last night and got her settled in a hotel. She's meeting with Matt Coles at nine."

Marcus nodded. "That's good. How long before the story breaks?"

"Monday, I think. The evidence is compelling. There are several Pentagon officials and a couple of congressional leaders on tape. George had e-mails and confidential memos between Rudd and his Pentagon contacts that imply the White House had given its approval."

"But you don't know who the contact was at the White House?"

"That's still the missing piece of the puzzle. I'm hopeful that Ramiro had communicated that to Coles—or at least pointed him in the right direction."

"What if he didn't?" Marcus asked. "Then what?"

They reached a hill on the path, and Brad lengthened his stride to keep pace with Marcus. "Once the story breaks, someone's going to be willing to make a deal. Whether Rudd, his people, or his conspirators crack first remains to be seen, but I'm confident we'll get the name of the White House contact in the end."

"Is the president going down for this?"

"I don't think so. George warned him. From my conversation with him the other night—" Brad shrugged—"I think Fitz might have known Rudd was involved in something, but I don't think he had the details, and I don't think he condoned it."

The sun had risen higher, warming the day. The morning dew was beginning to evaporate into a hazy cloud that bound with the pollen and dampened the air. Brad wiped a line of sweat from his forehead with the back of his hand. He shot a glance at Marcus. No matter what he said, Marcus was not himself this morning. "Tell me what's going on," he prodded. "Something's wrong."

Marcus didn't respond for several seconds. They had

crested the hill and entered a small copse of trees. "I'm under spiritual attack," he told Brad.

"What?"

Marcus nodded. "Yesterday afternoon, I finished my sermon for Nero's service. I've been under spiritual attack ever since."

"What kind of attack?"

"I can't sleep. I'm sick. I feel like I have the flu."

"Maybe you do," Brad said.

"No," Marcus said firmly. "It's spiritual warfare. I'm sure of it."

"Marcus—"

Marcus held up a hand and indicated a familiar bench where they'd had many conversations. "Let's sit."

Brad raised an eyebrow, but said nothing as Marcus led the way to the bench. He virtually collapsed onto it. His breathing sounded harsh and shallow. Brad watched him as he braced his elbows on his knees and buried his head in his hands. "I'm not sure I can make it through that service," he said. "I'm running a fever."

"Do you need a doctor?"

"A doctor couldn't help."

Brad was beginning to feel out of his league. Marcus had spoken often of the concept of spiritual warfare. He had warned his congregation in his sermons that with the Rapture of the believers had come a heightened presence of evil on the planet. Certainly the global spike in crime supported the theory, but Brad's experience with what Marcus called spiritual warfare was limited to the strange, disquieting sensation he'd felt the morning Marcus had led him to Christ and baptized him. Then, he'd felt uneasy and oppressed—but the sensation hadn't manifested itself physically as it appeared to be doing in Marcus. "How can you be sure—," Brad began.

"Because I saw it," Marcus told him.

"What?" Brad sat next to him on the bench. "Saw what?"

"The demon. I saw it."

"Oh." Brad didn't know what else to say.

Marcus looked at him through reddened eyes. "I sound crazy, don't I?"

"No," Brad said carefully. "If you say you saw a demon, then I believe you."

"Don't you want to know how I knew it was a demon?"

Brad shrugged. "I guess it's the kind of thing you just know when you see it."

Marcus managed a slight laugh. "I guess. It wasn't anything I was prepared for, I'll tell you that much." Quickly, he told Brad about his experience yesterday. "It kept reappearing," Marcus finally said. "The more I worked on my sermon, the more potent the presence became."

"Did you feel physically ill from the beginning?"

"That came in the night. I couldn't sleep. I could feel it moving about in my room."

"Marcus, you should have called me."

He shook his head. "I can't explain it. I knew I had to wrestle with it on my own." He looked at Brad. "It was *my* demon."

"I don't understand," Brad confessed.

"I'm not sure I do either, but by the time the sun came up, I knew that there was only one way I was going to make it through this sermon today. I've been getting progressively sicker. I'm fighting it, but I'm sure my temperature is spiking. My throat is sore; my blood pressure is too high." He shook his head. "I'm dizzy and a little disoriented."

"What can we do?"

"I'm going to need prayer," Marcus told him, "and a lot of it. The force of evil is mighty, but God is almighty. With His help, I can overcome this. I know I can."

"I think you should come back to the hotel with me and rest before the service," Brad told him. He placed a hand on Marcus's shoulder. His skin felt hot to the touch. "I can keep an eye on you there, and I'll make some calls. The service is being sent to the church via live telecast. There are some prayer warriors in that group, Marcus."

Marcus nodded. "I can't fight it by myself anymore."

Brad helped him to his feet. Marcus wavered slightly, but finally stilled. "Can you make it back to my car?" Brad asked him.

"I'm not going to give in to this," Marcus said, his voice strong and determined. "If it's the last thing I do for the Lord on this planet, I am going to deliver this sermon today. I'll make it."

Liza watched through the bedroom window as the sun finished rising over Manhattan. Boats moved on the Hudson. Cabs and utility vehicles rumbled along the streets. A distant siren wailed through the humid morning air.

She'd spent a sleepless night staring out the window at the city skyline wondering how she felt about all this. With a call to Daniel Berger, Mariette had made arrangements for Liza to slip quietly into the city. Randal had met her at the Alexandria Hotel with a new driver's license and instructions for her flight and arrival in New York.

When her shuttle flight touched down at LaGuardia, she'd gone swiftly through the Marine Air Terminal to the ground transportation area. Clutching a bag containing George's evidence and one change of clothes, she'd found cab number 4802 and handed the driver the business card Mariette had provided.

Wordlessly, he'd driven her here, to this apartment on

the Upper East Side, where Daniel Berger had been waiting. The apartment belonged to a longtime political supporter, he'd explained, who was currently traveling out of the country. The building was secure and hidden enough to offer her a level of protection no hotel could provide. Berger had left a two-man security detail that was, even now, sleeping in the living room. He'd given her his cell phone and home numbers, and left her alone. Liza had taken her bag, gone to the bedroom, and locked the door to wait for Matt Coles.

When she'd tried to call Coles yesterday, she'd been unable to reach him on the first several attempts. Finally, she'd left a cryptic message on his voice mail saying that she had information on Nuñez. She'd left her cell-phone number.

He'd called an hour later. He was in Los Angeles covering a story, and would take the red-eye back to New York to meet her this morning. Liza had spent the rest of the night locked in this bedroom, examining her evidence.

Coles's second call had come about a half hour ago. He'd landed at LaGuardia and was on his way. Liza had spent the past thirty minutes struggling with the idea that she was about to turn her life upside down. The conversation about witness protection she'd had with Brad still haunted her. She wasn't sure she was ready for this, and yet it seemed inevitable, as if she were being swept along in a river of events too strong for her to resist. Coles could, if she wished, protect her by not revealing her name, but it wouldn't change the fact that Victor Rudd and his very powerful allies knew she was involved. They'd burned her apartment building to the ground. They'd managed to breach White House security on a number of occasions in their attemps to murder Brad. They'd nearly managed to assassinate the president of the United States. They had brutally killed George Ramiro. And, no matter what the coroner said, they'd probably murdered Forrest Tetherton as well.

Liza knew Brad was right. Without the protection of a highly visible public profile like Brad's, she could never survive on her own. Rudd would kill her, and the terribly sad thing was that nearly no one would notice. The thought was frightening and depressing. She missed her father, she realized. She missed being able to turn to him for wise counsel and unqualified support. She missed his strength, his quiet confidence, and his unshakable peace.

Brad would tell her that those qualities came from the presence of Christ in her father's life. She saw the same qualities in Brad Benton, in Emma Pettit, in Randal and Mariette Arnold, and now in Daniel Berger. Despite the tumult around them, their lives were a sea of calm. Together, they'd mourned Nero's death, but they'd comforted each other, clung to one another, and found hope in their collective belief that he was, as they said, "at home" with the Lord.

Liza had watched with a feeling of envy. Since watching her apartment burn and knowing she'd lost whatever tangible connections she had to her former life, she'd felt adrift and unusually emotional. Even now she found herself fighting a fresh surge of tears.

Irritated with her lack of control, Liza pulled the curtains shut and switched on the lamp. There would be time enough to mope about her life in the days that lay ahead. She had a feeling that life in a safe house under the watchful eye of the U.S. marshals was not nearly as glamorous as it had always seemed in made-for-TV movies and romance novels.

She was reading George's notes for the umpteenth time when a soft knock sounded on the suite door. "Ma'am?" Liza recognized the voice of one of her security guards.

"Yes?"

"You all right?"

"Yes."

"There's a man here to see you. Says his name is Matt Coles."

Liza thrust the notebook aside and hurried to the door. She opened it to find Gasker, the larger of Daniel Berger's two security guards, watching her with concern. "You need something to eat or something. We didn't expect you to stay in there by yourself all night."

"I'm fine." She tried to peer around the man's wide shoulders. "Where is he?"

"In the hall," Gasker told her. "Mike's checking his ID."

"Oh." She wouldn't have thought of that. She'd have opened the door and let the man walk right in without bothering to confirm who he was. It was becoming painfully obvious to her that, left to her own devices, she'd last about twelve hours if she were in charge of her own survival. "Thanks," she said, "but I know what he looks like. I can give you a visual."

Gasker shook his head. "Daniel said don't take any chances. Mike doesn't like to take chances. It'll only take a minute."

Liza exhaled a long sigh. "What's he doing, running a cornea scan?"

"Something like that," Gasker said without batting an eyelash. "Sure you don't want breakfast?"

Liza folded her arms and gave him a speculative look. "Do you have a sense of humor, Gasker?"

"Not when it comes to my job," he said. "Breakfast?"

"Yeah. Sure. A bagel or something. And whatever Mr. Coles wants."

"I'll take care of it." Gasker tipped his head toward the

living room. "You want to meet this guy out here instead of in the bedroom? Mike and I can stake out the hall for you."

The mental image of Large and Larger standing with arms crossed outside the door of the apartment helped her find a reluctant smile. "Whatever you think's best. Just give me a minute to freshen up."

"Sure." She was glad Gasker chivalrously refrained from mentioning that it was going to take longer than a minute for her to look like she hadn't been hit by a freight train.

Five minutes later, Liza found herself in the living room with a man she'd admired professionally for most of her life—the legendary Matt Coles. He was tall, silver-haired, and sophisticated looking, a respected icon in a profession now dominated by the young and beautiful who could draw television ratings on looks alone. Coles had broken more history-making stories than Liza had forgotten in her lifetime.

She tried not to fidget. She felt like a high school newspaper reporter at a National Press Club meeting—jittery, excited, and totally out of her league. "I'm Liza Cannely." She held out her hand.

"Matt Coles."

"Thank you for coming."

"Brad Benton speaks very highly of your work," he said.

She managed a slight grin. "Yeah, well, he says the same about you."

That won a laugh. The warm chuckle broke the ice. Liza handed Coles the envelope. "Everything's in here. I don't know how much you already know."

Coles sat in one of the stuffed chairs and placed the envelope carefully on the coffee table. "Conrad Dishun called me a few weeks ago and asked if I was willing to meet with George Ramiro to talk about a story Ramiro had been working on. I still believed there was a story in the Nuñez fiasco, despite the Pentagon's position, and Dishun said that Ramiro could shed light on it for me. I agreed to the meeting, and never heard from them again."

Liza dropped into the chair across from him. "George Ramiro was murdered," she told him. "Probably Conrad Dishun as well."

That raised Coles's white eyebrows into his hairline. "You're sure?"

"More or less. I've got proof of Ramiro's murder. Dishun's disappearance is too much of a coincidence for me to discount it as foul play."

He nodded, thoughtful. "Then what do you need me for? I assume the *Los Angeles Times* would be interested in running this story."

"This story is going to take down a lot of very powerful people, Mr. Coles. Frankly, Brad Benton and I both felt that there was no way my editor could get it to press. It's going to take someone of your stature and reputation. Thirteen months ago, when the Hizb ut-Tahrir al-Islami killed those thirteen marines on the border of Turkey, you were one of the first reporters to break the story that the Muslim extremists had used U.S. weapons against our troops."

"That's when the Nuñez operation began to surface. The story went nowhere."

"The story was covered up by a conspiracy in the White House, on the Hill, and at the Pentagon," she told him. "The evidence in that envelope implicates three top Pentagon officials, a handful of congressmen, a U.S. senator, and Victor Rudd. It also indicates that a high-ranking official at the White House is involved. We haven't figured out who that is yet. Some efforts were made to frame Brad Benton in the event that the story came out, but it was just a smoke screen. Brad and I both hoped you might be able to shed some light on that."

"My contact with Ramiro never got that far," Coles confessed.

"Brad believes if we break the story with what we have, we'll eventually uncover the White House source."

Coles steepled his fingers beneath his chin. "If these men are as dangerous as you say, it could be risky. For both of us."

"I'm aware of that. The attempts on my life have already started."

He hesitated, then reached into his breast coat pocket and produced a small recorder. "Do you mind?" he asked her.

"No."

He pressed Record and set the unit on the table next to the evidence envelope. "Why don't you start by telling me what you know; then we'll see if we can fill in the rest of the pieces. . . ."

"The Nuñez operation," she began, "started when Admiral Tom Breaux, General Mitchell Bain, and Undersecretary Gordon Custis learned that the Hizb ut-Tahrir al-Islami had taken control of the former Soviet nuclear research facility in Abkhazia. They recommended a U.S. military intervention to the Joint Chiefs and the president, but Kolsokev assured the U.S. that he could handle the situation. When the Joint Chiefs decided to send intelligence operatives into the area in lieu of a military strike, Bain took matters into his own hands."

Liza reached for the envelope and dumped out the contents. Briefly sifting the papers until she found the confidential memo she wanted, she handed it over. "They approached Max Arnold first, with the idea of diverting congressional funding to a covert operation to overthrow the rebels, but he turned them down. Using an inside source at the White House, Bain initiated contact with

Victor Rudd. They developed a plan to divert gold reserves from the South Range facility through Rudd's freight operation to international ports. Kostankis's ships then picked up the gold and distributed it to rebel forces, who used it to purchase black-market technology and weapons. Bain's objective was to retake the facility at Sukhumi and establish whether or not the uranium had fallen into the hands of the Hizb ut-Tahrir al-Islami.

"The entire thing might have gone unnoticed until a soldier named Nuñez was killed on the Turkish border." The capture and subsequent brutal death of the Special Forces operative had drawn international attention when the Hizb ut-Tahrir al-Islami had broadcast a videotape of the torture and slaying of the stalwart marine. Public outcry had demanded a swift and powerful U.S. response. The skirmish had killed thirteen marines and several hundred of the Muslim extremist group that took full credit for Nuñez's death. Marines who'd survived the attack had sworn that the enemy had been armed with U.S. military weapons, prompting an investigation. After months of pointed questions by reporters and the public, the official Pentagon position had been that the rebels had stolen the weapons. Hearings by the Senate Armed Services Committee had failed to yield any additional information, and after a concentrated media campaign by the White House and the Pentagon, the issue had finally died, though many had felt that it remained unresolved.

Liza fished through the envelope contents again. This time, she handed Coles a copy of an e-mail message George had sent to General Dave Marsden, asking for an update on the issue that was now referred to as the "Nuñez matter" by White House insiders. "Marsden's response," she told Coles, "makes it fairly obvious that the Joint Chiefs wanted the matter closed."

Coles scanned the e-mail. "Ramiro wasn't able to let it drop."

"And eventually he began to turn up information on Victor Rudd." Briefly she told him about the evidence she and Brad had discovered from Federal Transportation Commission records that indicated Rudd's freight trucks had been shipping overweight deliveries out of the South Range facility to where they rendezvoused with Kostankis's ships to transfer the gold to the rebels in Abkhazia.

"Is there any proof that the gold reserves at South Range have been violated?"

"There hasn't been an inspection in over a year," Liza told him. "We believe Rudd's plan was to procure the gold bullion back through the international market with the sale of the uranium from Sukhumi, then replace it at South Range before the next audit."

"Probably."

"But George kept asking questions, and by the time he contacted Dishun, he had almost enough evidence to expose Rudd, Bain, and the others. He was going to bring the story to you first, instead of the FBI, because he suspected that Rudd had to have an inside source at the Justice Department in order to avoid FTC inspection and prosecution for the suspicious shipments."

Liza picked up another piece of paper from the table and handed it to Coles. It was a communication from the FTC commissioner to a local weigh station cautioning that three of Rudd's shipments were for contracts of the U.S. Army and should be waved through weigh points without comment. "No one could have arranged this without access to the Justice Department. They coordinate any interstate fraud investigations directly with the FTC."

Coles nodded, his expression thoughtful. "This is more than I hoped for, even from Ramiro."

She handed him the pictures of George's body. "Brad received these two days after the disappearances. The L.A. county coroner inspected them and will testify that, in his opinion, George Ramiro was murdered. This was no suicide. We have reason to believe that Forrest Tetherton was murdered as well."

Matt Coles leaned back in his chair and stroked his chin. "This is quite a bombshell," he admitted. "I can see why you've been running scared."

"No matter what the White House says, Brad doesn't believe the attempts on his life have been random acts of political protest." She deliberately lowered her voice. "Victor Rudd isn't about to go to jail for this without putting up a fight."

"It's hard to believe Rudd would commit murder just to cover his tracks. He's ruthless, but not a killer. And if Rudd didn't instigate the operation, he could probably turn state's evidence for the Justice Department and strike a deal," Coles argued.

"Maybe, but someone's desperate enough to keep this quiet to murder Brad." She told Coles about Brad's near miss on the MAC flight from California. "But no one had a record of the flight leaving LAX or making an emergency landing. When Brad asked Colonel Wells to investigate, he turned up dead. Brad first learned about Nuñez by securing Wells's computer files after his death. That was the morning of the assassination attempt during Carpathia's visit to Washington."

Coles picked up the documents and photos and looked at them carefully. "What's on the microcassettes?"

"One is a recording of Ramiro talking to Fitzhugh two days before Ramiro's murder. The president's answers don't implicate him, but it's clear he has his own suspicions. The other is a phone call from Bain to Rudd insisting on the urgency of a transfer. In the call, Bain indicates that an arms dealer in the Balkans has a shipment ready to send, but is waiting on the monetary transfer from the rebel government in Abkhazia."

Coles continued to study the wealth of evidence. After a few moments, he looked at Liza and said, "You've done award-winning work here."

"I had help," she said, leaning back in her chair. "Brad did most of it."

"You have enough concrete evidence here that we can run the story on Monday morning."

"The president will be out of the country," she pointed out.

"Yes. And so will Brad Benton."

"That worries me. I'm not sure what's going to happen when Rudd's White House conspirator sees the story break."

"Oh," Coles said with a half smile as he produced a cell phone from his breast pocket, "I think we'll have his name long before then."

★   ★   ★

"I don't have a lot of time," Randal told his father as they stood beside the Capitol fountain. "The memorial service is at 11:00."

Max nodded. "I know. Thank you for seeing me."

Randal thought his father had aged ten years in the last month. The man who stood before him had a slight stoop to his shoulders. His eyes looked slightly bloodshot, and his hair was mussed. Randal had expected to see his father's familiar, unflappable calm and polished public face. "What's going on?"

Max handed him a small leather portfolio. "Is it true that Benton's about to leak the Nuñez story to the press?"

"How do you know that?" Randal asked as he cautiously accepted the portfolio.

"News travels fast in this town," Max said. "My sources tell me that he managed to get his hands on evidence that is going to bring down Rudd, several Pentagon officials, and some insiders at the White House. Is it true?"

"I can't say. I haven't seen the evidence."

His father looked at him narrowly for several long seconds, then nodded. "Benton's smart. He knows that the smaller he keeps his circle of insiders, the more control he has over the trail of evidence."

Randal shrugged. "I think he's just protecting us." He flipped open the portfolio. "What is this?"

"Every shred of documentation I have on Nuñez," Max said.

Randal scanned the printed e-mails. "How deeply are you in this, Dad?"

"Not deep enough to go to jail," he said. "Maybe deep enough to get indicted depending on how the Justice Department proceeds. Bain will try to take me down with him."

"Did you do anything illegal?"

"No," Max said carefully, "but I knew Bain was involved in illegal activities and I didn't report it. I violated the code of ethics, but not the law."

Randal slapped the portfolio shut. "Then why are you telling me this?"

His father looked at him, and for the first time in his life, Randal thought he saw a hint of vulnerability in Max's gaze. "Because," he said softly, "I've disappointed you a lot. I know you think I failed you as a father—"

"You failed Mom," Randal said. "That's what I couldn't forgive you for."

"Your mother and I—"

Randal held up a hand. "Don't tell me things were complicated. Whatever you do, don't try and explain what you did to Mom by telling me it was all so complicated that it got away from you."

"Okay." Max exhaled a harsh sigh. "I cheated on your mother."

"A lot."

"A lot," he concurred.

"And mostly with Helen."

"Helen was convenient. She made me feel powerful. Your mother—she never liked the game in Washington. She was never impressed by it, and somehow, I felt like she was never impressed with me. My ego needed more," he admitted.

"You didn't have to publicly humiliate her," Randal insisted. "That wasn't necessary."

"I'm not going to defend myself."

"Good. I wouldn't buy it."

Max nodded toward the portfolio. "But this story Brad is going to break—it's huge, Son. If it weren't for Carpathia and these disappearances, it would be the story of the decade. A lot of heads are going to roll over this. Some people are going to jail. Some will end up dead."

"Some already have."

"I know." His father shook his head. "And whatever happens in the next few months, I'd like to get rid of that disdain I've seen in your eyes for the last few years." He managed a harsh laugh. "Maybe I'm just getting old; I don't know. But I'm tired of the thought that my only son holds me in utter contempt."

Randal's eyes dropped to the portfolio. How was he

supposed to answer that? *"You gotta let go, man,"* he could almost hear Nero telling him. *"You can stay bitter and angry all you want, but it ain't hurting nobody but you. You're the one that's gonna lose if you keep holding on to this anger against your father."* "I don't know what to say," he admitted.

"I suppose it would be too much for me to ask if you could see your way to forgive me."

"Three days ago," Randal admitted, "I would have told you that yes, it's too much to ask. But then Nero Jefferson died." He met his father's gaze. "He was a friend of mine. He may not have been very educated, but Nero was one of the smartest guys I've ever known. He was the first person besides Mom to really take me to task for resenting you so much." He shook his head. "I'm not sure I know how to put it behind me. But I don't think it's unreasonable for you to ask me if I can."

"I'm glad to hear that."

"I can't give you an answer right now."

"I understand."

Randal held up the portfolio. "I'll give this to Brad. My advice is, if you're approached by the FBI, tell them everything you know."

"I intend to."

"This probably means your political career is over, you know."

"It might."

"Can you live with that?"

Max shrugged. "I may have to."

"What will you do?"

"Become a highly paid consultant at a Washington law firm—that's the usual retirement plan for senators with excellent political contacts."

Randal hesitated for a moment, unsure how to end the conversation, and, for the first time in years, unsure he wanted to. "I'm going to be a pallbearer at the funeral," he announced.

"I'm sure that will be meaningful for you."

"Are you coming?"

"I thought about it. I have a pass."

"I think you should," Randal said. "I think you should come, and I think you should listen very closely to what the pastor is going to say."

Max's eyebrows rose. "Are you still holding out hope for my soul, Randal? I thought you gave up on it a long time ago."

"I did," he confessed. "But Nero helped me see that it's never too late—not for anyone. Not even for you, Dad. I know I haven't been much of an example of a godly person, but Nero was. If you can make yourself look at the way he lived—" He broke off with a slight shake of his head. "Just promise me you'll come to the funeral."

Max hesitated. "I suppose if it means that much to you—"

"It does."

"Then I'll do it."

★   ★   ★

"Obviously," Agent Elliot Mills said as he leveled Matt Coles a calculating look, "a criminal investigation requires a little more concrete evidence and time than a front-page story that slings a little mud."

If the comment was meant to intimidate or offend Coles, it failed dismally, Liza noted. He was watching Agent Mills with a look of amusement and admirable tolerance. His editor, on the other hand, was pacing the small conference room at the *New York Times* office with his hands shoved in the pockets of his trousers and a cigar butt clamped between his teeth. The flush on his face suggested that he was less than amused with the responses they'd received since Agents Mills and Carradine had entered the room.

"Gentlemen," Coles said lightly, "the simple reality is this: On Monday morning, the *New York Times* is going to break a story that is going to expose criminal activities on the part of Victor Rudd, Admiral Tom Breaux, General Mitchell Bain, Defense Undersecretary Gordon Custis, three members of Congress, and a U.S. senator. By the time we're done with this story, the attorney general is going to be calling for a slew of high-profile indictments. The way I see it, you can either cooperate with us, which will garner you the appreciation of your bosses, or you can refuse to assist Ms. Cannely, in which case the story will appear without any on-record comments from the FBI. It seems relatively simple to me."

Agent Mills swore and rose to his feet. He stalked angrily out of the room. Agent Bill Carradine leaned back in his chair and folded his hands over his stomach. He looked at Liza. "Ms. Cannely—" his tone patient but firm—"you have to understand that what you're asking for isn't really possible. Even if we could get approval to offer you protection until the trial, we don't have the budget to—"

"Agent Carradine," Coles interrupted, "you are the Federal Bureau of Investigation. You have the resources of the Justice Department and the federal government at your disposal. In light of the fact that Ms. Cannely has saved you millions of dollars and hours by gathering the evidence for you, I don't think her request is unreasonable."

"That's why we need to know exactly what evidence you have," Carradine shot back.

That won a harsh laugh from Coles's editor. "You're either the most naïve federal agent I've ever met, or you think I was born yesterday. We show you the evidence, you report it to the federal prosecutor's office, and by the time I can say, 'Stop the presses,' you've got a court order preventing us from releasing the story."

"We need time to make the arrests and compile enough evidence to make the charges stick," Carradine protested.

"You have until Monday morning," Matt Coles shot back. "The story is written."

Carradine sighed heavily. "I'm going to have to run this by my boss."

Coles's editor grabbed a phone from the console by the door and slammed it down on the table in front of Carradine. "With any luck, you can reach him now."

The agent looked from Matt Coles to Liza to the editor, then reached for the phone. "It's going to take a little time," he warned.

Coles's editor looked at his watch. "You've got three hours before we go to layout with the piece."

14

Marcus stood in the cool shadow of a limestone pillar and prayed for strength. The verger had led the procession into the cathedral where Nero Jefferson's casket, draped in an American flag, was prominently displayed on the main floor in front of the altar.

In less than five minutes, Marcus would step into the pulpit and preach the sermon he'd prepared yesterday. His flulike symptoms had been increasing for the better part of the day. After their run Brad had taken him to his hotel room, where Marcus had rested for most of the morning. Knowing that his congregation was praying for him even now strengthened his resolve, but he still felt feverish and flushed. His knees felt weak. And he saw the shadow. If he hadn't known better, he'd have thought he was losing his mind. He closed his eyes. *Lord, just get me through the next hour. If I can make it through the next hour, I can say what You want me to say.*

The organ prelude ended. The sudden cessation of noise left a strange void in the large cathedral as the lingering strains of the huge pipe organ reverberated in the vaulted ceiling.

Marcus gripped his Bible and headed for the stage. He scanned the audience as he stepped into the pulpit. Randal and Mariette sat several rows back. Randal's head was bowed. Mariette held his arm with her eyes closed. Brad was seated on the other side of the central aisle. He, too, appeared to be praying—for him, Marcus knew.

Marcus opened his Bible and laid it on the pulpit. He fought the sudden surge of dizziness that threatened to send him to his knees. "Brothers and sisters, ladies and gentlemen," he said, "we are here today for two reasons. First, my brother in Christ, Nero Jefferson, was slain while defending the life of a friend. Today, we are here to celebrate his life. His life as he lived it here on earth, and the life he now lives in heaven with the Lord Jesus Christ."

Marcus no sooner said the words than he felt his throat begin to tighten and his breathing turn shallow. On the front row, he saw the president squirm uncomfortably and give Charley Swelder a pointed look. Marcus gripped the edges of the pulpit to maintain his balance. "The other reason we are here is to share a moment in our national collective grief for the events of the past few weeks. There are few among us who have remained untouched by these events. Many of us have lost loved ones and friends. All of us have looked for answers to why and how this could have happened."

He turned to a passage in his Bible. "Today, I'm going to share with you the answers that Nero Jefferson found. My text this morning is from the fourteenth chapter of John, the first through the sixth verses." He paused to wipe the sweat from his brow. The shadow now loomed large across the standing-room-only crowd. *In the name of Jesus Christ,* Marcus silently prayed, *I cast you from this place. You cannot be where there are praise and admonition of the Most High God.*

He felt a surge of strength as the shadow wavered and

began to break up. "It will interest many of you to know,"
he told the crowd, "that three weeks ago, Nero Jefferson
walked into my office devastated at the loss of his young
wife and baby daughter. Grieving and afraid, Nero begged
me for answers. I directed him here," he pointed to his Bible,
"to the fourteenth chapter of the Gospel of John."

Marcus noted the increasingly uncomfortable looks he
was receiving from the dignitaries. Brad was watching him
closely, his expression full of confidence and encourage-
ment.

Marcus read: "Jesus answered him, 'Don't be troubled.
You trust God, now trust in Me. There are many rooms in My
Father's home, and I am going to prepare a place for you. If
this were not so, I would tell you plainly. When everything is
ready, I will come and get you, so that you will always be
with Me where I am. . . . I am the way, the truth, and the life.
No one can come to the Father except through Me.' "

Marcus set the Bible down and looked at the people. A
hush had settled on the large audience. "My question to
each of you this morning is whether or not you can claim
the promise that Nero Jefferson claimed—is Jesus preparing a place for you in heaven?"

A murmur spread over the crowd. On the front row, the
president crossed his arms and scowled at Marcus. A sudden burst of sunlight flooded through the large, stained-
glass rose window and bathed the congregation in a wash
of light. Marcus drew a cleansing breath as he felt his heart
rate begin to stabilize. *Thank You, Lord,* he prayed before
continuing. "There are many who have tried to explain the
event that forever changed our world. I am here to tell you
today that there may be many theories, but there is only
one truth. A third of the world's population was swept
away in an event that God foretold in the Scripture. That

event, which Christians call the Rapture, marked the beginning of God's timeline for the end of the present world.

"According to the Bible, we have entered the age of the Tribulation, which precedes the promise Jesus made in the book of John—that He will come again. Nero Jefferson did not live to see that Glorious Appearing. The Bible says that many of us will not, but in His infinite mercy and grace, God has provided the way for our salvation. That way is faith in Jesus Christ as the spotless Lamb of God who alone can cleanse us from unrighteousness and make us acceptable to a just and holy God."

At the back of the long basilica, he saw the enormous wooden door crack open. Sanura Kyle entered from the narthex. Though she was too far for Marcus to make out her expression, he sensed her gaze on him as she picked her way through the heavy crowd toward the back of the sanctuary.

That's when Marcus made the decision to set aside his notes. This was a topic he knew well, had preached countless times. Today it meant more to him than it ever had in the past, because today he preached it from a contrite and repentant heart that had accepted the truth of it. Acutely aware of the glare of the television cameras, Marcus concentrated on the faces of his congregation as he prepared to preach what might easily be the most important sermon of his life.

Liza had pages of notes spread on the conference table at the *New York Times* office as she sought to put together a timeline and flowchart for Matt Coles. The essential questions—who had known what when—were buried within the mounds of evidence. A quick glance at the TV monitor told her Nero Jefferson's memorial service had begun. Marcus, looking a bit pale beneath the harsh lights of the television cameras, was standing in the pulpit of the Washington National Cathedral. Liza set down her pencil and reached for the remote. She wanted to hear what he had to say about the brave young man who had saved her life.

★ ★ ★

"The politically correct thing for me to say," Marcus told his congregation, "is that all God requires of any of us is a good life, a commitment to decency and humanity, and an effort to live honestly and purely. I know preachers who would tell you that. I spent hours this week at a meeting in New York with a group of religious leaders who issued a public statement to that effect.

"Many of you have taken notice of the secretary-general, Nicolae Carpathia. His promises of global peace and harmony are alluring when we have just experienced an international tragedy of unimaginable proportions. Yet as persuasive as the secretary-general is, he fails to offer the truth. His vision is rooted in deceit, and his promises are built on falsehoods."

President Fitzhugh shot a telling look at one of his aides. Then the aide stood and began to make his way through the narrow pew to the long aisle that ran to the back of the basilica. Brad, Marcus noted, was watching the man carefully.

"The secretary-general is a charming man," Marcus told the audience, "and it is natural that we want to believe him, but I have to direct your attention again to John 14:6: Jesus said, 'I am the way, the truth and the life. No one can come to the Father except through Me.' Christ alone took the form of a man, came to earth as the Son of God, took upon Himself our sins, died on a cross for our salvation, and rose again on the third day to offer each of us the promise of eternal life. Only through faith in Christ and acceptance of His redemption can any of us hope to be acceptable to a holy and just God.

"As charming as Nicolae Carpathia may be, I must point out to you that Satan himself is a charming deceiver. He is not some cartoonlike devil that is confined to hell. The apostle Peter says in his letter to the early church: 'Be careful! Watch out for attacks from the Devil, your great enemy. He prowls around like a roaring lion, looking for some victim to devour.'

"Satan's greatest lie is that all roads lead to heaven. We don't need a Savior, he tell us. We live a good life. We're devout. We're sincere, and that should be enough. Satan wants you to believe that you can make it on your own, that you're not a sinner in need of salvation. 'There is a path before each person,' the Scripture says, 'that seems right, but it ends in death.'

"In his letter to the Romans, Paul says, 'all have sinned; all fall short of God's glorious standard.' And 'the wages of sin is death, but the free gift of God is eternal life through Jesus Christ our Lord.' So in His divine plan to provide salvation for us, God gave us His Son as the sacrifice to pay our debt. The prophet Isaiah said it like this: 'All of us have strayed away like sheep. We have left God's paths to follow our own. Yet the Lord laid on Him the guilt and sins of us all.'

"So when Christ died upon the cross, He took onto Himself the sins of a fallen and hopeless man. Through the cleansing of His holy blood, He washed us clean and made us acceptable to God."

★   ★   ★

Brad watched as Jordan Trask, the president's personal aide, began making his way through the crowd toward him. Most of the congregation remained riveted on Marcus's sermon, but the shoulder-to-shoulder seating forced Jordan to pick his way through crammed aisles and seats as he honed in on Brad.

Brad slipped from his seat and made his way swiftly toward the aisle to head off Trask. He knew exactly what this was about. Fitzhugh wanted Marcus out of the pulpit. Fast. But with dozens of television cameras trained on Marcus, there was little the president could do as his invited guest shared an unpopular but true gospel with an international audience.

Soon, Brad knew, Trask would begin appealing to the television networks to shut off coverage of the service. With the president scheduled to depart from the cathedral and head directly to Andrews Air Force Base where *Air Force One* would fly him to Jerusalem, the last thing Fitzhugh wanted was the distraction of the media storm that was sure to follow Marcus's shocking message. Brad saw the bishop standing in the shadows having a heated discussion with cathedral security.

Jordan saw Brad moving toward him and froze, his expression set in a harsh frown. Brad made his way into the shadowy corridor.

"What's going on, Benton?" Trask demanded.

Marcus's voice had risen to the strong and steady rhythm Brad had come to recognize from Sunday mornings spent in his church. "Each of us is accountable to God," Marcus was saying. "Each of us must answer the question: Is Jesus preparing a place for *me*?"

"He's preaching the gospel." Brad folded his arms and looked at Jordan Trask. "I'm sure you've heard of it."

"This wasn't the agreement," Jordan said through clenched teeth. "The president asked you to arrange a memorial service. Not a right-wing crusade."

"Nero Jefferson," Marcus was saying, "answered that question for himself. He looked into the face of a holy God and realized that he was a man in need of a Savior. He humbled himself before the Lord and admitted that he had sinned. He became a believer. This is the memorial service he would have wanted."

"Dumont is embarrassing the president."

"How do you figure that?"

"You know what the fallout is going to be over this, Benton."

Behind him, Brad could hear Marcus continue to explain to the congregation how Nero had confessed his sin and asked for God's forgiveness, how he had called upon the name of Jesus for deliverance.

Jordan leaned closer to Brad. "You've got to put a stop to this."

"No," Brad said.

"Benton—"

"If you want him to stop, you're going to have to pull him out of the pulpit."

Jordan's expression darkened. "If I were you, I would seriously consider the political ramifications—"

"You should know by now that I don't particularly care about political ramifications." He glanced back at Marcus, who was now expounding on the realities of the coming Tribulation.

"The president took a considerable risk in recommending you to head the Disarmament Committee. That offer could be withdrawn."

"I'm not going to intervene," Brad said again. "I don't care what you threaten me with." From the corner of his eye, he saw the nervous movements of the Secret Service detail as they prowled the perimeter of the cathedral communicating through their ubiquitous earpieces and collar-clipped communicators. "If the president's uncomfortable, then maybe he should listen more closely."

★ ★ ★

Liza watched the television in the conference room at the *New York Times* office, transfixed by Marcus's sermon. Minutes after he'd begun to preach, she'd sensed the rising level of activity in the newsroom. *Times* staff members had begun to file into the conference room seconds later. They'd turned up the volume, and Liza now watched the extraordinary event with thirty or forty others who, despite the Saturday morning, had been hard at work on the Sunday edition of the *Times* until Marcus had begun to preach and drawn the attention of the world.

He spoke of sin and redemption, the fall of man and the grace of God. Liza heard all the things her father had told her and watched the fire in Marcus Dumont as he told the story of Nero Jefferson and how he'd come to accept what Marcus called the truth of Jesus Christ. The words began to take root somewhere in her heart.

★ ★ ★

"On this point the Bible is clear," Marcus was saying. "Each of us is faced with a choice. We can accept the hand of grace, put our faith in Christ, and be afforded an eternity in heaven, or, we can turn away from God's offer of salvation and face eternal condemnation because of our sin. We were created in God's own image for perfect fellowship with Him. He gave us life, and with that life, He gave us a will and free choice. Because of our sinful nature, we choose to disobey God and go our own willful way. 'Your sins,' says the prophet Isaiah, 'have cut you off from God. Because of

your sin, He has turned away and will not listen anymore.'
So if we want Jesus to prepare our place in heaven, we have
to accept God's redemption through the gift of His Son.

"God provided the Cross to bridge the gap between our
sin and His holiness. Make no mistake: it is the *only* bridge
for that gap. In his letter to Timothy, Paul writes, 'For there
is one God and one Mediator who can reconcile God and
people. He is the man Christ Jesus.'

"In 1 Peter 3:18, we read: 'Christ also suffered when He
died for our sins once for all time. He never sinned, but He
died for sinners that He might bring us safely home to
God.' And in Romans 5: 8, we read: 'God showed His great
love for us by sending Christ to die for us while we were still
sinners.' "

Jordan Trask cast a quick glance at the pulpit, then back at
Brad. Charley Swelder had risen from his seat and was making his way to the back of the room where the media cameras were rolling. "We're going to cut him off," Trask told
Brad. "Mr. Swelder's headed to take care of the cameras."

Brad made eye contact with Marcus over the heads of
the crowd. His friend now held his Bible in his hand.
Limned in the flood of sunlight from the rose window, he
looked every inch the avenging angel wielding his sword of
truth. "Good luck," Brad muttered. Something told him
that the fervent prayers of Marcus's friends in a small,
crowded church sanctuary three miles away would keep the
cameras on and their pastor's voice strong as he delivered
God's message of redemption.

"And that is the choice," Marcus said. "In Romans 10:9
and 10 we read: 'If you confess with your mouth that Jesus
is Lord and believe in your heart that God raised Him from
the dead, you will be saved. For it is by believing in your
heart that you are made right with God, and it is by confess-
ing with your mouth that you are saved.'

"Friends, that is the choice I give you today. According to the Bible, the future holds unimaginable challenges, terror, and fear. But I was asked to offer you hope this morning, and the hope I offer is the sure and certain knowledge that God is in control, that He has a plan, that He has a plan for you, that He loves you and no matter what you've done or haven't done, no matter who you've been or haven't been, He is holding out His hand to you and offering you grace."

Brad saw Charley begin a heated conversation with a network reporter. *A few more minutes, Lord,* he prayed. *Just a few more minutes.*

Marcus's voice rang clearly through the vaulted cathedral. "I am not going to tell you it will be easy or without sacrifice. That's another of Satan's lies. Jesus exhorted His followers to leave all they had and follow Him. Nowhere are we promised that giving our lives to Jesus will mean a free ride through life. But Jesus did promise that we would have life, abundant life when we choose to forsake our sinful way and follow Him.

"Nero Jefferson made that choice, as have I, as have dozens of other men and women who may have missed or rejected the opportunity before the Rapture but have seen the truth since and been willing to sacrifice for it. Joshua, the great commander of the Israelites, stated it this way: 'Choose today whom you will serve. Would you prefer the gods your ancestors served beyond the Euphrates? Or will it be the gods of the Amorites in whose land you now live? But as for me and my family, we will serve the Lord.'

"That's the choice that Nero Jefferson made. And that's the choice every one of us is faced with today. For your sake—" Marcus looked across the audience with chilling determination—"I pray to God Almighty that you make the right one."

After several seconds of stunned silence, the cathedral erupted in noise. The president leaped to his feet as reporters rushed forward, yelling questions at him, at Marcus, and at the church leaders who were looking on in stunned disbelief.

Brad saw Randal shouldering his way through the crowd toward the front of the church. Ignoring Jordan Trask's demands for an explanation, he turned to move swiftly to join Marcus. In seconds, he had his hands around Marcus's upper arm and was moving him off the stage. "You know how to create a stir, don't you?"

Randal stumbled through the crowd and appeared at Brad's elbow. "Not that way," he said. "There's an exit through here." He pointed between two of the limestone columns toward the apse.

"You're sure?"

Randal gave Brad a nudge. "I went to school at St. Albans," he said, citing the boys' school affiliated with the cathedral. "I'm sure."

★   ★   ★

Liza stared at the television as the melee erupted at the cathedral. She caught a glimpse of Brad pushing his way toward Marcus a second before the picture cut away to the network correspondent covering the service.

"In an event that stunned the audience," the woman said, "the Reverend Marcus Dumont delivered a strongly evangelical message in sharp contrast to the recent initiative coming from New York."

Behind the reporter, chaos ensued. The Secret Service was quickly moving the president through the crowd as his aides tried to head off the media frenzy.

"Can you believe this?" one of the reporters in the conference room asked.

"Fitzhugh's bound to be furious," another said.

Liza's heart thumped hard in her chest as she sat motionless, wrestling with a feeling that this might very well be her last chance. Her father used to talk about what he called "conviction," a compelling need to make a decision, to act on a matter of the heart. He claimed that it was the Holy Spirit's way of moving in the life of man to get God's work done. Whatever the case, she realized that in less than forty-eight hours, her life was going to turn upside down, and she was sure she didn't want to start the new chapter on her own.

As the staff in the conference room began flipping channels to see additional television coverage, Liza reached for her cell phone and rushed from the room. She had to talk to Brad.

15

Brad walked across the tarmac at Andrews Air Force Base with purposeful strides. He carried one small suitcase with a change of clothes for tomorrow's treaty signing in Jerusalem. He'd already made arrangements for a commercial flight back to Washington. He had no intention of staying in Israel any longer than necessary.

The last few hours had passed in a blur of activity, and even now he was uncertain what kind of reception he'd find aboard *Air Force One*. The confusion and chaos at the cathedral had allowed him and his friends to make a hasty escape. Mariette had driven the car around from the Woodley Road parking area. When Randal, Marcus, and Brad emerged onto the grounds of the Close, they'd had only a brief sprint to the car.

She'd managed to merge into the heavy traffic on Wisconsin Avenue and guide them quickly out of the area before Marcus could be spotted by the overeager media. The four friends had celebrated the triumph as Mariette drove them to Marcus's church. There Marcus had been welcomed by his congregation who'd prayed diligently for him throughout the service.

The Word of Jesus had been broadcast to the world.

But Randal had pulled Brad aside to discuss the issue of Nero Jefferson's body. Neither of them felt comfortable leaving the body at the cathedral untended. Nero deserved to be laid to rest in consecrated ground. Randal had come up with the solution. Solomon Grady, the former Metro system mechanic who now served as the church custodian, was among the congregants who'd gathered to pray for Marcus. Recently retired, he still had ample contacts in the D.C. public and private transportation circles. After a brief conversation with Brad, Solomon had made a few phone calls. Within half an hour, he had located a delivery van, recruited five other church members, and was on his way to the cathedral to ensure that Nero's body was safely transported to the cemetery.

Randal had insisted on going along. After all, he'd pointed out, as a former St. Albans student, he was the best equipped to move the unlikely band of brothers in and out of the cathedral grounds. St. Albans boys, he'd explained, always dated National Cathedral School girls. He'd sneaked on and off the Close more times than he could count.

Brad had waited for the crowd at Marcus's church to ebb slightly before attempting to talk to Marcus. Marcus had excused himself to take Brad to his office, where they had spent twenty minutes on their knees thanking God for His mercy and asking for His protection as Brad prepared to leave for Israel. Both men were acutely aware that Brad still had no idea who Rudd's conspirator at the White House was. There was a reasonable chance that Brad was going to be boarding *Air Force One* with a killer.

While they were there, Liza had phoned to update Brad

on her meeting with Matt Coles and tell him she'd watched Marcus's message at the memorial service.

"I gave my heart to Jesus, Brad," she'd said. "I'm not exactly sure what comes next, but I know that while I was listening to Marcus, I finally understood what I'd been reading in the book of John. I wanted you to know that before you left."

Brad had rejoiced with her as a sense of relief rushed through him. Knowing Liza was now a child of God had gone a long way to alleviate his anxiety over her future. He knew they still weren't out of the woods, and that, even with the story breaking on Monday, they still had a trial to get through.

"Be careful, Brad," Liza had warned him.

"You, too."

"I'm safe. The FBI agreed to Coles's terms. I'll be in protection until the trial."

"Will I hear from you?"

"I don't know. I don't think so. I'll try to write."

"I'll contact you," Brad promised her. "Just be careful."

"I will. Brad?"

"Yes?"

"Thank you for everything. I owe you so much."

He had smiled broadly. "Welcome to the family, Liza."

Now, as he approached the plane, he braced himself to face the barrage of media questions that he knew awaited him. The official White House statement after the memorial service had directed all questions regarding Marcus's sermon to Brad. Charley Swelder had called to inform Brad that once the plane was in the air, the president would demand an accounting for what had happened. Already in crisis mode, the president had decided to withdraw Brad's name from Carpathia's short list to head the Disarmament

Committee. Reportedly, Nicolae was furious over what had happened at the cathedral.

Brad could only imagine the reaction at the UN, where Carpathia had watched the service via closed-circuit television. His public-relations staff had, no doubt, kicked into overdrive to determine how much damage had been done. The viewing audience, the White House knew, had spanned the globe, and the ceremony had certainly drawn national attention.

The media finally noticed Brad's approach.

"Mr. Benton, did you approve the text of Reverend Dumont's sermon?"

"Did you know he intended to insult Secretary-General Carpathia?"

"Did the president have any prior knowledge about the speech?"

Brad exhaled and held up a hand. "I can take questions until the president arrives," he said. "So make it count."

★   ★   ★

President Gerald Fitzhugh was in a foul mood. His staff had been whispering about it since they'd boarded the plane two hours ago. Usually he spent the first hour or so of a flight chatting with the press corps in the back section of the plane. Today, he'd boarded, given his pilot the call to take off, then headed directly for the office where he'd been sequestered with Charley Swelder and his new communications director.

Brad had been left out in the open to stew in his own juices. He had assured the press corps that the president had not had any foreknowledge of Marcus's sermon, but they wanted a statement directly from the top and the president wasn't going to give it to them. When the media had finally decided they'd gotten everything from Brad they could, they'd lost interest in him and left him in peace. He'd spent the last couple of hours in relative seclusion reading his Bible.

Finally, Jordan Trask came to inform him that the president was ready to see him.

Brad entered the office to find the president alone behind his desk. Fitzhugh was watching a cable news show on which commentators were hashing over the effects of Marcus's message. When Brad entered, Fitz glanced over his shoulder. "Shut the door," he said. He reached for the remote and turned up the volume. "Watch this."

Brad shut the door so the two of them were alone, then moved into the interior of the office.

"What I can't believe," a well-known liberal commentator was saying, "is that the president is claiming he didn't know this was going to happen. I mean, Dumont has been preaching this kind of sermon for most of his career."

The comment brought a predictable response as the other four commentators began talking at once as they argued one another into silence. Fitzhugh hit the Power button and switched off the TV. When he swiveled around to face Brad, his expression was unreadable. "This is one big mess you've gotten us into, Benton."

Brad sat in the chair across from the desk. "Yes, sir."

The president leaned back in his chair and regarded him speculatively. "Did you know Dumont was going to do this?"

"He told me early this morning."

"And you didn't think you needed to warn us."

"No, sir."

Fitzhugh pursed his lips. "Hmmm. You believe all that rot, don't you, Benton? That's why you didn't try and stop him."

"I didn't try to stop him for two reasons," Brad told him. "First, I believe every word of what Marcus said this morning in his sermon. I haven't tried to make a secret out of the fact that after the Rapture, I accepted the Lord Jesus as my personal Savior."

Fitzhugh waved a hand in dismissal. "Right, right. We've all heard that."

"And the second reason is that I live in a country where, the last time I checked, we still embraced the personal liberties of free speech and the free practice of religion. Our country was founded on those freedoms. You pledged to support them when you were sworn in. It's your job."

The president snorted. "Not for long," he said.

"Sir?" Brad said, shocked.

"In case you haven't heard, Nicolae Carpathia's latest scheme is to buy up all the major media outlets so he can control the press."

"Isn't that against the law?"

"That's what we told the FCC, but they say they don't see the conflict of interest. Can you believe that? Can you imagine what would have happened if I'd tried to buy the *Dallas Morning News* during the last presidential election? They would have flayed me alive."

"Then that's all the more reason for us to fight for the fundamental right we have for free speech. Since Nicolae Carpathia came to power I've begun to notice a rising pressure for politically correct speech. To agree with the secretary-general is considered laudable, but to disagree with him—" Brad shrugged—"haven't you noticed that the few people who have expressed doubts or even a lack of enthusiasm for some of his initiatives seem to suddenly disappear?"

"Don't tell me you're buying into some conspiracy theory."

"No, sir. I've just been paying attention. I think it's very telling."

Fitzhugh's half laugh was derisive. "The truth is, it just costs too much to disagree with the man." He indicated the office with a sweep of his hand. "Here I am, the most powerful man in the free world, and I'm making this flight on this outdated piece of junk because the golden boy is flying in my new jet." He swore softly. "And I gave in without a squeak of protest. The press is in love with Carpathia. The public thinks he's infallible. And if that's not enough, I've heard rumors that they plan to change his title."

"Oh?"

"Yeah. Grand Potentate of the Universe, or something equally ludicrous. You know, somebody should remind that guy of what happened to Louis XVI when he started spouting all that divine-right nonsense. The French whacked his head off for it." He shook his head. "That was back when politics was about people and not about media campaigns. Think how different things would be in this country if the winner got to be president and the loser was guillotined. That would keep things interesting, at least."

Brad managed a slight smile. "I suppose it would keep the random thrill seekers from jumping into the race."

"I could get a lot of pleasure out of watching Max Arnold get his head whacked off; I'll tell you that much." Fitzhugh shook his head and leaned forward to brace both his hands on the desk. "But that's not the way it works in this country, and unfortunately, even when we're not in an election year, we're running for office. So that brings us back to what happened today."

"I understand."

"I don't want to do this, but Charley says I have to."

Brad wanted to ask him if he always did what Charley Swelder told him, but he thought better of it. "I understand."

"There was no way I could have told you not to come on this trip. It would have caused too much speculation. But as soon as we get back to the States, I need your resignation."

"Yes, sir."

"You'll take responsibility for that whole disaster to-day—including an apology to Carpathia. That way, we can downplay it in the press, and, with any luck, the media will find something more interesting to pay attention to." He gave Brad a narrow look. "I've got to tell you, Benton, I don't get it."

"Sir?"

"I pegged you for a smart guy. We might not have always agreed, but you didn't get where you are without some po-litical instincts. With this nuclear disarmament thing, you were poised to take on one of the most powerful positions in the world. We still don't know how all this is going to shake out, and as far as I'm concerned, I don't give a mon-key's tail what the UN does as long as the interests of the United States aren't compromised."

"I realize that."

"But you bought into this whole religious thing kind of hard, Benton. You had to know that was going to have a serious effect on your future."

The irony made Brad's lips twitch. Gerald Fitzhugh had no idea just how true that was. "You could say that," he said.

"Was it worth throwing away your career?"

"Yes, sir," he said without hesitation.

Fitzhugh's expression clearly showed his confusion. "Like I said, I don't get it, Benton."

"I'm sorry to hear that," Brad said. "All I can tell you is that my faith in Christ is the most important thing in the world to me. I don't expect everyone to understand that, but I won't compromise it."

"I hope it turns out to be worth it," the president told

him. "In the meantime, until we get through this treaty signing, let's just keep this quiet. I don't want to be distracted answering questions about whether or not you're going to resign." He reached for the remote.

Brad recognized the dismissal and stood to go, but as his hand closed on the doorknob, he realized he couldn't let the opportunity to speak with the president alone pass without warning him once again that there was a traitor and potential killer in their midst. "Mr. President," he said, "there's one more thing."

★ ★ ★

Brad pulled back the curtain of his hotel room in Jerusalem and glanced out at the city. He'd sat up most of the night and prayed for his friends, for his country, for his world.

Today promised to be one of the most stressful days of his life. In less than four hours, the Monday morning edition of the *New York Times* would hit newsstands containing two front-page stories. The first would outline Nicolae Carpathia's historic signing later today of a treaty with Jerusalem that would pave the way for the rebuilding of the Jewish temple on the Temple Mount, the site of Arab-Israeli bloodshed for hundreds, even thousands, of years.

The second story would break the tale of Victor Rudd's illegal arms operation in Abkhazia. With that story would come federal indictments that would destroy countless lives and careers—and possibly mark the beginning of the end of Gerald Fitzhugh's presidency.

In his conversation with Fitzhugh aboard *Air Force One*, Brad had warned the president about the story. He'd told the commander in chief that they still had no idea who Rudd had relied on within the administration. He still couldn't finger the person who'd actually pulled the trigger that ended George Ramiro's life. Given the recent attempts to put Brad out of commission and the assassination attempt on the president himself, Brad didn't think it was beyond the pale of reason to think the killer might try to strike again.

Brad believed the killer's motivation was not only to save his own skin but also to maintain and increase the power of the American war machine that had made Victor Rudd a billionaire. What better forum for the political statement of an assassination of the president of the United States, Brad had pointed out, than the treaty signing in Jerusalem? The chaos and international outrage that would ensue would seriously inhibit Nicolae's ability to persuade the U.S. to fully cooperate with his plans. If Nicolae was unable to bring everyone safely to the table for the treaty signing, what hope did he have of playing out his plans on the world stage?

Fitzhugh had listened, but Brad had not felt that the president shared his sense of urgency. Though the president expressed his own concerns about Victor Rudd, he was not prepared to believe there was a conspirator inside his White House.

Brad knew that some things had to be left to God. He'd done what he could and his conscience was clear. Brad finally left the president to his meetings and the counsel of Charley Swelder.

At least, Brad thought, Liza was tucked away safely somewhere under the protection of the U.S. marshals. Rudd's people would not be able to get to her, and Brad took comfort in that.

Yesterday after they'd arrived in Jerusalem, he'd gone on a sort of spiritual pilgrimage. Christine had always wanted to see the Holy Land, but until Brad had accepted Jesus as his Savior, the trip held no appeal for him. Now, the opportunity to walk where Jesus had walked, to touch the stones He'd touched, to see the places where His Lord had spent the last days of His life, all those things had profoundly affected him.

Brad had gone to the Wailing Wall and watched at a safe distance as the two witnesses, Eli and Moishe, appeared to fend off an attack by incinerating a gunman. Horrifying though the scene was, Brad had watched, transfixed, by the sheer power of it. How anyone could witness something like that and not recognize the awesome power of the Most High God he didn't know.

The image of the gunman going up in flames had haunted him far into the night. A part of him longed to return to the Wall and ask the two witnesses for answers, but after yesterday's incident, the Israeli police had moved the crowd back an additional one hundred feet. No one could approach the two men without running into a wall of security personnel.

Instead, Brad had contented himself to sit at a distance during the evening hours and listen to the two witnesses testify. One of the miracles of their presence at the Wall was that their words were understood by all the people listening to them in whatever language they spoke. Despite the fact that the men were speaking in ancient Hebrew, a language he had no knowledge of, Brad had clearly understood all they said. The prophets railed against Carpathia and the treaty, calling it blasphemy and a defilement of the temple that Nicolae was allowed to desecrate the Holy City in the name of peace. The treaty was a pact with the devil himself, they said. That, Brad imagined, made Nicolae furious.

A knock on his door pulled his attention from the view. He strode across the room to find Jordan Trask waiting in the hallway. Jordan's attitude toward Brad had been cold and reserved since the memorial service yesterday. "The president wants to leave for the Knesset in thirty minutes. Don't miss the motorcade."

Brad nodded. "I'll be there."

★ ★ ★

At his mother's home in Silver Spring, Maryland, Randal sat straight up in bed, his T-shirt and shorts drenched in sweat. In the nightmare that had pulled him from a fitful sleep, he'd seen exaggerated images of Nicolae Carpathia seated on a throne at the top of the world. He'd seen the gaunt and drawn faces of countless people who'd fallen under Carpathia's control. And he'd seen Brad underwater, drowning, helpless and unable to pull himself from the vast, black sea that held him captive. The image was so vivid in his mind that his heart thundered and his breathing felt labored and forced.

Randal squinted at the digital clock on his nightstand. Just after 1:00 A.M. He wiped a hand through his damp hair and tossed off the covers. His legs felt shaky and unsteady, but he forced himself to pace the confines of his room as he struggled to clear the lingering disquiet from the dream.

God, he prayed, *keep Brad safe. Watch over him. Give him wisdom.* Randal checked the clock again and admitted he wouldn't be going to sleep anytime soon. He searched briefly until he located the remote control and turned on the television. Cable news might have some early coverage of the events in Jerusalem. Maybe he'd catch sight of Brad.

★ ★ ★

Brad paced the confines of the small, hot office near the back of the Knesset Building and checked his watch for the thousandth time. The closer the treaty signing came, the more sickened he felt. A part of him wanted to try and shake sense into the Israeli leaders who were putting so much faith in Nicolae Carpathia. How could they not know, he wondered, that they were ushering in the Great Tribulation? The *Last Terrible Week of the Lord*, the Bible called it.

Outside the door, he heard the cacophony of the press corps demanding access to Gerald Fitzhugh. The president was in another room where he'd pulled prominent *Global Weekly* reporter Cameron Williams aside for an unscheduled personal interview. The interview, Brad knew, was making Charley Swelder chew nails as he paced in the corridor and tried to hold the media at bay. No one knew why Fitzhugh had signaled Williams out, other than a long-standing relationship between the two and Fitzhugh's frustration at a round of meetings he'd had with Nicolae this morning.

Among other concessions, Fitzhugh had agreed to permanently consign the new *Air Force One* to the UN—which Carpathia had all but renamed *Global Community One*. At that meeting, Carpathia had also revealed his intention to move the UN headquarters from New York to Babylon. Though the president had been mostly pleased to move the UN and its affiliated problems off U.S. soil, Carpathia's proprietary handling of the issue had infuriated him.

Frustrated and humiliated, Fitzhugh had sent Jordan Trask to find Cameron Williams. Brad supposed the president wanted a final interview on record before the deal was struck.

He checked his watch again. Less than ten minutes remained before they were all supposed to report to the dais for the signing. In the hallway, the noise suddenly escalated. He heard reporters calling the name of the president seconds before the door opened. Jordan Trask stuck his head inside. "The president is going to meet with Carpathia. He's requested you," Jordan told him.

Brad raised an eyebrow but followed wordlessly. The crush of the press was so intense, the Secret Service had to move him through the melee toward the holding area where the secretary-general awaited them. Ahead, Brad made out the wide shoulders and distinctive bald head of the Secret Service agent they called Pudge. He was one of Fitzhugh's favorites, and Brad was certain he was on the president's security detail in the Knesset.

Three minutes later, he found himself in a room with Gerald Fitzhugh, Charley Swelder, Harmon Drake, Pudge, two other agents in the president's security detail, and Jordan Trask. The look Charley gave Brad was nothing short of hostile.

"What's this about?" Brad asked.

"We thought you could tell us," Charley said. "Carpathia asked for this meeting. He insisted you should be here."

Brad tugged lightly at his tie. "Beats me," he said. He took a seat near the edge of the room.

They waited in tense silence until Nicolae Carpathia came into the room flanked by a small entourage of advisors. Brad watched in amazement as everyone, even the president himself, leaped to their feet as if Carpathia were royalty.

★　★　★

Randal's eyes had begun to grow heavy. The late-night news he'd found, for lack of activity at the early hour in Jerusalem, had focused on the details of the treaty and its effect on U.S. foreign policy. The long discourse of several constitutional experts was having a predictable effect on him.

Then one of the commentators mentioned the whisper of a scandal about to break in the Fitzhugh White House and captured Randal's attention. On the screen, several pictures of Fitzhugh and Rudd demonstrated the close political relationship between the two. The final picture was a grainy black-and-white news photo with Rudd's and Fitzhugh's faces circled in the midst of a crowd. According to the commentator, the picture was taken in Witchita, Kansas, at a fund-raising event sponsored by the Small Farmers of America.

Randal studied the photo a moment, then froze when he spotted the man immediately behind the president. Harmon Drake was on the platform as part of then President-elect Fitzhugh's security detail.

Suddenly, Randal's eyes widened at a moment of insight so precise and so chilling he had to chalk it up to divine intervention. *Kansas.* The day of the explosion in the presidential limousine, Harmon Drake had mentioned that Brad had returned from Kansas. No one was supposed to know about Brad's unscheduled stop in the middle of the sorghum fields of Kansas, and there was only one way Drake could have that information.

Randal reached for the phone. He had to contact Brad.

Brad remained in his seat as he watched his colleagues pay homage to Nicolae Carpathia.

"Gerald," Carpathia greeted the president.

It had to gall Fitzhugh, Brad thought, that Nicolae used his first name in that condescending tone. The president looked him straight in the eye and said, "What's this about, Nick?"

The corner of Nicolae's mouth twitched. Brad couldn't

tell whether Carpathia was irritated or amused at Fitzhugh's familiarity. "My sources from New York tell me that a very damaging story about your administration is about to hit the newsstands," Nicolae told Fitzhugh. "The FBI is already poised to make several arrests."

That took some of the wind out of Fitzhugh's sails. "We're tracking the story," he said, ignoring the shocked look he received from Charley Swelder.

Brad felt a slight buzzing at his side and reached for his cell phone. He'd set it to Vibrate earlier, not wanting the ring to prove bothersome. The caller ID made him frown. It was two o'clock in the morning on the East Coast. Randal wouldn't be calling him if it wasn't important.

He started to answer, then realized his young friend was sending a text message. Brad shook his head with a slight smile as he realized that he would never get used to the easy familiarity young people had with technology. He had barely adjusted to having a cell phone, much less to text messaging. He found the small keys annoying and preferred the old-fashioned way of verbal communication. He glanced at the small LCD screen as Randal's message began to take shape.

Nicolae had crossed his arms over his chest. "I am concerned," he was telling the president, "that this could diminish the impact of the treaty signing today. If your credibility is damaged in the United States—"

"It won't be," Charley said. "No one in the administration is going to be implicated in the scandal."

"Then you know who is responsible?" Carpathia asked.

Charley slid a finger under his collar and tugged. "It's hot in here," he muttered. He met Nicolae's gaze. "We're going to fully cooperate with the FBI, yes. We believe a few renegade officers at the Pentagon are behind this."

"Victor Rudd claims he will name a source at the White House," Carpathia said.

Fitzhugh thrust his hands into his pockets and muttered a dark curse. "Victor's going to do whatever he has to do to save his skin. If he was stupid enough to get himself involved in an illegal arms deal, he'll be prosecuted."

"He's a friend of your administration," one of Carpathia's aides pointed out.

Brad's eyes widened as Randal's message flashed on the small screen of his phone. He glanced quickly at Harmon Drake, who was leaning against the wall watching the conversation with interest.

"He's not that much of a friend," Fitzhugh told Carpathia. "I'm not going to lose the presidency because a campaign contributor got in over his head. The White House had nothing to do with any of this."

Carpathia seemed to think that over for several seconds. He turned and gave Brad a look. "I understand you were instrumental in bringing this to light," he said.

Brad felt a chill slide down his spine. The light in Carpathia's blue eyes looked like sheer evil. "I believe the assassination attempt on the president's life during your visit to Washington was linked to the scandal," he said. "In the course of our investigation of the assassination attempt, we uncovered some information that led us to examine significant illegalities at the Pentagon and on the Hill in an operation to support the rebels at Abkhazia. I turned the information over to the proper authorities." He glanced at Harmon Drake. "The Secret Service and the FBI have both been involved in the investigation."

Drake's eyes narrowed. "We believe we're onto something," he told the group.

"Do you think there is a conspirator at the White House?" Carpathia asked Brad.

Brad sensed the sudden heightening of tension in the room. He stood and moved toward Nicolae. "I do," he said.

Drake swore loudly. "Benton—"

Nicolae held up his hand. "I would like to hear what Mr. Benton has to say."

Brad looked around the group of White House insiders. "Someone had to be working on Victor Rudd's behalf. I believe it's only a matter of time before we know who it was. When the conspirator's name is known, we will prosecute him to the fullest extent of the law."

"It's an internal matter," Charley Swelder said through gritted teeth. "It doesn't have any bearing on what's happening here."

"I am not so sure," Carpathia interjected. He looked at Brad again. "You have no idea who it might be?"

"No. It's someone who had access to the highest level of classified information, though. Someone who could move anywhere in the White House without arousing suspicion. Someone who knew where and when key decisions were being made and how to coordinate the pipeline of information so that no one noticed what was happening." Brad glanced at Charley Swelder. "For a while, I suspected you."

Charley appeared stunned. "Benton—"

Brad shook his head and began to pace in the room. "But I rejected the idea. You're powerful. You've got unprecedented access to the president, but if you'd been moving too much paper on your own or meeting independently with Rudd you'd have drawn fire for it. You're too high profile for that."

Brad glanced at the president. "I'm ashamed to say, sir, that for some time I thought you might have been involved in George's death. I was glad to realize that wasn't the case either." No one spoke as Brad continued to pace. "I've been racking my brains for weeks trying to determine who it might be. I knew that whoever it was had played a role in trying to kill me. I never believed that MAC flight I took out of California actually went down. Someone would have noticed. So someone knew I was going to be on that plane. That someone tried to kill me by having me pushed out of the plane.

"The same someone," he continued, "realized that Forrest Tetherton had access to George Ramiro's files and could have stumbled on George's notes about the investigation. By that time, the circle of conspirators had grown so large that no one trusted anyone else. Forrest was murdered simply because someone was afraid he *might* know something—not because he actually did."

"What the—" Fitzhugh burst out. "What are you saying, Benton?"

Brad looked around the room again. He felt as though a puzzle were slowly falling together inside his mind. Piece by piece a picture was emerging. "Rudd's source at the White House knew the system and the administration, but with the president in office for only two years, the person would have needed established contacts in Washington. The crisis in Abkhazia began nearly a year ago. There wasn't time for anyone in the administration to set up the network of communication that allowed Rudd to smuggle the gold out of South Range and transfer it to the rebels."

Brad looked at Charley Swelder. At Jordan Trask. At the president. And then his gaze swung to Harmon Drake. "It was you," he said.

Drake's expression turned thunderous. "That's absurd."

"Benton!" Charley demanded.

"No," Brad said. He took a step toward Harmon Drake. "It was you. That's how you knew where I was all those times you tried to kill me. That's how you put a sniper in the White House garage to kill Emma. That's how you murdered Ramiro and got his body out of the White House. That's how you got to Forrest Tetherton." He paused. "And that's how you knew I was almost murdered on my trip from California when your associates shoved me out of a plane in Kansas."

Drake's face reddened in fury. "I don't have to listen to this."

Brad took another step closer. "You had access to everything and everyone. You never made any secret that you didn't like the current administration's foreign policy, nor of your distaste for the handling of the Abkhazia matter."

From the corner of his eye, Brad saw two agents begin to move toward Drake.

Drake glared at him. "That doesn't make me a traitor, Benton," he ground out. "And I'll have your head for accusing me of this."

Brad shook his head. "I don't think so, Harmon. I think that right now Victor Rudd is planning to make a deal with the FBI. You're about to go down for this."

Drake stood still and silent, too shocked to speak.

"Is it true, Drake?" Fitzhugh asked.

The two agents took another step toward the head of the Secret Service. Drake looked from one to the other, then took a hasty step backward. "You can't prove any of this," he said wildly.

"We will soon enough. It all fits." Brad stared at the man in amazement. "I can't believe I didn't see it before."

Nicolae Carpathia put a hand on Gerald Fitzhugh's shoulder. "If this is true, it has to be dealt with."

"Sir—" Drake gasped, looking at the president—"you can't believe—"

Fitzhugh glanced from Brad to Drake and back again. "About twelve months ago, you and I had a conversation about Victor Rudd," he told Drake. "I didn't think much of it at the time. You asked me how much I trusted him. Do you remember it?"

"Sir—," Drake began.

Fitzhugh ignored him. "Remember what I told you? I told you Rudd was a valuable supporter but that when it came right down to it, I knew Victor's interests lay in his own ambitions. If he found it expedient to turn on me, he would. Remember that?"

"Mr. President—"

"You should have listened to me then, Drake. I could have spared you a jail sentence."

Drake's expression changed from disbelief to pure fury. As the two agents advanced on him, he slid his hand inside his coat pocket and produced his firearm.

"Gun!" one of the agents yelled.

Another agent tackled Fitzhugh and pulled him to the floor. The entire scene seemed to unfold in slow motion before Brad as Drake leveled his gun on Nicolae Carpathia and said, "I've given my life for the interests of the United States of America, and I'm not going to let you or anyone else sign it away."

One of Nicolae's aides dragged him aside as a Secret Service agent launched himself at Drake.

Drake fired the gun. The agent tackled Drake and wrestled him to the floor, but not before Drake fired two more shots into the room. Brad felt a searing pain rip through his shoulder. The force of the blow knocked him to the floor.

There was a brief skirmish. Another shot was fired. And then, silence fell on the room. Harmon Drake lay dead on the floor with a pool of blood pouring from his throat. Pudge still held his smoking firearm. He'd fired the shot through Harmon Drake's jugular vein.

Brad grabbed his shoulder and felt the warm spill of

blood where one of Harmon's bullets had clipped him. It hurt like fury, but he could tell it was just a flesh wound.

"Mr. President," another agent was saying. "Mr. President, are you all right?"

Fitzhugh swore and rose to his feet. "I'm fine," he muttered, issuing another stream of profanity as he brushed off his clothes. "Just fine."

Nicolae's staff was buzzing around him in apparent distress, but Carpathia, too, rose from the floor untouched by the bullets. One of his aides frantically searched his boss for signs of blood. "Are you sure you weren't hit? I was sure I saw you get hit."

"I was not harmed," Nicolae said. He smoothed his tie as if nothing significant had happened. He glanced at Brad, who was still clutching his bleeding shoulder. "I believe Mr. Benton caught the shot meant for me," he said. "I owe him a tremendous debt of gratitude."

Brad felt physically sick. The pain in his shoulder was excruciating, but it was worse realizing that Nicolae had escaped unharmed, thanks to him. *Forgive me, Lord,* he prayed silently, *but You could have killed him just then. I don't understand. . . .*

"We need a medic," Jordan Trask said. He moved swiftly to the door and jerked it open. "Get a medic," he told the Secret Service agent outside the door. "And do it quietly."

As two other agents dealt with Drake's body, Charley Swelder and Jordan Trask helped Brad to his feet. Nicolae came to him with a look of humility and gratitude that turned Brad's stomach. "I owe you a tremendous debt, Mr. Benton," he said.

"We all do," Fitzhugh added.

Nicolae folded his arms and regarded Brad closely. "I wanted to be cross with you over your friend's sermon yesterday," he said, "but I admit that I have a liking for men who speak their minds."

Brad didn't respond. He accepted a handkerchief from Charley Swelder and pressed it against the wound in his shoulder.

"How bad is it?" Jordan asked him.

Brad shook his head. "Flesh wound." He glanced behind him. "The bullet's probably in the wall."

"We are grateful to you," Nicolae said. "And as angry as I was yesterday, I have had some time to think about it. Just like your friend, Marcus Dumont, you are a man who fights for what he believes in. That is the kind of man I want on my team."

Brad looked at him, wide-eyed. Fitzhugh clapped a hand on Nicolae's shoulder. "What are you saying here, Carpathia?" he demanded. "I already told Benton I'd have to have his resignation by Monday."

"Then reject it," Nicolae told the president. He took a step away, forcing Fitzhugh to drop his hand. "I have decided I want Brad Benton to head the Disarmament Committee. I may not agree with him on everything, but I think he is just the man for the job. He is someone who is trusted by the people—they will believe anything he tells them."

"Yeah, I noticed." Fitzhugh said under his breath.

That won a slight laugh from Nicolae. "My apologies, Gerald, if I have caused you any problems, but the truth is, we have got too much work to do to lose such an honorable man."

"Fine," the president muttered. "Fine. Let's just get this over with."

Carpathia shot a look at his watch. "Indeed. It is time. Let us go and change the world."

As Brad watched the other occupants of the room file out, leaving him with several Secret Service agents who were still hovering over Harmon Drake's body, he felt his blood run cold. The Last Terrible Week of the Lord—the Great Tribulation—was about to begin. And he had it on the word of the Antichrist that now he'd most likely be in the middle of it, with a ringside view.

Brad took a deep breath and followed Nicolae and Fitzhugh from the room.

Be with me, Lord Jesus, he prayed. *I'm going to need You more than ever.*

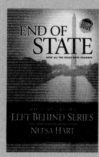

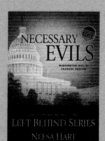

IN ONE CATACLYSMIC MOMENT
MILLIONS AROUND THE WORLD DISAPPEAR

Experience the suspense of the end times for yourself. The best-selling Left Behind series is now available in hardcover, softcover, and large-print editions.

1
LEFT BEHIND®
A novel of
the earth's last
days . . .

2
**TRIBULATION
FORCE**
The continuing
drama of those
left behind . . .

3
NICOLAE
The rise of
Antichrist . . .

4
**SOUL
HARVEST**
The world
takes sides . . .

5
APOLLYON
The Destroyer is
unleashed . . .

6
ASSASSINS
Assignment:
Jerusalem,
Target: Antichrist

7
**THE
INDWELLING**
The Beast takes
possession . . .

8
THE MARK
The Beast rules
the world . . .

9
DESECRATION
Antichrist takes
the throne . . .

10
**THE
REMNANT**
On the brink of
Armageddon . . .

11
ARMAGEDDON
The cosmic battle
of the ages . . .

12
**GLORIOUS
APPEARING**
The end of
days . . .

FOR THE MOST ACCURATE INFORMATION VISIT

www.leftbehind.com

ABRIDGED AUDIO Available on three CDs or two cassettes for each title. (Books 1–9 read by Frank Muller, one of the most talented readers of audio books today.)

AN EXPERIENCE IN SOUND AND DRAMA Dramatic broadcast performances of the best-selling Left Behind series. Twelve half-hour episodes on four CDs or three cassettes for each title.

GRAPHIC NOVELS Created by a leader in the graphic novel market, the series is now available in this exciting new format.

LEFT BEHIND®: THE KIDS Four teens are left behind after the Rapture and band together to fight Satan's forces in this series for ten- to fourteen-year-olds.

LEFT BEHIND® > THE KIDS < LIVE-ACTION AUDIO Feel the reality, listen as the drama unfolds. . . . Twelve action-packed episodes available on four CDs or three cassettes.

CALENDARS, DEVOTIONALS, GIFT BOOKS . . .

FOR THE LATEST INFORMATION ON
INDIVIDUAL PRODUCTS, RELEASE DATES,
AND FUTURE PROJECTS, VISIT

www.leftbehind.com

Sign up and receive free e-mail updates!

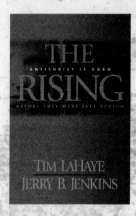